THE FEELGOOD

FALLACY

Hugh Morison

For all my friends and former colleagues in the late lamented Scottish Office.

Hugh Morison worked for 27 years in the Scottish Office before jumping ship to become Chief Executive of the Scotch Whisky Association. He divides his time between Edinburgh and the North West Highlands of Scotland.

CHAPTER 1

In which, as a result of a bureaucratic error, the right man is sent to the wrong place and vice versa.

'You fucking did what?'

Sir Terence Mould's eyes bulged beneath his grizzled brows. 'You sent Donald Macdonald to Tokyo?'

'In accordance with your instructions, Sir Terence.' Maurice Dibbs, Principal Establishment Officer and Director of Human Resources at the North British Office, glared at Sir Terence. Long experience had taught him that you should never admit an error to the Permanent Secretary of the North British Office and that, if his temper was short, so was its duration. But today was an exception.

'I told you to send Donald MacDonald to Tokyo, not Donald Macdonald. He was to be transferred to North Uist.'

The PEO looked blank. He had not been so confused since, following the establishment of the Scottish Parliament two years ago, they had added the words Human Resources to his title and told him that he had to be nice to the staff. 'I confess that I am at a loss...' he began. But the Permanent Secretary cut in.

'Donald MacDonald with a capital 'D' was to go to Tokyo. He is, according to your reports, the most intelligent man we've got, present company excepted, and I don't mean you. If we are to win the Feelgood Project we need all the brainpower we can muster. Donald Macdonald, small 'd', was to go to North Uist to work on the Minister's plans for local government reform. He is, again according to your reports, about as stupid as we've got, present company excepted, and I don't mean me. If we're going to save the Minister from himself and prevent the amalgamation of the North Uist and

Benbecula Urban District Councils, we need all the stupidity we've got. And you've sent the wrong man to the wrong place!'

'The wrong man to the right place, Sir Terence. Or, if you prefer it, the right man to the wrong place.'

Sir Terence Mould's face turned a dangerous shade of puce. 'Don't quibble with me, man. Through your quite overwhelming incompetence you've fouled up a strategy which...'

'I followed your instructions to the letter, Sir Terence.'

'To the letter? To the letter? Nonsense! It was precisely the letter that you got wrong. If word gets around that the PEO of the North British Office can't tell the difference between a capital letter and lower case, we'll be the laughing stock of Whitehall. The Treasury always said things would go from bad to worse if they set up a Scottish Parliament, and this will prove them right.'

'With respect, a 'd' is still a 'd', whether it's majuscule or minuscule.'

'I'll fucking minuscule you! When I've finished with you, you'll be so minuscule your wife will think you've joined a fleas' circus. You've got to get them back.'

'It's too late.'

'What do you mean, too late? They can get a plane back. Or in Macdonald's case, a MacBrayne's ferry, if they're not on strike.'

'MacDonald, Sir, not Macdonald.'

The vein in Sir Terence's temple throbbed ominously. 'Whichever the hell it is, get them back!'

'But it's too late. The Minister has already met Donald MacDonald, and was so impressed with him that he's given him *carte blanche* to do whatever he thinks appropriate to secure the amalgamation of the Councils.'

'Carte blanche? What the hell's Blanche got to do with it?' Sir Terence was not well versed in the liberal arts.

'White cart, Sir Terence. It means that MacDonald can put whatever he likes in it. And if you withdraw him now, the Minister will not be well pleased.'

Sir Terence leant back in his chair and swore volubly. 'So be it. But if either of those two foul up my plans you'll be picking mussels on Portobello Beach. The North British Office needs to win the Feelgood Project if it is to retain any credibility in Whitehall, and local government in the islands will be reformed over my dead body. Now get out.'

'There is on other small thing, Sir Terence.'

'Well, what is it?'

'Is it Carter Brown or Carter Browne you wish to have posted to Water and Sewerage Division?'

'Get out', yelled Sir Terence, losing his rag at last.

* * *

CHAPTER 2

In which a civil servant wonders at his luck and confusion is confounded.

Donald Macdonald, meantime, sat in the Executive Departure Lounge at Heathrow Airport waiting for his flight. He wasn't used to small luxuries, and he was quite unperturbed by the fact that his flight had already been delayed by fog for two hours and there was as yet no departure time noted on the monitor. There was a well stocked bar, and no one had asked him for payment. In addition, a number of pretty girls and attractive women of maturer years were within eyeshot, and Donald Macdonald was keenly speculating on whether any would be prepared to help him join the Mile High Club. For, though he had never flown before, he had acquired a detailed knowledge of international flight through studying the works of Capt. WE Johns, Malcolm Bradbury and David Lodge when he should have been processing Scottish Highland Agricultural Grants at his desk in the North British Department of Agriculture, Fisheries and Training.

All the flights South the previous evening had been cancelled due to what the airline called adverse weather conditions and the rest of the world fog, and Donald had travelled to London by sleeper. Between speculating as to how a mobile wagon for insomniacs had acquired such a name, he had spent the hours of darkness wondering how he had been offered such a glamorous job. An undistinguished career at Larkhall High School had led to a pass degree in moral philosophy at Glasgow. He had spent more time in the Union beer bar playing snooker than in studying philosophy; and his knowledge of morality had been developed, not so much by reading the works of Kant and Hegel, as osmotically, through practical experiments in cheating at poker and trying unsuccessfully to poke the nurses from the Home round the corner. From Glasgow he had progressed to the Executive Class of the Civil Service, where he had been given a thorough grounding in the arts of filing papers, counting paper clips against the possibility of an enquiry by the National Audit Office, and writing memos of a style whose turgid obscurity marked him out for the higher reaches of grant administration.

'The secret', his first boss had instructed him, 'is never to offer a grant at first request, and never to make clear why you have refused it. Your job is not to give money to help undeserving farmers buy their Volvos and Jaguars, it is to save taxpayers' money. And especially the taxpayers of other parts of the European Community. Never forget that.'

It was a lesson that he had taken seriously. In his first five years of service, despite enquiries by the Ombudsman, questions in the House, and articles in the *Sunday Post*, he had awarded only one grant – to a small farmer whose son had shared digs with him in the Byres Road. His head of department had defended his decisions robustly before the Public Accounts Committee; and he had recently been promoted to run the Scottish Highland Agricultural Grants Scheme (SHAGS) set up by the new Scottish Parliament to complement their work on land reform. He had a budget of £2m, which was almost entirely earmarked to cover the expenses of the SHAGS Inspectorate (who required to stay in the most expensive Country House Hotels, as befitted servants of the North British Office). In six months the agriculturalists of the Highlands had not enjoyed a single SHAG. He was looking forward to a further five years of bureaucratic obstruction and country house hotels when he had received the call from the secretary of the Principal Establishment Officer and Director of Human Resources.

'Mr Dibbs would like a word with you. Can you be over at three o'clock?'

Calls from Dibbs' office were always potentially dangerous. 'What's it about?' Donald asked nervously.

'I am not at liberty to disclose.' Angela Thoroughgood did not know, but she had discovered that an air of mystery ensured respect. 'But don't be late. Mr Dibbs is a very busy man, and he doesn't like to be kept waiting.'

Donald had an uncomfortable hour reviewing his most recent grant refusals and his expenses claims – had somebody queried the blue movie he had watched in that hotel in Kinlochbervie? He bought a clean shirt in M&S and a new Glasgow University tie at Jenners: while the egg on his current model perfectly matched in colour the golden stripe of his graduate tie, it didn't match the shape. He polished his glasses, combed his lank brown hair over the spots on his forehead, and arrived at five minutes to three, to be met by Angela Thoroughgood and the sound of angry voices from behind the closed door of the PEO's office.

Ms Thoroughgood beamed her 50-megawatt smile and adjusted her miniskirt. 'I'm afraid Mr Dibbs is tied up at present' she breathed, in a tone of voice which suggested that the PEO was engaged in some exotic sexual practice. 'Won't you take a seat?'

Donald took the low chair opposite Ms Thoroughgood's desk and tried to remember the Office Notice on Sexual Harassment. Would it be contrary to the rules to invite Ms Thoroughgood out for a drink? It was certainly against the rules to try to peer up her skirt; but Ms Thoroughgood seemed not to mind. Indeed, by continually crossing and uncrossing her legs as she varnished her nails, she seemed positively to encourage it. He took off his spectacles to polish them.

At which point the voices in the office reached a crescendo and the door burst open. A short angry man emerged, his ginger hair and eyebrows bristling with rage, followed by the limp figure of Maurice Dibbs.

'And you can tell Sir Terence where he can put the North Uist bleeding Urban effing District sodding Council!' the short angry man was shouting.

'Hardly the kind of language one can use to one's Permanent Secretary, MacDonald,' said Dibbs. 'The Minister wishes to see you, and I suggest you arrange to meet him immediately. And I'll thank you not to use intemperate language in front of my secretary, contrary to Departmental Circular 47/1999.'

'I'll tell you where you can stuff your Circular,' shouted MacDonald. He stormed out, slamming the door behind him. Ms Thoroughgood did her best to blush, as required by the Circular, but failed lamentably and confined herself to a giggle.

Dibbs took a deep breath and made a visible effort to change gear. 'My dear chap,' he said to Donald, 'I do apologise for that. Most unseemly, most unseemly indeed. Now do come in and make yourself at home.' He beckoned Donald into his office with an expansive gesture, dislodging a tired looking spider plant from one of Ms Thoroughgood's filing cabinets. Donald stood up and, stealing a last regretful glance at Ms Thoroughgood's legs, entered the office.

Inside was a paradigm of chaos. (Donald was fond of the word 'paradigm'; it was useful in rejecting grants. 'I regret to inform you' he had written only that morning, 'that your application fails to meet the paradigm of the scheme.') Files and papers lay piled on every available surface. An overflowing ashtray stood on top of the most recent draft of the Department's anti smoking circular; Dibbs' deputy was a founder member of CND, the Campaign against Nicotine Dependency, and was keen to have the message widely disseminated. A half empty bottle of gin made rings on a similar draft circular banning drinking in office hours. A poster of the Queen on a white horse hung drunkenly from three blobs of bluetac, and the windowsill held a collection of dead and dying pot plants, a futile attempt by Ms Thoroughgood to soften the anonymity of the typical government office.

'Do sit down,' said Dibbs, throwing some papers from an armchair and making himself formal behind his desk. 'Now, who are you, and what can I do for you?'

'Donald Macdonald, Sir. Your secretary asked me to call on you at three o'clock.'

'You're not Donald MacDonald. I've just seen MacDonald.'

'I, Sir, *am* Donald Macdonald', Donald persisted. 'Your secretary asked me to call on you at 3 pm precisely. She said that you don't like to be kept waiting.'

'Well, you're late!' said Dibbs, looking at the clock on his wall, which was stopped at five past four. 'What did you say you wanted?'

'I don't know. It was you, or rather your secretary, who summoned me.'

'Well, we'd better ask Ms Thoroughgood, then. Why didn't you suggest that in the first place?' Dibbs glared impatiently at Donald and lit a Senior Service Navy Cut No 2 with a brass paraffin lighter. Then, having failed to find the buzzer to summon Ms Thoroughgood beneath the morass of papers on his desk, he bellowed for her to enter.

Ms Thoroughgood minced in on heels too high for her and

smoothed her diminutive skirt over her shapely hips. 'Tea or coffee, Mr Dibbs?' she asked. 'Or is it' – she looked at the clock – 'something a little stronger at this time of day?'

Dibbs gave her a basilisk stare. 'Neither and no. I want to know what this man, who calls himself Donald MacDonald, is doing in my office. Apparently you told him to come. But I've already seen Donald MacDonald.'

'You were to see both Donald MacDonalds this afternoon, Mr Dibbs.'

'What do you mean, both?'

'There are two MacDonalds, Mr Dibbs. One of them has a big D, and the other one,' she looked at Donald and giggled, 'a small. You were to post the one with the big 'D' to Tokyo, and the one with the little 'd' to North Uist. Sir Terence Mould's instructions. It's all in the file.' She looked hopefully at the piles of documents which littered the room.

'Show me,' said Dibbs.

Ten minutes later she was no closer to finding the relevant document. Dibbs sat behind his desk tapping a government issue biro against the side of the gin bottle, whose pitch steadily fell with the level of the contents. Macdonald, after a few desultory attempts at small talk, had taken to staring at the Queen's horse, which stared lopsidedly back. Ms Thoroughgood inclined herself over pile upon pile of papers and files, revealing shapely legs and a hint of black lace, but nothing of the file in question.

'It's no good,' she said at last. 'We'll have to try the computer.'

'The com-pewter,' snarled Dibbs, drawing the word out to make it sound like a particularly vicious breed of reptile. 'I have made it clear on many occasions that I will not have such a thing in my office.'

'Well you don't. It's in mine,' responded Ms Thoroughgood.

'I refuse to allow its use,' snapped Dibbs. 'The next thing we know, they'll have taken away our livelihoods. Not to mention our jobs.'

'Well I'm not spending any more time rooting around in this midden. And I dare say that Donald Macdonald has more important things to do than make eyes at the Queen's horse.' With which forceful words, Ms Thoroughgood flounced through to her own office and switched on the offending contraption.

'Such impertinence!' muttered Dibbs. 'I knew I should never have insisted she go on that assertiveness training course. But perhaps she knows best – she generally does.' With which weak words Dibbs, accompanied by Donald, followed her into the outer office and stared at the screen.

The screen remained blank for a few seconds while the Central Processing Unit built up a head of steam, then issued the curt instruction `Type Password`.

'What's this, some kind of game for Boy Scouts?' muttered Dibbs, while Ms Thoroughgood, using the one finger technique favoured by computer-literate secretaries who thought that touch typing was a means of telling men from women in the dark, keyed in the letters for – if Donald followed her aright – `effoff`.

The computer whirred, and then the screen filled with space invaders. `YOU HAVE LOST TO THE MASTER OF THE UNIVERSE` it said. `DO YOU WISH TO TRY AGAIN? PRESS [Y] OR [N].`

Ms Thoroughgood pressed 'N', and the space invaders were replaced with battleships. `DO YOU WISH TO TAKE ON SADDAM HUSSEIN OR GENERAL GALTIERI?` asked the screen.

'For God's sake, get on with it,' spat Dibbs. 'I've got to finalise the Departmental Circular on misuse of official property before close of play this afternoon.'

Ms Thoroughgood depressed a few more keys, and the battleships were replaced by an image of Ms Thoroughgood, dressed in a string of pearls and very little else. 'That bloody computing officer,' she swore. 'I'll flame his balls over the Internet, you see if I don't.'

'Why don't you press Enter?' asked Donald, eager to demonstrate his computer literacy.

'I'm not at all sure that's a good idea,' said Dibbs. 'What is supposed to enter what?'

Miss Thoroughgood pressed Exit. Her body remained on the screen, but her face was replaced in rapid succession with those of the Queen Mother, Nelson Mandela, Margaret Thatcher, Mother Theresa, Shergar, Tony Blair, Arnold Schwatznegger and finally Sir Terence Mould. Of them all, Sir Terence Mould looked the least ridiculous, perhaps because he clutched a red rose between his teeth. Finally, the succession of bizarre image disappeared, to be replaced by a file of text –

MacDonald, Donald.
Entered North British Office Department of Home Affairs (DOHA)
30 08 1985.
Educ. Winchester; New College, Oxford.
First Class Honours degree in Literae Humanores 1982.
Prize Fellow of All Souls 1983.
Publications: The Regeneration of Local Economies, Clarendon
Press, Oxford 1987; 'Dauphiné', Crowwood Press, Reading 1991;
'The Marquis de Sade: was he a Masochist?' Olympia Press,
Paris, 1993
Career: Assistant Principal, NBO DOHA 1985-88;
Private Secretary to Minister of State 1988-9;
Principal, NBO Dept of Economic Affairs 1990-
Achievements: successfully reformed local government in
Strathclyde 1995 (credit to Parliamentary Secretary); successfully
reversed reforms to Strathclyde local government 1997 (credit to
Secretary of State); introduced new Financial Management system
into NBO 1998 (credit to the then Mr Terry Mould, who received a
knighthood as a result).
Married 1990 Lady Lucinda Bowes Carter, elder daughter of the
late Earl of Auchtermurchty.   Twin daughters, Lorraine and
Alsace.
Note from Permanent Secretary: 'A career to watch. Could be a
strong contender for the Feelgood Project. Thereafter Treasury,
Cabinet Office or No 10.'

'There, Mr Dibbs' simpered Miss Thoroughgood, 'don't tell me computers aren't wonderful. It's all there.'

'But that's not me' said Donald, 'that's not me at all.'

'What do you mean, not you?' said Dibbs. 'It's on the computer, so it must be you. Or are you telling me,' he turned to Ms Thoroughgood, 'that these things are fallible?'

'Perhaps we didn't ask it the right question,' responded Ms Thoroughgood. She pressed a few more keys, and the paradigm of public service disappeared, to be replaced by the following –

Macdonald, Donald.

Entered North British Office Department of Agriculture, Fisheries and Training (DAFT) 29 09 1987.
Educ. Larkhall High School; Glasgow University.
BSc (not honours) moral philosophy with home economics.
Publications: letter to Larkhall Gazette complaining about declining standards of fast food outlets in Larkhall High Street 1980.
Career: Executive Officer, DAFT, 1987-90, responsible for grants for training fish farmers.
Higher Executive Officer, DAFT, 1990-93, responsible for SWILL (Swine and Related Species Introduction to Lowland Landscapes).
Senior Executive Officer and Head of Branch, DAFT 1993-1998, responsible for BOGS (Bovine Offal Grants Scheme).
Principal DAFT 1999, responsible for SHAGS (Scottish Highland Agriculture Grants Scheme).
Achievements: Commended by HM Treasury for infrequency of grants awarded. Criticised by Parliamentary Commissioner for Administration for obscurantism and obstructionism in relation to grant applications; the PCA's report led to a further commendation from HM Treasury.
Note from Permanent Secretary: 'A career to watch, if only for the potential impact on one's own back.'

Dibbs stared at the screen for a long moment. 'Are you telling me that this is you?' he said at last.

'Not exactly,' said Donald, who had vague recollections of his university classes on the difficulty of capturing the essence of being. 'But in outline, yes.'

'Christ,' thought Dibbs. Then, taking one of those snap decisions which had earned him a reputation for decisiveness and stupidity in equal proportion, he reverted to the full dignity of official language and said: 'I have it in charge from the Permanent Secretary to instruct you to proceed to Tokyo to take charge of the Feelgood Project. It is a project of great importance to North Britain, in particular because it will demonstrate that the establishment of the Scottish Parliament has not affected our capacity to attract inward investment, and this posting demonstrates the very great faith which Sir Terence and I have in your abilities, as exemplified by your exemplary administration of SWILL, BOGS and, er' – he stole a glance at the screen – 'SHAGS.'

'But I know nothing of Japan,' stammered Donald. 'I've never even been abroad.'

'Nor had Sir Francis Drake before he circumnavigated the globe. Nor had Marco Polo.'

'I've never even been to England.'

'That,' said Dibbs, 'is an advantage. Now you really must permit me to get on with my labours. Miss Thoroughgood will arrange for you to be fully briefed. Sir Terence expects you to be in Tokyo by next Monday.'

And Dibbs retreated into the chaos of his office, to take a consoling pull of gin and light a relaxing Navy Cut No 2.

* * *

CHAPTER 3

In which a scholar of Winchester meets a sinister sergeant and plots revenge.

While Donald Macdonald of Larkhall High School was drinking large gins and tonics in the Departure Lounge at Heathrow, Donald MacDonald of Winchester and All Souls sat in the bar of the MacBrayne's Ferry from Uig to North Uist plotting his revenge. It was not a pleasant day. Low storm clouds smudged a dirty grey on the horizon. Lady Lucinda had insisted on accompanying him to see him settled in, as she put it; and both Alsace and Lorraine had been sick. The tin ashtrays in the bar were sodden with spilt beer; and the few brave souls still attempting to stand upright at the bar counter were in a state of increasingly noisy inebriation.

'Large whisky, my man,' said Donald to the barman when at last he caught his eye.'

'Will that be a malt whisky, or chust a blend?' asked the barman.

'A blend,' replied Donald. His stomach did not feel up to the finer delicacies of a single malt.

'And will that be a Famous Grouse, a Chonny Walker, a White Horse, a Whyte and Mackay or a Pig's Nose?' asked the barman, who had been on a customer satisfaction course.

'A Johnny Walker,' replied Donald, beginning to lose patience.

'And will that be a Chonny Walker Red Label, a Chonny Walker Black Label, or a Chonny Walker Blue Label?'

'Just a Johnny Walker,' snapped Donald. 'I don't care which one. But get a move on, can't you?'

'All in God's good time,' said the barman. 'This nectar was 10 years in the making, and it won't be harmed by another few minutes in the waiting. Stornoway wass not built in a day, or were they not teaching you history at the fancy college where you wass having your education?'

The barman turned slowly to the gantry and with great reverence dispensed a double measure. 'That will be seven pounds and 45 pence,' he said.

'What?' spluttered Donald. 'Not even in the Hilton in Boston do they charge as much.'

'A fine whisky, like a faithful wife, is a pearl beyond price. But it iss all the fault of the new Parliament and that bloody North British Office. Since they took away our subsidies, it iss at the bar that we have to make our profits.'

Donald took his whisky to a table by the window and peered out through the rain-sodden glass. Seagulls were blown backwards through the sky. Huge waves broke over the rail, and the wind howled through the rigging. As he lifted his glass to his lips the vessel gave an immense lurch, spilling at least three pounds worth of the precious liquid beside the pearl pin in his tie. Pearl beyond price, indeed! What the hell was he doing here?

He blamed Sir Terence Mould, of course, Sir Terence and the Minister. Sir Terence had virtually promised him a glamorous posting to Tokyo. Lady Lucinda would have been in her element, calling on the Ambassador, learning flower arranging, calligraphy, zen archery. Even the twins could have been sent to an English language school, so that Lady Lucinda would have been forced to abandon her project for bringing up Alsace speaking French and Lorraine German to test her theory that linguistic differences were the root cause of wars. And here he was, in a squalid floating bar which charged more than Annabel's, on his way to oversee the forcible amalgamation of the North Uist and Benbecula Urban District Councils.

The Minister, to give him his due, had been charming – but then so had Ms. Thoroughgood, whom he had telephoned immediately on his return from his meeting with Dibbs, and while Donald Macdonald was beginning his. Ms. Thoroughgood had assured him that it was all an unfortunate mistake: he was to be posted to Tokyo to take charge of the Feelgood project, and the Minister wished to see him to discuss the matter 'at his earliest convenience'. She had not thought to tell him of the PEO's later snap decision to let sleeping Dibbs lie and his posting to North Uist stand; and with a light heart Donald MacDonald had taken 'Teach Yourself Japanese' out of the Office Library and mastered the first five chapters in an evening.

He had met the Minister the following day in his room at Bute House, the room where Lady Caroline Mouton, Byron's other mistress, was reputed to have clipped a lock of hair, but not from her head, to encourage her lover in the Greek war of independence. 'Ah Donald,' he had said, 'Good of you to come over to the Athens of the North.' (Since inheriting the room he had taken to peppering his speech with literary references.) 'Now I needn't tell you that I've asked you to undertake a task of considerable delicacy. But I have great expectations of you. I have to say that Sir Terence Mould opposes my plans; indeed, I have a considerable file of papers here setting out in tedious detail why I should not proceed. But, as I said to him, his opposition is based on little more than prejudice and pride, or should I say pride and prejudice? And I am certain that you are the man to bring all to fruition, so that at the next Party Conference I can make Brighton rock.'

'I am deeply honoured,' said Donald, thinking of geisha girls and sumo wrestlers, 'to have been offered this opportunity.'

'Excellent,' said the Minister, thinking of peat bogs and the votes of Benbecula crofters. 'Speak the lingo, do you? Language, truth and logic is what I always say: truth follows language and, er, logic follows truth.'

'I have a smattering,' replied Donald, 'though I still have to master the script.'

'Looks Irish to me,' said the Minister, 'but I expect that you'll get the hang of it in no time. Just requires a bit of sense and sensibility; and from your reports you've got that in plenty. It's a paradise lost, and our task is to regain it with as little Agonistes as possible. Well, I mustn't keep you: I need to get down to the Parliament for a division. Why they insist in having votes in the new Parliament I cannot understand! I expect great things of you, by middle March at latest. Oh, and give my regards to Torquil McCorquodale when you get there.'

'The Ambassador, Minister?'

'The Wee Free Minister. Good luck, dear boy, good luck.'

And the Minister ushered Donald MacDonald from the room, puzzled as to where was the paradise lost, and what a Wee Free Minister was doing in Tokyo.

Now he knew. And he would get his revenge if it were the last thing he did.

'This seat free, guv?'

The little man with the black beret and woolly pullover, clutching a plastic bag of comic books, didn't have the air of those with whom Donald MacDonald normally had social, or any other kind of, intercourse. But there was no one on the ferry who did, apart from Lady Lucinda, with whom intercourse, social or any other kind, was becoming increasingly rare as she pursued her linguistic experiments with the twins.

'By all means,' said Donald, inclining his head at the empty chair opposite. 'Care for a drink?'

'Don't mind if I do. I'll 'ave a beer, if that's all right with you.'

After a lengthy exchange with the barman, who offered him a choice of Tennants, S&N, Bass, Dryboroughs and Caffreys, broken down into tinned and bottled and lager, ale and stout, Donald returned to the table to find his acquaintance deep in a comic book.

'Donald MacDonald,' he said, placing the beer unsteadily on the table. 'North British Office Department of Economic Affairs.'

'Sergeant Alf Stripe,' responded the little man, laying the comic book between the pools of beer and less mentionable liquids on the table. 'Special Air Service. I run the fucking range on Benbecula. Leastwise, I does when Major Prendergast is away, and 'e spends most of 'is time in London. And when 'e's not there 'e spends 'is time killing fish and birds with the gentry. Dunno why people join the fucking army if all they're interested in is killing things.'

'And you, what interests you?' responded Donald.

'War, of course,' said Sgt Stripe, waxing lyrical. 'Diplomacy by other means. The thing to do when politicians fail. The noblest pursuit known to man. The source of all 'onour, all courage, all technological progress, all development. I'm making a special study of the war in the Pacific in World War II. Fucking Japs. See what they did at Pearl 'arbor.' He gestured at the comic book. 'It's all in there. I'd 'ave loved the chance to 'ave a go at them.'

'Bit old hat, isn't it?' said Donald. 'I mean, it's over 50 years ago, and the Japanese are among our most important trading partners.'

'Trade,' spat Sgt Stripe. 'Fucking war, guv, innit? See those Yanks, they're giving them what for. Trade's just war by other means. If I had 'alf a chance I'd sort the lot of them.'

'Well, I doubt that you'll have much chance here' said Donald. 'I doubt whether they've seen a Japanese in these parts since the beginning of time, and certainly not since Pearl Harbor.' But already an idea was forming in his head.

'Alsace, *dépêche toi! Beeil dich*, Lorraine,' shouted Lady Lucinda as the twins made for the gangplank. The twins, laden under their burden of Lady Lucinda's hat boxes and the baskets which contained her two Pekinese dogs, Mao and Tse Tung, did their best to oblige.

'*Excusez moi, Monsieur*,' said Alsace to the fat and bearded harbour master as she reached dry land. '*Où est le Syndicat d'Initiative ou l'Office de Tourisme? Nous cherchons un hotel de grande luxe.*' Lorraine pushed her sister towards the edge of the quay. 'Stupid girl,' she said, 'he doesn't speak French. *Entshuldigen Sie mich bitte, wo ist der Touristen-informationsbüro? Haben Sie ein Doppelzimmer für die Nacht?*'

'Girls, girls,' shouted Donald, 'do try to behave yourselves. There should be someone to meet us from North Uist Urban District Council. Go and help mummy with her trunks.'

He strode down the storm-lashed quay. Vicious looking black and white dogs snapped at his heels and snarled at each other. Small boys, dressed in navy shorts and pullovers, threw stones at the twins and each other and yelled in a language that made German sound mellifluous. Old men, their raincoats held together with string, took surreptitious swigs at quarter bottles of whisky and rolled bloodshot eyes on the look out for the Wee Free Minister. Old women wrinkled their noses and their brown woollen stockings and glared at Lady Lucinda, whose fur coat, six-inch heels and wide brimmed hat failed, in some inexplicable way, to live up to the North Uist dress code. Behind her, six quay hands cursed and sweated under the weight of her trunks.

'Donald MacDonald of MacDonald, iss it?' The man was half hidden behind a rain sodden notice saying '*Ceud Mile Fàilte*:

Welcome to North Uist, Britain's Foremost Holiday Destination', and at first Donald didn't see him.

'Or do you prefer the patronymics? Donald son of Donald son of Archibald son of Alastair son of Kevin son of Wayne. Welcome back to land of your fathers, on behalf of the North Uist Urban District Council.'

He moved crabwise into the rain and grasped Donald's hand in a vice like grip. 'I am Hamish McTurk, the Chief Executive of the North Uist Urban District Council. I am come to take you to your lodgings. Then, tomorrow, we can get down to God's work in chastening those heretics in Benbecula. Come, it is but a short step across the peat bog.'

And Hamish McTurk strode off into the rain, followed by an increasingly bedraggled procession of Donald MacDonald, Lady Lucinda MacDonald, Alsace and Lorraine (still squabbling loudly in their two languages) and five native porters, the sixth having abandoned Lady Lucinda's heaviest trunk to a soft part of the bog and slunk back to the quay, where Sgt Stripe was briefing his platoon for the long march to Benbecula.

'Keep yer guns cocked and yer eyes peeled. They could be anywhere – behind a rock, in a cave, up a tree...'

'Please, Sarge, there ain't no trees.'

'Where the Japs are concerned, you can't take nuffink for granted. They'll provide the bloody trees if they think that will give 'em global advantage. 'Eard of Bonsai trees, ain't you? Easily portable, and quite big enough to hide a little yellow Jap with murder in his 'eart and a rifle between his teeth. Now get a bloody move on and stop arguing. By the front, quick march!'

* * *

CHAPTER 4

In which there is a search for contraceptives.

Three hours and five large gins later, Donald Macdonald was no closer to leaving the International Executive Departure Lounge at Heathrow Airport. At irregular intervals the departure of one or other international flight to exotic locations – Los Angeles, or Delhi, or Caracas, or Cape Town – was announced; but no word of Tokyo. Enquiries at the Desk elicited no more than that an announcement would be made when an announcement would be made. The time of such an announcement would be announced at the proper time, and not before. Making a mental note to ensure that British Overseas Airways were denied any grant they might apply for under the Scottish Highland Agricultural Grants Scheme, Donald Macdonald returned to his gin.

'Mind if I join you?'

She was mid twenties, blonde, petite and shapely, and in her hand she carried a copy of David Lodge's *Small World*. Donald could think of worse ways of killing time that conversing with a young lady with such a figure – and if she was on the Tokyo flight she looked a fair bet for membership of the Mile High Club, or David Lodge was the author of the encyclical *Humana Vitae*. Things were beginning to look up.

'Be my guest,' he said in his best Kelvinside accent. 'You off to Tokyo?' He tried to hide the eagerness in his voice.

'That's the general idea, when they get us off. I was to have flown Virgin, but I lacked the qualifications.'

Donald Macdonald, hardly believing his luck, was wondering how to formulate a question about hymens in a way which would not offend a young lady whom one had met only two minutes before, when she continued: 'Air Miles, you know. Daddy didn't have quite enough for Virgin, so I am having to go BOA. Quite a bore, really – Virgin show much better films. Why are you going to Tokyo?'

'Business,' replied Donald curtly. 'Government business.' In fact, despite several attempts at mastering the brief, he had only the vaguest idea why he had been sent to Tokyo. Something about a major industrial project promising hundreds of jobs that Sir Terence Mould wanted to attract to Scotland. But how he was to do it he hadn't the foggiest idea. 'I can't really talk about it. Official Secrets Act, you know. What about you?'

'Oh, nothing as glamorous as that. I've a year's sabbatical at the University of Kyoto. I'm just completing my doctoral thesis on Lacan and feminism in 20th century Japan.'

'Feminism,' said Donald Macdonald, whose earlier unhappy contacts with the creed had led to bruised egos and aching balls. 'You a feminist?'

'We don't all dress in dungarees, wear our hair in crew cuts, and have names like Irma Klutz. I'm called Pussy Galore.'

'Pussy Galore?' gasped Donald.

'Daddy was a James Bond fan. But I do believe in the essential need, as T S Eliot put it, to purify the language of the tribe so that sexist, racist, handicapist, sectish and sizist language is abolished. The only way to abolish discrimination is to abolish discriminations. Take our air hostpersons, for example.'

'Air hostpersons?' Donald was finding it difficult to reconcile the shapely feminine creature sitting opposite him with the language of feminism and political correctitude which slipped so easily through her perfectly formed lips. And hadn't T S Eliot said something about the need to make discriminations, or was that F R Leavis?

'Yes, don't you see how the word air hostperson discriminates against hostpersons who work on boats and trains and buses, leading to lower pay and a lesser social status. The only way round it is to call them transport hostpersons.'

'I see,' said Donald, who didn't. 'And how does David Lodge fit in?' He was eager to test whether a radical feminist was a likely candidate for membership of the Mile High Club, or whether he should transfer his attention to the formerly married women of size who were sitting amongst their carrier bags and knitting on the other side of the departure lounge.

'I shall be writing to David to suggest how he might recast his work to remove offensive nuances. But he does, in my view, give a very true picture of international air flight.'

Donald Macdonald had his answer. He began to wonder about contraceptives. His thoughts were interrupted by the Public Address system.

'British Overseas Airways regret to announce the cancellation of Flight 007 to Tokyo Narita International Airport, due to fog. All passengers on this flight will be rescheduled onto Flight BOA 008 to Tokyo Narita, which will be retimed to depart at the revised time of departure for Flight 007. Passengers on Flight 008 should await a further announcement. Relevant passengers should proceed immediately to gate 47.'

'That's us' said Pussy Galore. 'Flight 007.'

'No it's not' said Donald Macdonald. 'Flight 007's been cancelled.'

'But all passengers on Flight 007 have been put on Flight 008, which will leave at the same time as Flight 007. So it amounts to the same thing.'

'I think that we should seek clarification' said Donald, whose powers of textual analysis did not match those of a post structuralist feminist proponent of the politically correct. But at that point a further announcement was made.

'British Overseas Airways regret to announce that their previous announcement regretting the cancellation of Flight 007 to Tokyo Narita erroneously referred to the wrong flight. British Overseas Airways regret the cancellation of Flight 008 to Tokyo Narita. All passengers on this Flight will be rescheduled to fly on Flight BOA 007, which will now be rescheduled to fly at the former time of Flight 008. Passengers holding Economy Class tickets for this Flight will be upgraded to Club, and passengers in Rows B through G of Club will be regraded to Economy. Any passenger who wishes not to be rescheduled should proceed immediately to the boarding gate for tomorrow's Flight 008, which will depart today.'

There was a rush of confused and angry passengers to the Enquiry Desk brandishing Gold Cards, First Class tickets, and Yves Saint Laurent hand luggage. Donald Macdonald, whose bureaucratic expertise consisted in the creation of confusion rather than its clarification, decided to delegate. Besides, he had urgent business in the gentlemen's lavatory.

'I say,' he asked, handing Pussy Galore his tickets and boarding card. 'You couldn't check out what flight and seats we're actually on? I've got a little matter to attend to.'

The Gentlemen's Lavatory, as one would expect of the world's second favourite airline, was spotless. White electric hand dryers glistened above gleaming wash hand basins. Perfectly rectangular bars of white soap waited at precisely the right angle in their soap dishes at the corners of the basins. Empty waste paper baskets awaited the paper towels that were no longer supplied (electric hand dryers being more hygienic, if less effective). Every closet offered a choice of three kinds of paper, meeting the requirements of those who preferred the soft, the crisp or the medicated touch. And, beneath a large poster encouraging voyagers to 'TRAVEL SAFELY ABROAD! REMEMBER THAT MOST FOREIGNERS DRIVE ON THE RIGHT', was the bank of slot machines that Donald was seeking.

The choice offered was even greater than the choice of paper. There were smooth condoms for greater sensitivity and ribbed condoms for greater pleasure. There were French Ticklers for those whose partners, like Queen Victoria, needed to be amused. There were coloured condoms for use at Christmas parties and condoms that glowed in the dark for those whose sense of touch left something to be desired. There were enough flavours to grace a banquet at Marlborough House – smoked salmon, pâté de foie gras or marmite for starters, steak and kidney pudding for main course, and a choice of chocolate (dark or milk), banana, raspberry or strawberry for dessert. Finally there was cheese, though for some reason Stilton did not feature; and the feast could be rounded off with Scotch Whisky McCondoms.

But what condom to employ in the seduction of a feminist post structuralist deconstructionist follower of Lacan? Feminists were not noted for their sense of humour, so it was unlikely that she would be impressed by a French Tickler, even though Lacan was French. He did not know whether the precise object of his attentions had a sweet or savoury tooth, or indeed any teeth at all, which rather ruled out the flavoured condoms. A condom that glowed in the dark would not be wise for an attempt to join the Mile High Club in a crowded aircraft, and coloured condoms could be regarded as discriminatory. He was debating between the ribbed condom which would give *her* greater pleasure, and the smooth condom which would give *him* greater sensitivity, and coming down selfishly in favour of the latter, when it struck him. A feminist would not use a condom at all. She would use a femidom.

'Will Donald Macdonald, last remaining passenger on Flight BOA 007 to Tokyo Narita, report immediately to Gate No 42, where his flight is ready to depart.'

Donald Macdonald cowered in a stall of the Ladies' Lavatory in the BOA International Executive Departure Lounge at Heathrow Terminal Four waiting for liberation. Outside, an angry old lady with a furled umbrella and a moustache rapped on the door.

'I know you're in there, young man, and I know what you're up to. Perverts like you should be locked up.'

Donald, who tended to agree and who, in any case, was locked up as effectively as if he were in Dartmoor, made one more attempt. Wrapping some of the crisp (not medicated) toilet paper around his comb, and sounding like one of the less intelligent Muppets, he said falsetto: 'Madam, I am a woman of post feminist lesbian tendencies. And if you do not go away at once I shall call the police.'

His quest for a femidom had not been a success. He had started in the Duty Free, where a giggling attendant informed him that since Femidoms were zero rated for VAT they didn't stock them. The bookstall contained a selection of magazines designed to make the use of doms, whether femi or con, redundant, and of the small objects of desire there was none to be had. The Pharmacy, which might have been the logical place, told him that since the Femidom had yet to receive the approval of the US Food and Drugs administration, its policy was not to sell them lest one should find its way into the hands, or rather some other part, of a returning US citizen, who would then sue them in the Philadelphia courts for every penny they possessed. And the Medical Centre told him that they only dealt in emergencies such as broken bones – unless he proposed to use a femidom as a splint they could not help.

Finally, Donald decided to try the Ladies' Lavatory. Wrapping a scarf round his head, and looking steadily at the floor, he walked resolutely through the door which, like the gates of the Temple of Diana, should remain resolutely shut to the stronger portion of the human race, at least in times of peace.

Fortunately the lavatory was empty. Donald took a deep breath and looked around. The interior was not dissimilar to the Gentlemen's Lavatory. True, it was pale pink; and for some reason there were no urinals and a smaller choice of condoms. Those that *were* available were flavoured with a more feminine taste, such as strawberry, peach and plum, and offered in more feminine colours, such as strawberry, peach and magenta. There were boxes of pink and blue tissues, and wads of cotton wool, and bunches of dried flowers. On a long marble table by the mirror was a selection of potions, unguents, scents, perfumes, fragrances, lotions, creams, moisturisers, demoisturisers, depiliatory devices, tweezers and driers such as would take a further two decades off an aging film star so that she could star in a remake of Lolita. And finally there was the object of his quest – or Donald Macdonald assumed that it was, the users of femidoms being no doubt of greater linguistic sensitivity than their male counterparts. In solitary splendour by the door was a pink slot machine. And in bold capitals were imprinted on the pink the words 'FEMININE HYGENE'.

Donald inserted his coins, retrieved the packet from the dispenser, and unwrapped it eagerly. It was not a first sight easy to work out how the device was used. He could see how it could be inserted, but not how anything could be inserted into it. And surely cotton wool, however tightly compressed, was not the most effective barrier to the overpopulation of the globe.

It was then that disaster struck. So intent was he on his biological investigations that he did not notice the door opening. Indeed, the first he knew that he was not alone was a sharp pain across the shoulders as he was struck by a furled umbrella. With the same instinctive behaviour as drives a rat up a drainpipe or a ferret up a trouser leg, he rushed for cover. And, twenty minutes later, he was still wrestling with two mysteries – how the femidom worked, and how the hell was he going to catch his flight.

***

CHAPTER 5

In which an aristocratic lady experiences Hungarian hospitality.

Lady Lucinda MacDonald stared incredulously at her new quarters. The long whitewashed building sat low in the peat bog. Green moss grew in damp abundance on the walls; and the door hung half open on broken hinges, secured with a piece of string. A wisp of smoke emerged from a blackened chimney at one gable. Two windows were deeply recessed into the walls by the door; and sheep grazed placidly on the turf roof.

'I cannot possibly stay here,' she expostulated.

'It iss the finest black-house on the island, Ma'am,' said Hamish McTurk. 'And it iss-er snug as a bug-er in a rug-er.' Her anger had made him stammer. 'You will be chust so inside, when the g-gales howl and the rains lash and the thunder roars from p-pole to p-pole.'

'I don't care for buggers, and I don't play rugger. Take me to the Hotel at once.'

'But that will not be possible. The North Uist Hydro Hotel is booked solid with the members of the South Carolina Ladies' Highland Games Team, here for the North Uist and Pabbay Highland Games, and there iss no other lodgings to be had on the island. But my mother, Mistress McTurk of McTurk, will look after you handsomely. No expense will be spared, I assure you, to make your visit a memorable one.'

Lady Lucinda MacDonald was not in good humour. Her heels had sunk into the black peat; and her sheer stockings had snagged on the abundant bushes of gorse and furze. The twins had released her Pekinese dogs *'pour faire pipi'* as Alsace had put it; and the local collies had vociferously objected to this invasion of their territory and chased them off into the gloom. Donald MacDonald had been too busy quizzing Hamish McTurk about Sgt Stripe to pay any attention to domestic details; and the quay hands had, one by one, abandoned Lady Lucinda's trunks to the softer parts of the bog and slunk off to the Public Bar of the Hotel to slake their thirst on pints of beer and large whiskies.

'About the only memorable thing about this visit,' she replied, casting a glance at McTurk which would have turned anyone less rigid than a local government official into jelly, 'will be its brevity.' She looked for support from Donald or the twins; but Donald had been persuaded by Alsace to pursue the dogs, and they were lost somewhere in the bog. So, as a fresh flurry of rain swept in from the Atlantic, she stooped low and entered the dwelling.

There was an overpowering reek of peat smoke and odours of damp woollen socks, long boiled cabbage and rotting fish. As her senses grew accustomed to the gloom she made out three mangy cats, deficient, in varying degrees, in eyes, ears, tails and legs. In a rocking chair by the fire sat an elderly though still elegant woman knitting what looked like Balaclava helmets for the Crimean war.

'Come in, my dear, come in,' she croaked in a voice which Luciano Pavarotti would have eaten whole oxen for, and in an accent which would not have been out of place in the Gellert Hotel, Budapest. 'Make yourself at home, and draw up a chair to the fire. Vere are your vonderful husband, about whom my son has told me so much, and your charming children?'

Donald MacDonald was in fact at that moment pursuing Lorraine across the peat bog; Lorraine was pursuing Mao (the younger of the Pekinese), Mao was pursuing Tse Tung (the elder); and Tse Tung was pursuing Donald. Alsace, who had moral objections to chasing one's tail, was sitting on a peat hag rolling a cigarette and mouthing the words *'espèce de chien'* at a particularly hungry looking collie that was snarling at her feet.

'I have no idea,' said Lady Lucinda, a tear escaping from the corner of her eye despite all the training of Roedean and Girton. 'Donald was following me across the park with the twins and the trunks and the hatboxes and the dogs, and now they're lost in the gloom and I am left like Niobe amid the alien corn or like Ruth, all tears.'

'The other vay round, my dear', said Mrs McTurk, who had a doctorate in English Literature from the University of Hajduboszormeny. 'And it is barley that they grow here for the visky, not corn for the flakes. But never you vorry. Vy don't you come and look at my photographs vile ve vait. This is Hamish at his christening, and this is him at his first communion, and this is him at his bar mitzvah, and this is him in the Robes of Grand Master of Lodge 666 (North Uist), and here he is in the saffron robes of Hare Krishna, and here he is on his appointment as Depute Chief Executive of the Achiltibuie Rural District Council, and here he is after his divorce, and here he is again as a baby. Lovely boy, though I say it myself.'

'Mother, put those away,' said Hamish, who had lifted his kilt and was warming the backs of his knees at the fire.

'Mrs McTurk, I am not interested in your son's rites of passage. I am interested in finding somewhere comfortable to stay.' Lady Lucinda gave Mrs McTurk her most withering stare, like Lady MacBeth wondering whether to offer Duncan another spoonful of porridge at the feast.

'But here are some photographs of his vedding. Such a fine figure of a man he was then, with his kilt and his sporran and his Magyar waistcoat. It was such a pity about his bride. Sharon vas not good enough for him in any vay, vas she Hamish? She refused to let him near her, even on their vedding night. I always told him that if he couldn't find someone like his mother he'd be better to remain a bachelor. But he wouldn't listen; always vas a headstrong boy, even ven he vas little. I remember the time ven...'

But even Mrs McTurk's flow of language could not carry over the noise of two yapping Pekinese, three barking collies, the twins (each yelling in her own adopted tongue) and a swearing Donald MacDonald, who fell through the door simultaneously into a sprawling heap on the floor. *'Ta gueule'* yelled Alsace, who was making a study of French argot but who as yet had an uncertain grasp of registers. *'Halt deinen Mund!'* screamed Lorraine.

'Silence, the lot of you!' Hamish McTurk had decided to take control, and he imbued his voice with all the authority of the Chief Executive of the North Uist Urban District Council. 'I have never seen the like of it, and in my mother's house too! Donald MacDonald of MacDonald, I expected more of you as a senior representative of the

North British Office, and as the younger son of a chiefly family.'

'Hamish, get those lions out off here!' shouted Mrs McTurk, who was suffering from category confusion and had mistaken the Pekinese for animals altogether less fierce.

'They are but dogs, Mother,' replied McTurk, kicking one into the fire. 'We will find them quarters in the byre in a moment. But first, we must offer hospitality to our guests. Never forget that this is a Highland home, despite your Hungarian ancestry.'

To forget that this was a Highland home, and a wee one at that, would not have been easy. Over the peat fire hung a black iron cauldron in which there seethed and bubbled a glutinous liquid from which two or three chicken claws emerged. Above the black leaded mantleshelf was a framed sampler embroidered with the legend 'Hame sweet Hame'. A massive oak sideboard carried an array of bottles and flasks, among which Grolsch, Ouzo, Tequilla, Champagne, Anise and Polish Vodka did not feature. And a selection of ancient armchairs shed horsehair and broken springs into the air.

'You will be having a dram, MacDonald,' commanded McTurk. 'And a cup of tea for your Ladyship, and some lemonade for the children.'

'The children do not like lemonade,' hissed Lady Lucinda, 'it is bad for their teeth. And I myself would prefer a G and T – before, that is, I transfer myself to the Hotel. A large G and T, with ice and lemon.'

'Will you hold your wheesht, woman. You will have tea and like it. Chin and Tonic hass neffer been drunk in this house, and neffer will so long as there's grouse in the heather and herring in the sea. Now drink up, MacDonald, and I'll show you the fax machine. We have every modern convenience in this house, every modern convenience.'

* * *

CHAPTER 6

*In which an inexperienced traveller is terrified by a safety video
and attempts to join the Mile High Club.*

'Will Mrs Hermione Badger please report immediately to the Enquiry Desk on the First Floor, where her son is waiting to meet her.'

For Donald Macdonald, incarcerated in his cubicle by the actions of a manic old woman who was over enthusiastic about the works of Angela Dworkin, it was at least variety. The same message had been repeated five times over the public address system, with increasing urgency and at decreasing intervals: 'Will Donald Macdonald, last remaining passenger to Tokyo, please report immediately to Gate No 42, where his aircraft is waiting to depart.'

The banging of the old woman's umbrella on Donald Macdonald's stall suddenly ceased. 'My son!' Donald heard her say. 'I'd forgotten all about him! Wait here, young man, I shall be back. I want your word of honour that you won't try to escape, you pervert.'

'I give you my word of honour, Mrs. Badger' said Donald in his most unctuous tones. And at last he was free.

Pausing only to retrieve his hand luggage from the Executive Lounge and to take a large slug of gin to steady his nerves, Donald Macdonald rushed headlong in the direction of Gate 42. It was not his day: the escalator was out of order, and Donald had run five yards along the reverse travellator before he realised that his progress was counter-directional as well as counter-intuitive. Heavily laden travellers of all nationalities formed impenetrable knots of humanity in his path, dressed in saris, shell suits, jeans, anoraks, and even the odd three piece suit with watch chain and Panama hat. He only avoided a long argument with an oversized American girl with long blonde hair and a ring in her nose, whose shapeless legs he had grazed with his briefcase, by addressing her as Joan Baez.

'Donald Macdonald,' he announced breathlessly to the transport hostperson at the Gate. 'You've been paging me.'

'Where the hell have you been?' asked the representative of the worlds second favourite airline, scowling at him. 'Do you realise that you've kept 350 people waiting for an hour. We were about to take your luggage off and send the plane without you. Where have you been?' she repeated.

'In the loo,' replied Donald Macdonald truthfully. 'Stomach trouble,' he lied.

'If you are suffering from dysentery, diarrhoea, dysphasia, dyspepsia, dislocated hip, constipation or any other diseases of the lower intestinal tract, British Overseas Airways cannot fly you, and nor will the Japanese allow you to land.'

'I'm not. It's just that I suffer from fear of flying.'

'In that case, you need a stiff drink. Here.'

She handed him a hip flask. 'Take a pull of that. It's cask strength Highland Park from the Scotch Malt Whisky Society. Now where is your boarding card? We're late enough as it is.'

Donald Macdonald took a hearty pull at the flask and choked on the fiery fluid. He reached into his inside pocket for his boarding card. It wasn't there. Nor was it in his other pockets, briefcase, wallet or handbag.

'I...I...er...' he stammered when he had recovered the power of speech. 'I don't appear to have it.'

'What do you mean, you don't appear to have it? Everyone must be in possession of a valid boarding card to progress to the aircraft. Otherwise all kinds of stowaways, highjackers and terrorists might get on board.'

Donald took another pull at the flask. Things were beginning to get on top of him. 'Do I look like a stowaway, highjacker or terrorist? I am a senior civil servant from the North British Office on government business, and I demand to be allowed on board.' His speech, possibly as a result of his last large gin and the slugs of malt whisky, was becoming increasingly slurred; and for some reason the representative of the world's second favourite airline had developed another body about half an inch to the right of her first. She must have been drinking.

'I cannot help that,' her left hand body said. 'No boarding pass, no board. Now either you find it pretty damn quick, or I get your luggage thrown off the flight and it goes without you. What's it to be?'

'Pussy!' Donald said suddenly, remembering that he had given his Boarding Pass to Pussy Galore so that she could check the flight while he went in search of contraceptives.

'Don't you swear at me,' said the right hand version of the representative of the World's second favourite airline.

'Not bloody swearing,' swore Donald. 'Pussy Galore – she's got my boarding pass.'

'And my name's James Bond! If you think I've got time to discuss your fantasies about some dated film from the sixties they show every Christmas... I've got a plane to get airborne.'

'Pussy Galore is a passenger on this flight. I met her in the lounge. She's got my boarding card. At least, I gave it to her to check on the time of the fight.'

'You let your boarding pass out of your possession? And gave it to a complete stranger? How do you know she had a Boarding Card herself? She may have used yours to get on the plane. So we could have a terrorist, highjacker or stowaway.'

'She didn't look like a terrorist or highjacker,' Donald said to the average of the two transport hostpersons. 'And if you can't tell the difference between someone called Pussy Galore and someone called Donald Macdonald, no wonder this isn't the world's favourite airline! Why don't you ask her?'

Five minutes later, Donald Macdonald was ushered with profuse apologies towards the Boeing 757 bound for Tokyo Narita International Airport. As he went through the gate, he saw out of the corner of his eye an angry old woman waving a stick and pursued by a large florid man in a trilby hat and a policeman.

'He gave me his word of honour that he would stay in the cubicle, the despicable pervert!' she was shouting. 'There's no time to lose – there's no knowing what filthiness he might be up to.'

It was then he remembered that he had left the Femidom on the floor of the ladies' loo.

The view that it is better to travel hopefully than to arrive is not, apparently, shared by the 350 passengers of a delayed Jumbo jet which has been held back by a further hour by the non appearance of a single passenger. Or perhaps the 350 passengers were simply wishing for the opportunity to travel hopefully, rather than sitting motionless on the tarmac listening to the excuses of the Captain and the cabin staff, particularly as the air conditioning was not working and the champagne, for First Class passengers only, was warm.

Donald stumbled up the aisle. He had not been conscious of such hostility since he had faced the House of Commons North British Affairs Committee on the great pig grants scandal. Japanese passengers, whose eyelids made glaring impossible, nevertheless contrived to give him looks of considerable malice. The British relaxed their normally stiff upper lips to snarl. An Italian, judging by the cut of his suit, went so far as to shake his fist; and several Frenchmen threatened, in fluent though heavily accented English, to secure Britannia's removal from the European Union (an organisation which Donald was in the habit of calling the Foreign Market) for having sought to veto the departure of the Flight.

Only Pussy Galore seemed pleased to see him. She had managed to secure them two seats together at the very rear of Business Class, next to the bulkhead. A perfect place for an attempt on the Mile High Club, if only he had remembered the Femidom.

'Shorry,' he slurred as he lowered himself into his seat. 'Unavoidably delayed. Needed to shend an urgent fax to headquarters.'

'That's OK,' she replied 'though the Captain's being getting a little impatient. I've had a chance to catch up on my reading.' She showed him her copy of *Small World*. 'Very funny book, and Howard Ringbaum is particularly finely drawn. His attempts to join the Mile High Club are hilarious.'

'Mile High Club?' asked Donald, whose insobriety had not, as yet, over-ridden his deviousness. 'What on earth is that?'

'It's not on earth at all. It's a club for persons who've done it in the sky.'

'Done what?' asked Donald, feigning innocence.

But her response was interrupted by the Captain. 'We should like to apologise once more,' he announced in the educated cockney favoured by airline pilots around the globe, 'to all our passengers bar one on this flight to Tokyo Narita International Airport, for the delay in departure. This was caused by events beyond our control: fog, and the failure of one of our passengers to show. But everyone is now on board, and we are about to close the doors and the hatches and push back for takeoff. Could you please watch the Safety Video carefully, ensure your seats are in the upright position, and fasten your seatbelts.'

Despite, or perhaps because of, his increasing intoxication, Donald found that his attempts to fasten his seatbelt were hampered by the fact that something other than his seat was in the upright position.

'Can I help you, Sir?' British Overseas Airways, being an equal opportunities employer, recruited their female transport hostpersons for their delicate beauty and femininity and their male transport hostpersons, or stewards, as the males themselves insisted on being called, on the same principles. The steward, whose tight uniform enhanced the lissom grace of his body, and whose blond hair and eyebrows and neatly trimmed moustache enhanced a tan which could only have been acquired on some tropical island or the sunbed of the Barnsley Gymnasium and Massage Parlour, leaned over Donald and reached for his buckles.

'Ooh!' he gasped, 'Sir is in something of a state!' He gazed at Donald with baby blue eyes. 'Flying takes some of us like that. If Sir would like to come to the Galley after takeoff, I'm sure we could find something to relax him.' He deftly buckled the belt, and minced forward in search of other conquests.

Donald glared at his retreating back and settled in his seat to watch the safety video. Unlike most passengers, who had seen it many times before and used the time to read their newspapers, pick their noses, boot up their laptops in defiance of airline regulations, and complete their crosswords, Donald viewed it with the freshness of the first night of a Hollywood disaster movie. He saw himself struggling to release his seat belt as the plane slid off the runway in flames. He saw himself removing his fountain pen and other sharp objects from his pockets and sliding down the inflatable escape shute before rushing from the exploding aircraft. He saw himself stubbing out his cigarette as the aircraft decompressed and reaching for the oxygen mask which materialised mysteriously and automatically at his nose, before tugging firmly three times to release the oxygen and reaching over to assist a small child beside him. He saw himself struggling to find the lifejacket beneath his seat, tying it with the regulation double bow, and bobbing about on the vast ocean while he blew on his whistle to warn fishermen of his presence and the little light flashed to attract passing satellites. But there was one thing that he didn't understand. He pressed the Call Button and the steward hurried to his side.

'Can I be of assistance, Sir?' he lisped, glad of the opportunity to further their acquaintanceship so soon.

'Yes,' said Donald, 'Where are the parachutes?'

'Ladies and Gentlemen,' announced the public address system when the safety video had finished. 'This is the Captain speaking again. I'm afraid that I have some bad news for you. I had been hoping that we'd be airborne within five minutes. But when we closed the luggage lockers a red warning light came on. I'm afraid that we've got to ask the engineers to check it over. We'll push back from the stand; and I've asked the cabin crew to open the bar and serve you with drinks. We'll get you off as soon as we can.'

Three hours later the aircraft was at last on its way. The transport hostpersons had plied their passengers with beverage alcohol; and Donald Macdonald's steward, no doubt with some ulterior motive of his own, had been eager to offer him the selection of champagne, claret, brandy, calvados and Scotch whisky which Donald felt appropriate to a senior civil servant in Business Class. Pussy Galore, having told Donald that a couple of glasses of wine always made her feel randy, confined herself to a half bottle of Burgundy and a further study of Small World. Dinner, served shortly after takeoff, was criticised by Pussy as the usual airline pap and praised by Donald as a gastronomic experience such as he had rarely encountered; he had been particularly impressed at the assiduous way in which the steward smoothed his napkin over his lap and kept his glass filled with a delicious red wine from the Napa Valley. As the liqueurs came round – Donald had settled for a very large Drambuie – Pussy leaned over to him and whispered 'You know, it might be rather exciting to join the Mile High Club. I've got a contraceptive in my bag.' But the lights were already dimming for the first feature film, and Donald Macdonald was blissfully, drunkenly asleep.

* * *

CHAPTER 7

In which the plot thickens.

It was eight thirty in the morning, and Donald MacDonald was not at his best. He had spent one of the most uncomfortable nights of his life in a bed which contrived at the same time to be too soft (at the edge) and too hard (in the middle), and which, in Hebridean style, he had been compelled to share not only with Lady Lucinda, but also with the twins and the Pekinese dogs. The twins had kept up a conversation all night in the curious mixture of French and German which they used for private conversation. The Pekinese had been relatively peaceful, as befitted well-trained lap dogs, except on the frequent occasions when Mrs McTurk's cats had tried to join them. And Lady Lucinda had alternated between weeping (which made the bed even damper than it was before) and rehearsing the names of all the divorce lawyers with whom she was on Christian, or rather fore name terms. What little sleep Donald had was broken by the rattle of rain against the cracked glass and the howl of dogs chained in the yard. At five o'clock he abandoned all thought of rest and fled to a chair by the now dead peat fire, where he finished Hamish McTurk's bottle and gave further thought to his revenge.

Sir Terence Mould, assisted by the incompetent Dibbs, had posted him to North Uist instead of Tokyo. Sir Terence was determined to win the Feelgood Project – a major Japanese investment which would create many hundreds of jobs in the medical electronics sector – against strong opposition from the Irish, the Welsh, the French, the Americans and, for all Donald knew, the Basques. Sir Terence Mould was equally determined that the Minister's proposed amalgamation of the North Uist and Benbecula Urban District Councils should not proceed, presumably because Sir Redbreast Footman, the Secretary of the Cabinet, was concerned at the precedent which this would set for England and Wales. And in both cases Sir Terence was inspired, if that was the word, by Lady Mould's ambition. For Lady Mould wished to revisit the Palace to see her husband invested with the Grand Cross of Knighthood of the Order of the Bath.

It followed that in neither project should Sir Terence be allowed to have his way. And it was also essential that he, Donald MacDonald, should be seen as entirely innocent of any attempts to thwart Sir Terence's ambitions. Donald Macdonald, the rude mechanical from DAFT who had been posted to Tokyo in his place, and Sgt Stripe, the sinophobe from the SAS whom he had met on the ferry, would provide both the mechanism and the alibi. Together, and entirely unwittingly, they would abort the biggest inward investment project that Scotland had ever known, secure the amalgamation of the North Uist and Benbecula Urban District Councils, and destroy the career of Sir Terence Mould. And he, Donald MacDonald, would be an innocent and a happy man.

Donald reached for pen and paper and began to compose a long fax to Donald Macdonald, care of the Origami Intercontinental Hotel, Tokyo.

Hamish McTurk locked the door of his office and gestured Donald into a faded leather chair. 'You'll be having a wee refreshment before we get down to work?' he asked.

A wee refreshment was the last thing that Donald wanted. After plotting his revenge he had fallen into an uneasy sleep in Mrs McTurk's armchair, and had dreamed feverishly of Sgt Stripe chasing Japanese sumo wrestlers across the machair while the twins attacked small black dogs and Lady Lucinda attacked him. The Pekinese had wakened him with the dawn; and Mrs McTurk's breakfast of porridge, black pudding, white pudding, gulls' eggs, mushrooms, steak, chips, fried potatoes, Arbroath smokies and kippers lay heavily on his stomach. What he could do with was half a gallon of black coffee.

Hamish McTurk turned to his safe and, after three abortive attempts and a considerable amount of swearing, succeeded in opening it. The safe, like McTurk's desk, was entirely innocent of paper – unless you counted the labels on the whisky bottles which filled every corner. McTurk selected a bottle with care and placed it in his empty in-tray.

'Speyside,' he said. 'A good breakfast whisky.'

'Actually,' said Donald, 'I'd like a coffee.'

'Coffee!' spluttered McTurk, taking two tumblers from his desk drawer. 'Don't you paper pushers from Edinburgh believe in supporting local products?'

McTurk, to judge by the hairiness of his tweed suit, the mounted and stuffed trout, salmon, grouse and deer on the panelled walls of his office, and the size of the drams which he poured into the two glasses, was a staunch supporter. Donald looked at the glass with something approaching horror. He habitually drank grapefruit juice at breakfast, G and T before lunch, dry sherry before dinner, claret during and port or brandy after, and whisky only on MacBrayne's ferries. But he would have to humour McTurk if he was to use him as a tool in his plot. He lifted the tumbler. 'Do you have any ice?' he asked.

'Ice!' repeated McTurk in incredulous tones. ' Of course I have no ice. Where do you think you are, the cocktail bar at the Ritz?'

Donald could not think of a better place to be. 'I believe in supporting local products,' he said.

'I will thank you not to insult your hosts,' said McTurk. He swallowed his whisky angrily and refilled his glass. 'Now, I think that you should explain precisely what your mission is.'

Donald MacDonald took a minute sip and felt the warmth flood down his gut and begin the third world war on his breakfast. He composed his voice into bureaucratic mode and sought the appropriate words to convey with appropriate dignity the Minister's proposals for the amalgamation of the North Uist and Benbecula Urban District Councils.

'I have it in charge from the Minister to explore the possibility of securing an amalgamation of the two Urban District Councils in this area. To that end, the Minister has asked me to report on your finances, your activities, and your efficiency. Having made a report on the situation that pertains in North Uist, I am instructed to proceed to Benbecula to do the same there.'

Hamish McTurk sat through this speech in silence while his face turned first pink, then magenta, then purple, and he took short angry gulps of his whisky. 'But this iss preposterous,' he said at last. 'There hass been an Urban District Council in North Uist since the days of Bonnie Prince Charlie. The Council's silver dates back to the time of the Spanish Armada. We have the lowest Council Tax in the whole of Scotland, and have assiduously carried out government policy in privatising our refuse collection and school meals – my brother-in-law hass both contracts. And besides...' McTurk paused dramatically, '...the Kirk would never allow it. In Benbecula they are Catholics.'

'I hear what you say,' said Donald, employing one of the looser phrases from his armoury. 'But I fear that you are overlooking one vital point.'

'What iss that? We will never accept the immaculate contraception in North Uist.'

'When the Councils are amalgamated there will only be one Chief Executive. And anyone who doesn't cooperate with me will certainly not be in the running.'

By lunchtime, five members of the South Carolina Ladies' Highland Games Team had been rehoused in Mrs McTurk's black-house, and Donald, Lady Lucinda, the twins and the Pekinese had moved into sumptuous accommodation in the North Uist Hydro Hotel. McTurk, as required by Donald, had arranged a varied programme of visits and meetings to enable Donald to get the flavour of the work of the NUUDC and the BUDC. He was to start with a meeting with Provost Farquhar Urquhart, and would spend the afternoon as Guest of Honour at the North Uist and Pabbay Highland Games. The following day he would make some visits to Benbecula, where he would meet Dudley Scrope, the young and inexperienced Chief Executive. He would return to North Uist for varied confrontations with what McTurk described as 'local economic interests, mostly not economically active'. The twins would attend the local schools (Lorraine in North Uist and Alsace in Benbecula); and Lady Lucinda was to be entertained by Mrs McTurk.

'It iss sure that I am that this will meet your requirements,' said McTurk. After Donald had left, he spent a fruitful half hour on the telephone to Dudley Scrope explaining that the Minister did not trust Donald MacDonald and reversed every recommendation that he made, so that it was in all their interests to appear as inefficient as possible. Then he polished the final details of the North Uist programme and poured himself another large dram, confident that he would become the first Chief Executive of the new Benbecula and North Uist Metropolitan Council.

* * *

CHAPTER 8

*In which one of our heroes finds it difficult to pass water
and even more difficult to pass through immigration control.*

'Will you have another drink? We land in fifteen minutes.' The
steward bent solicitously over Donald, who was dozing fitfully at
15,000 feet above the Sea of Japan, and adjusted his napkin.

Donald jerked awake. A drink was the last thing that he wanted.
Two hours earlier, after sleeping deeply throughout two films –
Airplane I and *Airplane II* – he had woken with a raging thirst and an
incipient headache, and had concluded that champagne and honey
roasted peanuts would give him a lift. They had not. The four tiny
lavatories serving Business Class passengers were occupied; and
Donald had spent an uncomfortable ten minutes in the galley resisting
the blandishments of the steward and trying not to throw up.

'Airsickness takes a lot of people this way,' said the steward. 'I
always find that a gentle massage of the neck helps. Would you like
me to have a go – Mumsy always finds it a great comfort when she
flies with me.'

Donald declined. 'But we can't have you sick in the galley', the
steward insisted. 'Perhaps a tummy massage would be better, the
effect is quicker that way.'

At last one of the lights flashed from 'Occupied' to 'Vacant', and
Pussy Galore emerged with fresh pink lipstick and carefully coiffed
hair. 'I do feel fresher after freshening up,' she said tautologically.
Donald didn't stay to debate the point; and in the claustrophobic space
of the lavatory the battling fragrances of Chanel No Five, Eau de
Cologne, Gentlemen's After Shave lotion, and Ladies' toilet water,
combined to act as diuretic, enema and purgative combined. He

allowed nature to take its three courses, and passed out with his head on the bowl.

He was roused twenty minutes later by an insistent knocking on the door. For a moment he thought himself back in the ladies' loo of the Executive Departure Lounge, besieged by Mrs Hermione Badger; but the voice of the steward brought himself back to earth, or rather to air. 'I say, are you all right in there?' it asked gently. Another voice cut in, deeper and angry. 'I have been waiting twenty minutes while some wretched woman puts her face on. Why can't BOA provide separate facilities for men?'

'Ooh, that's a nice idea,' Donald heard the steward reply. 'Though I'm sure we want the ladies to look their best when they arrive in Japan. But we men like to look good too, don't we, Sir?'

Donald dragged himself upright, resisted without difficulty the temptation to put Gentlemen's After Shave lotion on his pulse points (why didn't they have Ladies' After Shave lotion? he thought), and glanced briefly at his reflection in the mirror. He certainly didn't look his best. His five o'clock shadow, or whatever was the equivalent in local time, enhanced the pallor of his skin; and the bags under his eyes would have been rejected as too large for hand luggage had he presented them at check-in. His incipient headache had blossomed into a steam hammer.

'Sleep well?' asked Pussy Galore when he regained his seat. 'I did, after the films, though the journey could have been made more interesting. You were miles away, although sadly not miles high.'

'It's not too late,' said Donald tentatively, although the prospect of joining an exclusive club seemed rather less attractive than it had the previous evening. Indeed, he was likely to require an injection of testosterone such as would disqualify him from the competition if he were to attain the requisite performance level. But at this point the lights came on and the Chief Cabin Attendant Hostperson announced that breakfast was about to be served.

'Tough cookie,' said Pussy Galore.

'Buck's fizz,' whispered the steward into his ear. At least he hadn't given up.

Donald consumed a breakfast of croissants ('They remind me of the Left Bank, where I had such a wonderful weekend with my friend,' said the steward); lightly boiled eggs ('Ooh, the yoke is running down your chin; would you like me to cut you some little soldiers?'); and about half a pint of Bucks Fizz ('It does wonders for your hormone balance'). He rejected the stewards offer to guide him through the in-flight exercises in the Galley ('They are so relaxing') but allowed him to fill out his immigration card, and fell into a fitful doze, interrupted at regular intervals by offers of more drinks.

Donald devoted the final fifteen minutes of the flight to putting on his shoes. For some reason they had shrunk; and the plastic shoe horn which shared the interior of his in-flight courtesy travel wash bag with after shave lotion, body lotion, toothbrush, toothpaste and shaving kit didn't seem to help. He trapped the fingers of his right hand behind his left heel, and he sent his shoe skittering down the aisle while trying to release them. 'Cinderella, I presume,' said the steward as he returned it. 'Can I be your Prince Charming?' Donald finally resorted to removing his socks and greasing his feet with the body lotion; and he squeezed his feet into his brogues at the moment when the plane touched down and the Chief Cabin Attendant Hostperson was saying, with as much right as a guest greeting another guest at a country house weekend, 'Ladies and Gentlemen, welcome to Tokyo Narita International Airport.'

Donald retrieved his hand baggage from the overhead locker, bade farewell to Pussy Galore, and made his way slowly onto Japanese territory. Everywhere there were bowing Japanese in immaculate uniforms or dark blue suits and white shirts. Everywhere there were strange symbols, as incomprehensible to Donald as the task for which he had come to Japan. Everywhere was the noise and bustle of an international airport, assaulting Donald's, by then, highly delicate sensibilities. He realised that he would need a lavatory – and fast.

Donald was of the school that believed that to communicate with foreigners, you needed simply to increase your decibel level. He searched out one of the uniformed Japanese, positioned his mouth about six inches from his ear, and shouted 'Excuse me, please – could you direct me to the nearest lavatory?'

The Japanese jumped a foot into the air, then recovered his composure and bowed politely.

'Solly?'

'Lavatory!' shouted Donald. 'Restroom! Bathroom!

Convenience! WC!'

A large woman in a Welsh bonnet and buckled shoes, arguing loudly with her companion about the performance of their National Rugby Team at the most recent International at Murrayfield, looked pityingly at Donald. The Japanese still looked puzzled.

'Please?' he said.

'Urinal! Bog! Jakes! Water Closet!'

The Japanese smiled with incomprehension.

'Toilet,' said Donald quietly. Since joining DAFT he had learned that the toilet word was never used in polite society; but desperate straits need desperate remedies, and things, if not entirely straight, were becoming desperate.

'*Hai*, toirettu,' said the Japanese, a smile of understanding lighting up his features. 'Toirettu shown by toirettu sign.' He pointed at the battery of graphic non-communication lining the walls of the transit corridor. 'Man has legs, no?'

'Thank you,' said Donald, attempting to return the Japanese's bow. But the pain in his bladder forced him to straighten up; and he rushed for a door with the relevant sign.

A tiny Japanese woman was standing inside the restroom. Donald retreated as fast as he had entered; perhaps, he thought, the signs were reversed in Japan. The referee in the sumo wrestling which he had watched on TV to brief himself for his visit did, after all, wear a skirt. Japanese women, unlike their Chinese neighbours, did not however wear trousers – so perhaps in Japan they used the same sign to distinguish between male and female lavatories. But if that was the case, they should surely use the skirt and not the trouser legs.

Donald wished that he had paid more attention to his logic classes at Glasgow University. That might help him solve an urgent problem in semiotics. But at that point a group of dark suited Japanese businessmen pushed past him through the door; and Donald decided that empiricism rather than logic should rule his actions and followed them in.

The tiny Japanese woman was washing the floor; and the Japanese businessmen positioned themselves strategically in front of the porcclain, still conversing in animated tones. The fall in the Tokyo stockmarket, Donald imagined, or the latest innovation in micro electronics. Donald stood beside them and tried to ignore the woman, and the flashing red electronic eye which for all he knew was photographing his performance, or rather non-performance, for purposes of medical research. Not being the product of an English public school, he had always found it difficult to pee in company, whatever the pressure on his bladder, and the difficulty was compounded by light-headedness caused, he presumed, by jet lag. At last he gave up the struggle and, hoping that none of the Japanese had noticed his failure, stepped back in embarrassment from the urinal. As he did so, the bowl was flushed automatically, and his bladder responded with a reflex action. He regained the porcelain with not a moment to spare, and violently emptied his bladder, splashing his trousers and shoes as he did so.

The Japanese woman looked up and him and grinned with toothless gums. She said a few words in a high pitched sing song tone, and the Japanese businessmen stared at him and giggled behind the backs of their hands. Not the most propitious introduction to his first foreign country, he thought.

'How long you stay in Tokyo?' asked the immigration officer. Donald had waited in line for fifty minutes as the Japanese bureaucracy painstakingly checked passports and visas to exclude those who wished to enter the land of the rising yen in order to smuggle drugs, foment rebellion, promote the views of the Red Brigade, assassinate the Emperor, join a sumo wrestling stable, or sell legitimate goods on the home market in competition with Japanese producers. He had spent the first five minutes mentally redesigning the layout of the Immigration Hall in order to increase the rate of throughput, and the next twenty wondering why, as usual, he had chosen the slowest moving queue. At last he had reached the head, and had waited a further twenty minutes while the Immigration Officer assured himself that the Phillipino Grandmother seeking permission to enter ahead of him was not Daniel Cohn Bendit or Carlos the Jackal. As a government official who was subject to continuous scrutiny under the Citizen's Charter, Donald did not take kindly to being kept waiting by officials of another State who seemed to be even less efficient than himself; and his patience was running short.

'One week,' he replied.

'But Immigration Form say one year,' said the Official. 'For one year you require visa and work permit.'

'One week,' repeated Donald, remembering that his Immigration Form had been filled out by the steward. 'There must be some mistake.'

'If form say one year, passport need visa and work permit for one year. You here for business?'

'Yes,'said Donald, 'government business.'

'Ah, so, government business. You Minister of the Crown? If so, you must go to VIP Suite.' Japanese officials were no less keen to pass the buck than their occidental counterparts.

'I'm a senior civil servant.'

'*So des ne*? But senior civil servants need work permit for stay of one year. Which no granted unless diplomatist. You diplomatist? Diplomatists usually wear socks.'

'I'm a home civil servant,' said Donald.

'If at home, why in Japan?'

'For discussions with a Japanese company about investment in Scotland.'

'*Ah so*, Scotlandu! Whisky, golf, fishing. Very beautiful country, just like Japan. We have paddy fields, you have Loch Nest! But why you need one year for your discussions?'

'One week,' stressed Donald, emphasising the point by raising one finger in the air.

'No need get angry,' said the Immigration Officer. 'Immigration Card say one year. Rook!'

Donald rooked down quickly at the card. What it gained in elegance it lacked in accuracy. The steward had filled it out in green ink and a large effeminate hand with many whorls, loops and exclamation marks. Donald had no interest in staying for one year, but nor was his home address the House of Lords and his Tokyo address the Imperial Palace. His business was indeed to talk to Japanese companies, but to describe it as developing closer relationships with senior executives on a deeply personal level ran at the least the risk of misinterpretation. Nor was he a trader in intimate leatherwear.

'I am afraid that there are some mistakes in this card,' he said.

'I... I was not feeling at my best when I filled it out. Perhaps I could fill out another.'

'Japanese not like mistakes. Japanese quality 100% right 100% first time! Your first time in Japan?'

'Yes,' said Donald. 'If, that is, you let me in.'

'Europeans learn by their mistakes. So you learn! Japanese not make mistakes. I lisk mistake if I let you in. Total Quality say keep out!' The immigration officer paused and looked at Donald through half closed eyes. There was a long pause. 'Howevah,' he said at last, 'on this occasion I take lisk. Next time, not so rucky!' He stapled the Immigration Form into Donald's passport, stamped it, and waved Donald onto Japanese territory.

Donald waited a further hour for his suitcase to appear on the carousel: it arrived second to last, still with its red 'Priority Baggage' label tied to the handle. He spent ten minutes explaining to the Customs Officials that the fact that he was sock-less did not mean that he was attempting to import prohibited vegetable substances such as chick-peas, lentils or nut cutlets. Finally, he emerged into the Arrivals Hall at six fifty pm local time, to find a tall Japanese in a chauffeur's uniform holding up his name on a pole.

'Mistah Macdonard,' said the Japanese. 'Mistah MacRerran from Tokyo Office of Locate in North Blitain sent me here to meet you. Mistah MacRerran hope you had preasant journey.'

* * *

CHAPTER 9

In which very little happens.

'Come in, Mr Mackenzie, come in,' said Provost Farquhar Urquhart, gesturing Donald MacDonald into his office. 'And you, McGurk, you'd better join us, I suppose.'

'MacDonald' 'McTurk' said MacDonald and McTurk simultaneously.

'What's that? Don't all speak at once! You first, MacTavish.'

'I am Donald MacDonald of the North British Office,' enunciated Donald slowly and distinctly, like Professor Higgins initiating Eliza Doolittle into the finer points of Received Pronunciation.

'Ah, the National Lottery Office,' said the Provost. 'And you, McSprent? Don't tell me. You are our Town Clerk.'

'Chief Executive. And the name's McTurk.'

'Chust so, chust so.'

The Provost was a man of venerable years, sporting a long and unkempt white beard, pebble glasses, a waistcoat resembling in colour and texture the peat bog whence it came, and a long coat of Harris Tweed inherited from his great grandfather. His office has last been redecorated in the year in which his coat was woven. Portraits of former Provosts lined the dark panelled walls. Each was of venerable years, and each sported a long, unkempt white beard, pebble spectacles, a waistcoat resembling in colour and texture the peat bog whence it came, and coats of a cut at least two generations before the subject had held office. A peat fire smouldered dully in the grate; and the stuffed and mounted heads of a herd of moth eaten deer glared balefully from the wall opposite the window. The grate and the good, thought Donald.

'It will be having a glass of claret that you will,' said the Provost. 'I do not hold with this crofters' habit of dramming from morn until nightfall. McFirk, you will be after finding a bottle in the clock.'

McTurk opened the door of the longcase clock by the Provost's desk and extracted a bottle of 1959 Chateau Margaux. 'Let no one suggest that the ratepayers of North Uist do not get value for money,' intoned the Provost, as if quoting from some ancient election address. 'You will find a corkscrew in the mouth of the third deer to the right.'

'Shouldn't you decant it and give it time to breathe?' gasped Donald, aghast at the Provost's treatment of one of the finest products of the oenological arts.

'Not at all, not at all,' responded the Provost. 'Never let it be said that we in the Western Isles do not act promptly when the time is ripe. It iss a calumny to suggest that in Gaelic we have no word to convey the urgency of the word *manyana*.'

McTurk splashed the wine into three half pint mugs which he took from the horns of the twelve pointer to the far right of the herd, and the Provost extracted a can of diet coke from his desk drawer and offered it round. 'I find that the diet coke brings out the bouquet better than the regular,' he explained, adding a liberal dose to his mug and stirring it with his finger.

'Not for me, Provost,' said McTurk. 'I prefer Ardbeg Single Malt from the Isle of Islay. Diet Coke iss not quite peaty enough.' He extracted a hip flask from an inside pocket and fortified his wine.

Donald sought to chambray the precious fluid with the warmth of his hands, and conjured up mental pictures of vineyards under the hot suns of Bordeaux. He'd get even with Sir Terence Mould if it were the last thing he did.

'Provost, I think we should get down to business,' he said. 'I am here to discuss proposals for the amalgamation of the North Uist and Benbecula Urban District Councils.'

'Ah yes, the railway,' responded the Provost. 'It hass long been my ambition to amalgamate the two islands with a system of railways such as they have between Kyle of Lochalsh and Inverness. But I am not sure whether we should have a tunnel or a bridge. What do you propose?'

Donald raised his voice. 'We are not here to discuss railways. We are here to discuss local government reform.'

'Absolutely,' said the Provost. 'We shall have to reform the track laid by my Great Grandfather, Proffost McPhee' – he pointed at one of the venerable portraits – if we are to take steam trainss of the weight required by a modern railway system.'

'Local government reform!' shouted Donald.

'Local stations are essential,' said the Provost. 'It iss not the TGV we are looking for, nor even the Bullet Train – they would not approve of that on Benbecula at all, at all.' He took a deep draught from his mug.

McTurk was looking increasingly uncomfortable. It was not the tradition in the North Uist Urban District Council for officials to contradict their political masters; and he owed his present position to vigorous support for the Provost's inter-rail project at his appointment interview. Yet he owed his future to Donald MacDonald, who was rapidly losing patience. He did a rapid mental calculation, then, under pretext of replenishing the Provost's mug, added a substantial quantity of Ardbeg.

'Mr MacDonald iss here to discuss the amalgamation of the Councils,' he said slowly and distinctly. 'The marriage, so to speak, of North Uist and Benbecula.'

The Provost smiled a broad smile. 'Ah, a wedding,' he said. 'There iss nothing like a Highland wedding. We were drunk for five days together at my great grand-daughter's nuptials. Except, perhaps for a wake.'

'So you favour the amalgamation?' asked McTurk.

'Of course, of course. Now, will you have another drink?'

* * *

CHAPTER 10

*In which a Scottish official is instructed in the rules
of Japanese business etiquette.*

'Welcome to Origami Intercontinental Hotel,' said the obsequious booking clerk at Reception. 'You have been assigned to Room 1826 on the eighteenth floor of the Tower. Many fine views await you there. Also, many messages. Management of Origami Intercontinental Hotel hope you have very nice stay.'

Donald Macdonald hoped likewise. He was feeling uncommonly tired with, he supposed, the effects of what his driver had insisted in calling jet rag. It made his surroundings appear clear as a spring day in the mountains, and at the same time slightly out of synch, like a view seen in a broken wing mirror. After a desultory attempt at conversation, in which he was baffled by his driver's fluent but incomprehensible English, he had spent the rest of the interminable crawl from Narita to Central Tokyo studying the briefing papers for the Feelgood Project and becoming increasingly apprehensive about the task which had been assigned to him.

The briefing papers, which had been prepared by the Tokyo Office of LOIN (Locate in North Britain), revealed that the Feelgood Project was a major industrial development which the conglomerate Omeiwaku Denki Corporation (ODC) wished to push offshore. While Scotland was thought to be in the running, there was major competition from the Welsh, the Irish, the French, the Spanish and the Californians. All were offering substantial subsidies, apart from the Californians who hoped to win the project through a combination of sun, surf, sex and the support of Omeiwaku Denki Inc (US), or ODIOUS as they were known to their competitors.

Faced with this competition, LOIN had little to offer but an environment scarred by years of industrial dereliction, a workforce marred through years of alcohol abuse, and so called state aids reduced to a minimum by a parsimonious Treasury. But the President of ODC was known to be an afficionado of golf, fishing and Scotch. And Sir Terence Mould had staked his career on winning the project for North Britain and for Albert Herring, the newly elected Scottish First Minister.

Donald turned again to the executive summary and conclusion:

> *'I do not rate the chances of our winning this project for North Britain particularly highly. Indeed, if I were a betting man, which I am not, I would not rate it at all. But we have strengths, and I recommend that we should play to them. In particular, we should*
>
> a) *emphasise the importance of Scotch Whisky, golf and fishing;*
>
> b) *offer a location as far as possible from industrial dereliction, but with good transport links to the South and Europe;*
>
> c) *undertake a programme of misinformation in relation to our competitors;*
>
> d) *offer grant at three times the level authorised by Treasury; we can sort out the details later.'*

'I agree,' Sir Terence had noted. 'The NBO must win this project in order to secure the approval of the Scottish Parliament to our proposals to raise income tax in order to fund the civil service pay rise. LOIN must win the project at all costs.'

The Director of LOIN had been even more direct. 'Win this project,' he had told Donald, 'or the new Trophy for the Scotland-Japan Golf Tournament will be made out of your balls.'

'Prease, this way,' said the Bellboy, grasping Donald's two cases in his hands and lodging his brief case and his grip under his armpits. 'Many walk to lift, no?' And he walked off at a rapid pace through the crowded lobby.

Everywhere, to Donald's surprise, there were Japanese. Japanese women in kimonos stood smiling beside dour men in dark suits and white shirts while their elderly parents took photographs. Salarymen with bulging briefcases rushed to meetings where they plotted world economic domination for their companies. Little boys in samurai costume burst into loud tears on being refused a fourth ice cream. Young women in western dress sat at tiny tables drinking coffee, their fat knees pressed tightly together below the hems of their mini skirts.

'Follow, yes please,' said the Bellboy, seeing that Donald was falling behind. 'Not far now!'

Their route took them along a thickly carpeted passage. On one side were store fronts, displaying in their windows all the riches of the occident – Cartier watches, Armani suits, Louis Vuitton luggage, Hennessy Cognac. One held a score or so of impressionist paintings, the points of light in the lavender fields or on the slowly flowing waters of the Seine echoing the rows of noughts on their price tags. To the other side of the passage was a coffee shop where yet more Japanese plotted world domination for their companies, or the next golf outing. Everyone had inscrutable eyes and black patent leather hair.

At last the passage narrowed and took a sharp turn to the right. A uniformed girl stood by the lift. As Donald and the Bellboy approached, she smiled insincerely behind her hand and bowed. Donald, eager to learn the social customs which would help him negotiate the Feelgood project and having been brought up to respect women, bowed lower. The girl bowed lower still. Donald, not to be outdone, bowed still further. The girl, who owed her position to the transfer of her predecessor from bootlicking to bootblacking for showing insufficient respect to the guests, bowed yet further, striking her head against Donald's stomach.

'Say, what is all this? You some nodding dawg on the back window of a Buick, or what?'

The American was, as his countrymen would say, a person of size. His neck bulged over the collar of his button down off white shirt. His stomach bulged over the belt of his off white pants. (Donald had always wondered why Americans called trousers pants, so that they had to call pants panties.) His chest bulged within his off white jacket. Little beads of sweat moistened his brow, which bulged over his bulbous eyes, and which he mopped from time to time with an off white handkerchief.

Donald straightened himself. The lift attendant and Bellboy bowed for a last time, then ushered Donald and the American into the lift.

'Quaint country,' said the American. 'Think they can dominate the world by bowing at it. Dwight Dildenschneider, CIA.'

'CIA?' asked Donald. 'I thought that you kept quiet about that kind of thing.'

'Hell no! Can't do the business if you don't advertise yourself. Only way we get the Japs on side is through plenty of sex, sand, surf and sun. If you've got it, flaunt it.' Dwight Dildenschneider shook his hips, as if to demonstrate the point. His stomachs wobbled ominously.

'But aren't you at risk of being shot? I mean, spies and all...'

'What do you take me for, Central Intelligence or something? I'm Director of the Californian Investment Agency. We attract Japanese companies to California. Not much risk of getting shot in that business, unless some goddam Limey's trying to steal a project from under our snatch. Say, where you from?'

'Donald Macdonald, from the...'

'Excuse, Sir,' interrupted the Bellboy. 'Your floor.'

'See you for a drink, Donald Macdonald,' said Dwight Dildenschneider. 'Have a good day.'

Donald left the lift feeling slightly annoyed. It would have been good to exchange notes with someone in the same business. Dwight Dildenschneider might even have been prepared to teach him a trick or two. But no doubt they would catch up with each other later.

Donald's room was smaller than he had expected. The Bellboy proudly showed him the switch to control the lighting, the panel to control the heating, the regulator to control the air conditioning, the remote control to control the television, the buttons to control the telephone, and the bell to summons the Bellboy. He opened and closed the curtains using the electronic sensor. Finally, he demonstrated that it was unnecessary to flush the loo – the simple action of sitting down and standing up was enough to do the trick.

'Many technology, no?' said the Bellboy.

'But what if I don't sit down?' asked Donald, wondering about the anatomy of the Japanese male.

'Solly,' said the Bellboy, perplexed. 'Don't all gaijin sit down?'

He had obviously been misinformed about the anatomy of the Western male.

'Never mind,' said Donald. 'I was told that there were messages for me.'

'*Ah so*, many faxes. Here on table, beside generous gift from management of Origami Intercontinental Hotel. Thank you, Sir, thank you.'

And the Bellboy departed, bowing his way backwards out of the room like an Ambassador taking his leave of the Sultan, and smiling behind his hand as he went.

The generous gift from the Management of the Origami Intercontinental Hotel was a bowl of exotic fruit such as Donald had never before seen, and several sachets of green tea. Beside them was a pile of envelopes. Donald took the top one and slit it open with his thumb.

> '*Management of Origami Intercontinental Hotel welcomes Donald Macdonald to Origami Intercontinental Hotel and hopes he will have a pleasant stay. Why not try massage (extension 324), room service (extension 325), room service massage (extension 69) or one of our excellent restaurants...*'

Donald put it aside, and slit open the next. It was from Stuart MacLellan, the head of LOIN's office in Tokyo, and said simply, '*Welcome, boss. Lobby bar. 8 pm.*' Next was a rant from Sir Terence Mould, impressing on him the imperative need for success in securing the Feelgood Project and threatening him with dire consequences if he failed. And finally there was a long telefax from Donald MacDonald, North British Department of Industry, care of the North Uist Hydro Hotel.

Donald Macdonald did not know Donald MacDonald well. In fact, he had only met him on two occasions, both of which had been mildly disastrous. He was, in Donald's view, the worst kind of product of the Northcote Trevellyan reforms of the civil service in the late nineteenth century – intellectually arrogant, making a virtue of detachment, and unwilling to allow the facts to interfere with his logical analysis of the problem, whatever it might be. Their first meeting had been when Donald was summoned to the Minister of

State's Office to explain a particularly neat grants scheme for fish farmers which he had devised after six months' agonising consultation with the industry. MacDonald, the newly appointed private secretary, had told the Minister that he could see how the scheme worked in practice, but not in theory. (Neither Donald nor the Minister had spotted the plagiarism from Garret Fitzgerald.) The scheme had been rejected, and Donald had spent a further six months developing an alternative which worked in theory but not in practice. Needless to say, it had been accepted.

So Donald was not expecting a fax from his namesake. Still less was he expecting a fax as helpful as that which lay on his writing table:

> 'Congratulations on your appointment to LOIN, and best wishes for the Feelgood Project. The Perm Sec has told me that only someone of your undoubted calibre can win it.
>
> You will be looking for a suitable location in Scotland to place a major Japanese manufacturing plant. My recent posting to North Uist has enabled me to locate just such a place. The environment is attractive. The natives are friendly. Communications with the mainland and with Northern Europe are excellent. There is ample land zoned for industrial development, and a well trained and highly educated workforce – North Uist has the highest proportion of Ph Ds among its unemployed of any comparable location in Western Europe. Finally, there are well developed leisure facilities – golf, fishing, hang gliding, surfing, water ski-ing and sailing.
>
> I strongly recommend a site visit by your Japanese contacts, and shall be happy to make the necessary arrangements.
>
> Kind regards
> D McD'

Donald lay back on his bed, and a warm glow suffused his tired limbs. Things were coming together. The American he had met in the lift would give him some tips on how to attract investment. Donald MacDonald had identified a suitable location. It simply remained to attract the Japanese on a site visit. While he had never been to the Hebrides, preferring to take his holidays in Troon, his youthful reading of *Whisky Galore* had given him a sufficient understanding of the general environment to make it sound irresistible. Once there, the Japanese were bound to decide in favour.

Donald began to muse on the rewards of success – a performance bonus, promotion, perhaps even a place in the Birthday Honours List (he would prefer the Birthday list, since his friends were likely to be drunk at New Year and wouldn't notice then). He fell into a reverie, in which images of Japanese golfers and Pussy Galore merged with those of faery lands forlorn amongst the farthest Hebrides, and hairy crofters hiding bottles of whisky in peat bogs. He slept...

'Say, good to see you again, Donald. What you doing here in Tokyo?'

Dwight Dildenschneider, the American he had met in the lift, had accosted Donald the moment he had entered the bar. He had wakened feeling somewhat fuzzy after two hours sleep; but a luke-warm shower, an alka seltzer, three ibruprofen and a whisky from the mini bar had restored him to something like equilibrium. He had toyed with the idea of keeping Stuart MacLellan waiting for him in the bar, so that he could effect a grand entrance and show who was boss, but he had concluded that his interests were better served by arriving early so that MacLellan felt upstaged and embarrassed. It was important, Donald had learned, to assert your superiority as a boss in the first moments of the first meeting with a subordinate, however much more your subordinate might know about your new job than you did.

So he arrived at half past seven and was promptly accosted by Dildenschneider.

'Take a seat,' he said. 'What you drinking? Scotch? Bourbon? Beer?'

'Beer,' responded Donald. The whisky from his mini bar had had an immediate beneficial effect; but the longer term impact was not so positive. His stomach was feeling decidedly raw, and the bright lights in the darkened bar were hurting his eyes.

Dildenschneider snapped his fingers, and a waitress glided over. She wore a skirt split to mid thigh and moved as if on casters.

'Two beers, honey.' Dildenschneider had either failed to learn the politically correct linguistic habits of his countrypersons, or regarded them as inappropriate to Japan, where women were thought to know their place.

The waitress smiled and bowed. '*Hai*,' she said. 'Asahi Dry, as before?'

'The very same.' He turned to Donald. 'You'll love this beer – like Bud served by the girl next door. But tell me, what're you doing here.'

'A bit like you, I suppose,' said Donald. 'Working for my country. I'm trying to win an investment for Scotland.'

'Say, that's what I call coincidence. You Limeys are quite good at that. Half the goddam corporations in Silicon Valley have set up plants in Scotland. Must be attracted by the rain and the people. It takes a lot to make a Californian look intelligent, but in contrast with the Scots they're all Einsteins.'

Donald debated briefly whether to challenge the jibe, but decided against. He had much to learn from Dildenschneider, and could not afford to annoy him.

'I'm meeting a company called Omeiwaku Denki,' he said. 'Have you heard of them?'

Dildenschneider's eyes narrowed. 'Can't say I have,' he lied. 'What line they in, the toy business?'

'They make conglomerates,' said Donald, whose study of the brief had done little to enlighten him on the intricacies of Japanese industrial structures, but who had once provided a grant for conglomerate to fill Wick Harbour. 'We're trying to get them to establish a conglomerate plant in North Uist.'

Dildenschneider sipped his beer. 'That sounds like a cute project,' he said at last. 'Who you meeting?'

Donald had only the faintest idea. He extemporised. 'Top brass, mainly. And of course the project co-ordinator. And I'm arranging to take the foreman golfing, along with the shop steward. But tell me, what in your experience is the best way to deal with the Japanese?'

Dildenschneider folded his hands over his ample belly. 'Well, I guess you hear a lot of bullshit about that,' he replied. 'Yeah, man, consultants'll tell you that the Japanese are very formal, that they like you to wear business suits and to bow and exchange business cards and call them Fujimoto-san and Inanaga-san and approach things very slowly and very indirectly. And they charge you five hundred bucks an hour for the privilege.'

'What, then?'

'Why, the most successfully guy I ever knew in dealing with the Japs just went straight in there. Straight off the bird, and still wearing Bermuda shorts and a shirt with a picture of Waikiki Beach on the back. He threw his business card across the table at the President of NEC, and wrote notes on the back of the President's business card until he'd run out of space. Then he tore bits off it and used it as a toothpick. None of that bowing nonsense – he just told them straight. Set up in California, which is God's own country, and we'll give you sun, sex, surf and the biggest market on God's earth. Or go to Europe, and Uncle Sam will ensure you never sell another widget in all of the New World. No, Sah!'

'What happened?'

'Landed a project with 5000 jobs worth $2000m, and a seat on the US Board. He's now in the Senate. There's success for you! He took no notice of the bullshitters!'

Donald peered at Dildenschneider across his beer. He had never had a good opinion of Americans, but this one topped the bill for naiveté. He had expected to have to work to extract Dildenschneider's secrets, just as he did with the fishermen of Peterhead; but Dildenschneider had revealed them all almost without prompting. In an unusual fit of generosity he decided to buy him a drink.

'I'll take a rain check,' said Dildenschneider to Donald's bafflement. 'I'm dining with the Head of Corporate Affairs of a major electronics company. Hang in there, Donald, I'll see you on the circuit.' And Dildenschneider levered his immense off white bulk from the sofa and went in search of riches.

Stuart MacLellan arrived, flustered, ten minutes later. 'Donald Macdonald?' he asked, somewhat unnecessarily since Donald was by now the only *gaijin* in the bar. 'Sorry I'm late – Tokyo traffic, and I got caught up with my Californian opposite number in the lobby. The biggest rogue in the business – you need a mighty long spoon when you sup with him. Let me know if he tried to get in touch; you can't trust him further than you can spit.'

But Donald kept his counsel. 'Beer?' he asked, since the first duty of a new boss is to offer refreshment to his subordinates.

'Later,' said MacLellan. 'I thought we'd go to the Ginza for dinner. Then we can discuss the project, and I can brief you on Japan. It's a strange place, and you need to know their little ways if you are to make a success of this business.'

'I shall look forward to that,' said Donald.

* * *

CHAPTER 11

In which quite a lot happens.

'*Maman!*' shouted Alsace.

'*Mutti!*' screamed Lorraine.

The twins were straining on each side of the Allt Burn drenched to the skin. Their floral dresses, the finest products of the Laura Ashley loom, hung shapelessly from their stooped shoulders as they hung on to the rope. Water dripped from their lank hair. Their shoes squelched in thick mud.

Both had been pulled unceremoniously into the burn as the Benbecula and North Uist Tug of War teams battled for supremacy at the North Uist Highland Games. So closely were the teams matched in size, weight and cunning that it was a full fifteen minutes before there was any movement at all. Then the North Uist Team Manager had sent one of the most beautiful of the island maidens across the burn to distract the Benbecula team. The Benbecula anchorman had temporarily lost concentration; and the first three of the team, including Alsace who had insisted in participating, had been dragged into the water.

Benbecula had tried the same trick; but the North Uist anchorman was a woman who, despite a substantial dose of testosterone and steroids, had refused to be distracted. Lorraine, however, had laughed so much at the plight of her sister that the fragile balance of power had been destroyed; and she too found her way into the Burn. But both teams redoubled their efforts, and order was restored.

The North Uist and Pabbay Highland Games were closely modelled on the Braemar gathering. True, no royalty was present – not even the estranged wife of a younger son. But there were piping competitions, highland dancing, caber tossing, clarsach plucking, and various exhibitions of highland skills. And like the Braemar gathering, the North Uist Highland Games were a truly international event, for this year they were graced with the presence of the South Carolina Ladies' Highland Games team and their redoubtable Chief, Ms Miriam Katzenellenbogen.

Ms Katzenellenbogen was at that moment preparing her team for a demonstration of Highland dancing under the watchful eye of Sgt Stripe, who had brought his platoon over from Benbecula for the day to give a demonstration of bayonet drill.

'Now, sisters,' she was saying, 'I want a good clean dawance, and dowant kiyick your legs too high in the air.'

'Why ever nat?' complained Mary Lou Krantz, who was in an argumentative mood as a result of having been relocated from the North Uist Hydro Hotel to Mrs McTurk's black-house .

'Because we want everything abaht the dancing to be authentic, even down to what you're wearing under your kilts. Mary Lou, dowant tell me that you ignored mah instructions?'

'That's right, you tell 'er,' interjected Sgt Stripe. 'You'll never win if you don't get it really authentic. Used to be an officer at the Royal Scots wot checked his platoon with a dentist's mirror on the end of 'is swagger stick. If your bollocks weren't on view, 'twas the 'igh jump for you. Beggin' your pardon, missis,' he concluded, noticing that Mary Lou, who was as wanting in the organs requiring to be covered as she was surplus in the vestments required to cover them, was close to tears.

'Darran would never have let me come,' she sniffed, 'if he knewed that ah had to dawance here nude. As a born again Baptist, ah am nat expected to cast mah bread upon the waters.'

'Wayell,' said Ms Katzenellenbogen, 'Ahm nat having you dressed up like a can-can dancer from La Vie Parisienne. Either you remove your pantyhose, or we dawance the eightsome one short. And ahm nat prepared to dawance the first sevensome on Scottish soil – Spartanburg would never stand for it. Get 'em off!'

'Can I help?' asked Sgt Stripe.

McTurk, meanwhile, was shepherding Donald around the sports field, or Plain of the Gathering of the Clans of North Uist and Pabbay, as it was called in the Gaelic, and briefing him on the superiority of

North Uist over Benbecula in matters relating to Highland Games as well as in the administration of local government. Donald was finding it difficult to pay attention. Sgt Stripe had caught his eye, and he was reflecting on the fax which he had sent to Tokyo that morning. If Donald Macdonald swallowed the bait and persuaded the Omeiwaku Corporation to send a project team to North Uist, all hell would be let loose when Sgt Stripe got to hear about it. Donald smiled a secret smile at the thought of Sir Terence Mould's wasted career.

But McTurk persisted. 'We shall beat them in the dancing,' he intoned. 'We shall fight them with the caber, we shall outpipe them with the great pipes, we shall outrun them in the terrier races, we shall never surrender.' He jutted his lower lip and wished that he had a Havana cigar to wave for emphasis.

'I dare say you may,' said Donald languidly. 'But I quite fail to see what relevance such victories might have on the Minister's proposals to amalgamate you and Benbecula.'

'Why, it iss obvious, man? If you breed good stock with bad, you lower the quality of the flock, at all. Even their dogs are puny wee things. Look!'

Donald stepped delicately through the puddles and looked around him. There was little sign of underbred anorexics. In the centre of the field a group of eight large women wearing kilts and tartan baseball caps danced an approximation to an eightsome reel, nervously holding down their kilts as they pranced. Beside them, an ancient man with patriarchal hair and beard herded a flock of ducks with two sheepdogs. The tug of war teams had regrouped across the burn and, dripping gently, were straining motionless for the advantage. Sgt Stripe's platoon stood stiffly to attention, awaiting the moment when they would demonstrate the latest techniques in bayonet drill and keeping a wary eye open for Japanese. And to the far right of the field, beyond the dancers and the ducks, preparations were in hand for the terrier races.

The terriers had not yet been metricated and, in accordance with tradition, ran a course of one hundred and twelve yards precisely. At each end was an inverted bicycle in the charge of an upright pensioner – unimpeachable integrity being the primary requirement for such employment. The rear wheels of the bicycles were joined by a continuous belt of rope, to which was attached, at about ten feet from the starting line, a damp woollen sock filled with malodorous rotting meat. When the starter, a retired army officer also of unimpeachable integrity, dropped his handkerchief, the pensioner guarding the further bicycle had to turn the pedals vigorously, dragging the sock along the ground. The dog handlers, who had bet large sums on their animals and whose integrity had been impeached on many occasions, were at this precise moment, and not an instant before, to let go of their charges, which would race after the sock. The pensioner at the near end had merely to ensure that his bicycle remained upright, or rather inverted, and that the rope did not snag. If the pensioner at the far end turned the pedals too fast, the dogs would lose interest in the sock and fight amongst themselves. If he pedalled too slowly, the dogs would catch up with the sock and fight amongst themselves.

'McTurk, a word if you please.' One of the dog owners beckoned to the Town Clerk. His animal strained at the leash; it had the ears of a collie, the head of a spaniel, the muzzle of a Doberman, the fetlocks of a greyhound, and the rump and tail of a whippet.

'What iss it, MacIlvenny? I am after looking after an important guest, Donald MacDonald of MacDonald, of the North British Office, who is here to examine the activities of the Council.' McTurk considered it prudent to effect an introduction. He waved his crook at the dog owner. 'Lachlan MacIlvenny,' he said, 'Chairman and sole member of the North Uist Chamber of Commerce, the North Uist Rotary Club, the Most Noble Order of the Buffalo, and the Businessmen's Discussion Group.'

'Pleased to meet you,' he said. 'It's about my terrier, Bran, at all. Major Campbell, the Starter, iss casting doubt on his pedigree and entitlement to race. Would you believe it – Bran has raced every year since he was a pup at his mither's teats, and it would break his doggish heart to be excluded now, so it would.' The dog looked up with limpid spaniel's eyes and gnashed its Doberman jaws menacingly.

'What's his height, shoulder to ground?' asked McTurk. 'The rules are quite clear. A terrier is a dog of less than 4 hands in height. If your dog iss less than that, he can compete. If not, not. Major, do you have a tape measure with you?'

The Starter strode over and raised his Trilby hat. 'I have indeed, and I can confirm that the dog in question is less than the relevant height as specified in the Bylaws, as passed by the Council on 1 January 1898.' He fingered his guards' tie, and the dog gazed up at him with approval. 'But I'm afraid that it's not quite as simple as that.' The dog began to foam at the mouth.

'It is sure that I am that this is the clearest Bylaw that ever wass passed by the Council,' said McTurk. 'Despite the fact that it wass considered on January the First.'

'But it has been modified,' said the Starter. 'By a Directive from Brussels. The Dangerous Dogs and Related Breeds Directive specifies that a terrier must conform to a number of criteria in which this dog is entirely lacking. For instance, its colour.'

'Perhaps I can help,' interjected Donald, who recognised in Lachlan MacIlvenny a potential ally in his battle against Donald Macdonald and Sir Terence Mould. The Chamber of Commerce, after all, would play a crucial part in attracting the Japanese to visit.

'Certainly, at all, at all,' said McTurk. 'There is no one better qualified to interpret the emanations from Brussels, whatever, than our eminent friend from the North British Office. Can we agree to let MacDonald arbitrate?'

Both Lachlan MacIlvenny and Major Campbell looked dubious, but the dog looked up and nodded, and the decision was taken.

Donald pulled at his ear and took a deep breath. 'While it is true,' he said slowly, 'that in the generality of cases a Directive made by the Council of Ministers acting on a recommendation of the Commission and with the advice of the Parliament and the relevant social or economic committee is binding on a Member State, or not.'

The disputants looked puzzled, apart from the dog, which gave every impression of having understood perfectly. Major Campbell removed his Trilby and mopped his brow with a large red spotted handkerchief. 'Or not what?' he asked aggressively.

'As the case may be,' smiled Donald. 'Particularly in the case of an island such as Madeira or, I suppose, North Uist. So you see,' he concluded, 'the dog is perfectly entitled to race.'

'Ah,' said the Major, who had served in the Royal Scots where intelligence disqualified one for a commission. 'Ah,' said Lachlan MacIlvenny. 'Aye,' said Hamish McTurk. 'Well, that settles it. The dog races with the rest.'

Lachlan MacIlvenny gave Donald a long wink. ' I will be after seeing you in the beer tent,' he said. 'But first I must see the Dog Bran win. Come, Bran!'

The protagonists took up their positions. Major Campbell checked the bouquet of the woollen sock and waved his hat at the pensioner at the far end. The pensioner adjusted his cycle clips and prepared to turn the pedals. The terriers, held firmly by the collar, yelped hoarsely. The owners glared at each other and calculated the chances of being outed in the *West Highland Free Press* for administering illegal substances to their dogs. And, across the field, Miriam Katzenellenbogen and the North Carolina Ladies' Highland Games Team continued to dance their eightsome, and the old shepherd herded ducks with his sheepdog, and Sgt Stripe prepared his platoon for a demonstrations of bayonet drill, and shifty looking bookies took illegal bets on the outcome of the race. And, over the Allt Burn, the tug of war teams strained motionless while Alsace and Lorraine hurled abuse at each other in their respective if not respectable languages.

It was a moment out of time. A lark wheeled in the cerulean, its delicate wings beating against the bright sky. A curlew's liquid note spun filigree strands of gold against the air. The blue hills and white sands were of a colour more intense than mere blue and white. In the corner of the field, a dog crapped.

The world held its breath. And Major Campbell lifted and dropped his red spotted handkerchief.

The pensioner pedalled. The dog handlers released their dogs from the traces. The sock of rotting meat bounced along the uneven turf, casting molecules of putrefaction to the still air. The terriers accelerated. The Dog Bran drew into the lead. Onlookers cheered. Dog handlers urged their dogs into even greater speeds. The smallest terrier collapsed and fell on its back in a cataleptic fit, waving its legs in the air. One of the bookies, who was relying heavily on a victory by the cataleptic, slunk off the field clutching a wad of greasy £5 notes. And then disaster struck.

The pensioner of unimpeachable integrity whose task it was to turn the pedals was not a man of unimpeachable sobriety. Perhaps it was the quantity of Ardbeg that he had consumed at breakfast. Perhaps it was the irresistible urge to adjust his right cycle clip, which had become twisted around his ankle. Or perhaps it was the swarm of midges which had landed on his neck the moment that his pipe went out. But, however it was, the pace of his pedalling slackened sufficiently to allow the Dog Bran to reach the sock.

Bran sunk his fangs into the rotting meat and dug his forepaws into the machair. Five other terriers leapt onto his back. The pensioner, unbalanced by the sudden check of the rope, fell backwards onto the sandy grass. The dog handlers rushed forward to separate their charges, their heavy tweed trousers flapping around their knees. And three of the dogs broke loose and rushed across the machair towards the flock of ducks, which the ancient shepherd was still attempting to corral with the help of his two myopic sheepdogs.

Mary Lou Krantz had been raised in one of the more remote quarters of South Carolina. Her grandfather's smallholding had provided barely enough produce for himself and his wife; and when his eleven year old granddaughter had come to live with him following the untimely drowning of her parents in the Chipaquidick Creek (where they were chauffeurs to one of the lesser scions of the Kennedy clan) he had been forced to diversify. He had introduced a flock of ducks into an area of swamp at the bottom of the farm; and it was Mary Lou's task to clip the wings, feed the birds, gather the eggs and, when the time came, wring the necks. Her psychotherapist dated her obsessive fear of ducks to that era, and to the juxtaposition of tiny eyes, snapping beaks, twisted necks and feathers matted with guano with her emerging pubescent sexuality. At all events, Mary Lou Krantz had a fear of ducks amounting to paranoia. When she saw the shepherd's flock streaming towards the highland dancing she let go of the hands of Miriam Katzenellenbogen, whom she was whirling in the final climax of the eightsome reel, and rushed screaming from the field.

As if to demonstrate the full force of centrifugal energy, Miriam Katzenellenbogen was hurled towards the outer ring of dancers, who were holding down their kilts with one hand while grasping the elbow of their neighbour with the other and orbiting the centre in a rapid anti-clockwise motion. She struck the dancers with all the force of Comet Hale Bopp hitting Jupiter, but with ten times the destructive effect.

Jasmine Kutzweil, who received the full impact of the blow, was knocked headlong onto the grass. The other members of the South

Carolina Ladies' Highland Games Team tumbled over her and each other in turn. Their kilts were displaced from the modest position in which they had so far been held, revealing the full extent to which they had, or had not, complied with their Chieftain's dress code. Apart from one lace garter and a pair of scarlet silk panties, they were immaculate. And that fact was not lost on the men of the Benbecula Tug of War team...

...who at last, and after a stale-mate of two hours, lost their concentration. A tremor ran down the line; and the anchorman, victor of so many such encounters, felt his knees begin to tremble as his flesh began to stir. The North Uist team who, like true gentlemen, had their eyes averted from the unseemly sight behind them, felt the scintilla of weakness and redoubled their efforts. Gradually, then with increasing momentum, they dragged the opposing force one by one into the Allt Burn. At last the line broke; and the North Uist team, all restraint gone, found themselves rushing backwards across the machair to collide with the beer tent, which collapsed with a mighty sound of breaking glass about the ears of the serious drinkers who had inhabited it since lunchtime.

Sgt Stripe was appalled. Not even the Japanese could cause such chaos. Weeping American matrons tried to restore their make up and their decency. Terriers were everywhere, fighting each other and everything else that moved on the ravaged field. The flock of ducks ran hither and thither, looking for their coops, a pond, anywhere where they could hide from the appalling cacophony of barking. The Dog Bran, waving his whippet's's tale and foaming at his Doberman jaws, had eaten the contents of the meat filled sock and had turned his attentions to the sock of the pedalling pensioner, who lay insensible on the ground. And Major Campbell had removed his Trilby hat and was looking unhappily around him, remembering the fate of his brother officer who had fouled up the start of a recent Grand National and wondering whether there would be a Jockey Club enquiry.

'Platoon!' shouted Sgt Stripe. 'Fix Bayonets! We've gotta restore order. And quick. Platoon, restore order!'

Trained killers all, the soldiers went about their task with a will. True, their training had been addressed at a different threat; and some at least were disappointed that they could not demonstrate their prowess at bayonet drill using the straw dummies which Sgt Stripe had tastefully dressed in Kimonos and Happy Coats. But this was the real thing.

Fifteen minutes later, an uneasy calm had been restored. The beer tent had been re-erected and its contents loaded onto a lorry for subsequent consumption in the Sergeant's Mess. All of the ducks and most of the terriers had been slaughtered, and their bodies were laid out on the grass outside the tent for later decision as to whether they should be sold to the butcher or buried in a mass grave as victims of war. The Dog Bran had, however, been rescued by Donald MacDonald, who had assumed the role of UN Observer and was still keen to secure the co-operation of Lachlan MacIlvenny in the matter of Japanese Inward Investment. Mary Lou Krantz had not been seen since the attack of the flock of ducks, and had been posted missing. The rest of the South Carolina Ladies' Highland Games Team had been taken prisoners of war, and were standing with their hands behind their heads under the keen eyes of Cpl Snodgrass. Major Campbell was talking to his solicitor from the public telephone in the bar of the hotel. And the pensioner whose dilatoriness had started the whole affair was waiting for a helicopter to fly him to the Craigmore Hospital, Inverness, to be treated for a lacerated leg, while Sgt Stripe's medical orderly practiced field dressings on his wounds.

'A most unfortunate turn of events,' opined Hamish McTurk to Donald MacDonald as he surveyed the scene. 'Such a thing has never happened before, at all, at all. Most unfortunate indeed.'

But Donald MacDonald did not agree.

* * *

CHAPTER 12

In which one of our heroes is offered a temporary wife.

'*Hai*, you want temporary wife?'

The Japanese who lurched at them out of the Ginza crowds was six feet six tall and had grey hair and orange lipstick. He or she grinned down at Donald Macdonald from his or her immense height and beckoned him with a gigantic hand.

In other circumstances Donald would have been tempted. His encounter with Pussy Galore had enflamed his imagination; and hangover and exhaustion always made him feel randy. But he had to impress Stuart MacLellan; and until he knew him better he could not risk gaining a reputation for lasciviousness. So he reluctantly decided to decline the offer. He had read somewhere that the Japanese signify a negative by nodding vigorously, so he nodded vigorously.

'Ah, *so des ne*,' said the Japanese, grasping his arm.

'No, no,' said Donald.

'So you like our *Noh* plays, yes?' said the Japanese. 'So first *Noh* play. Then *mikoh*. Very pretty.'

Donald, who had no idea what a noh play was, nor that a mikoh was an apprentice geisha, had a sudden and appalling vision of being involved in the making of a pornographic wireless programme.

'No, no!' he repeated with greater emphasis. 'Negative. Not. Never. Absolutely no how. No way.' He slowed as he ran out of negatives. But the message had got through.

'Ah, you not want girl. Like your Oscar Wilde, *ne*? I know very pretty boy...'

But Donald had had enough. He wrenched his arm away and rejoined Stuart on the sidewalk.

'Not tempted?' asked Stuart.

'Certainly not,' said Donald pompously. 'And I trust you don't indulge in such activities yourself. I cannot think why you brought me to such a place.'

'You have a lot to learn about Japan,' said Stuart. 'Let's go eat.'

They walked through the Ginza crowds, past innumerable bars, and past innumerable people all dressed alike in business suits and white shirts and with ubiquitous patent leather hair. The traffic crawled bumper to boot, blaring horns and flashing lights at the few jaywalkers, all of them European or American. Hotels advertised rooms by the half hour – 'Just-in-time technology applied to the art of love,' explained Stuart. Everywhere there were neon lights, proclaiming heaven knows what new-minted pleasures in their archaic script. The evening was balmy; and despite himself Donald began to be moved by the spirit of it all.

The restaurant was small and dark.

'I take it you like sea food,' Stuart asked. Donald, whose habitual evening meal was a fish supper from the Frying Scotsman Chinese Carry Out and Fish Restaurant in the Gorgie Road, Edinburgh, enthusiastically assented. He now sat peering through the gloom at a plate of suchi, on which raw fish was complemented with seaweed and one or two live shrimps still hopped, while Stuart speared his own shrimps expertly with chopsticks and briefed him on efforts to date to win the Feelgood Project.

'I've arranged a meeting first thing tomorrow with the Ambassador,' he said. 'He'll brief you on the general approach to Japanese investment in the UK. Afterwards we've got a meeting with Omeiwaku Denki. That's absolutely crucial, and I hope you've studied the Papers I sent you on Japanese business etiquette and on Omeiwaku's locational requirements.'

Donald secreted a piece of raw fish in his cheek and gestured with his chopstick. 'I have indeed,' he said, 'but I am bound to say that I don't entirely agree with you.'

Stuart's expression changed from enthusiasm to alarm. He had worked long hours preparing those briefs, and they encapsulated many man-years of experience. But Donald didn't notice. He moved into the epigrammatic mode with which he had in the past cowed, or rather piked, Buchan fishermen (or, to use a more appropriate metaphor, knocked them off their perch).

'Politeness is the courtesy of princes,' he intoned, 'but courtesy is the prince of virtues.'

'What the hell's that supposed to mean?'

'Just as the lion is the king of the pride, so pride comes before a fall.'

'I'm sorry, I don't follow you.' Stuart wondered whether Donald's suchi had included a piece of imperfectly prepared fugu – guaranteed to cause insanity within ten minutes and death within the hour. He was soon to regret that it hadn't.

The waiter refilled their beer glasses and brought more fish – this time prawns lightly fried in batter. One or two tails still flapped. Donald looked at his plate with distaste and took a large draught of beer. He decided to be clearer.

'What I am trying to say,' he said, 'is that courtesy is not a fixed star in the firmament. It is a moving planet that wanders around the drawing rooms of polite society, changing its spots like a leopard as it lopes.' He had gleaned his knowledge of the drawing rooms of polite society from watching Eastenders, and he warmed to his theme. 'If we don't track its every vacillation, we are likely to find ourselves stranded on the receding tide of fashion and make of ourselves utter prats.'

'So?' said Stuart.

'Well, you don't still sign your letters "I remain, my dear Sir, your most humble and obedient servant", or wear spats or address your best friend's wife as "Mrs Smith" instead of "Waynetta".'

Stuart, who had a secret hankering to do all three, demurred. 'But this is Japan.'

'And even Japan changes,' asserted Donald with all the authority of his one day visit. 'If you bow and exchange business cards and drink green tea and refuse to blow you nose they'll simply think that you're out of the ark and push the project elsewhere. It's self evident.'

'But...'

'I don't need to remind you of my hierarchical relationship to you. I have been given personal responsibility to win this project by none other than Sir Terence Mould and, to quote Shakespeare, "I'll do it my way". Tell me about locational requirements.'

'But...'

Donald glared through the gloom. Stuart abandoned his attempts to emulate a Japanese Miss Manners and switched into Knight, Frank and Rutley mode.

'Nothing complex. They need an initial 40,000 square feet with room for expansion, ready access to motorways and airports, a trained workforce and a substantial grant. Oh, and close to at least three pubs with karaoke machines, but we can get the Tourist Board to supply those. We thought about Bathgate.'

'Bathgate!' Donald spat out the word with contempt and the tail of a shrimp. 'It may have been built by Beau Nash and Capability Brown, but its the dimmest place in Scotland. Have you considered North Uist?'

Stuart looked anxiously at his plate. Now he knew that the sushi was off.

* * *

CHAPTER 13

In which Sergeant Stripe instructs his men, and the supremacy of London as the restaurant capital of the world is challenged.

Meanwhile, in North Uist, things had almost returned to normal.

The fax machine of the North Uist Hydro Hotel was working overtime sending messages to South Carolinian lawyers who might be prepared to sue the British Army, on a no win no fee basis, for voyeurism, indecent assault and cruelty to ducks.

Donald MacDonald had written a terse but vivid memo to the Minister confirming the incompetence of the North Uist Urban District Council and recommending a press release on the plans for amalgamation. While waiting for the fax machine, he composed a further fax to Tokyo confirming the support of the North Uist Chamber of Commerce for a substantial investment – he had spent a profitable twenty minutes in the bar with Lachlan MacIlvenny – and describing the proposals for a tunnel under the Minch to link the tramways of the Hebrides with the TGVs and *shinkanzen* of the Kyle line (Benbecula to Brussels in 5 hours provided the Belgian railways weren't on strike).

Lady Lucinda had retreated to her room with the twins and was trying to settle them with a story: Stephen King's *Misery* with alternate sentences translated into French and German

Hamish McTurk had repaired to the public bar of the Hotel and was well into his eighth large Glenmorangie.

And Sgt Stripe was debriefing his men.

'Well done, lads. You restored order calmly and efficiently, as per the manual. But there is lessons to be learnt. Corporal Snodgrass, tell them.'

'Yes, Sarge,' said Cpl Snodgrass. 'Like you say, there is lessons to be learnt. Brown, tell 'em.'

Lance Cpl Brown was not the quickest witted of the platoon, but he could recognise when his superiors were at a loss.

'Ducks, Corporal,' he said.

'Ducks, Sergeant,' repeated Cpl Snodgrass.

'Ducks?' expostulated Sgt Stripe. 'Why ducks?'

Cpl Snodgrass looked blank. 'Well Sarge,' said Lance Cpl Brown, 'They was Barbary ducks, what is well known for their violence, being of oriental extraction. We should 'ave liquidised them at the start. Then none of the carnal would 'ave started.'

'Correct,' said Sgt Stripe, grateful for having been let off a hook of his own making. 'If you 'ad reckernized them as barbarian ducks, you'd 'ave gone for 'em straight away. Anything else?'

'Triage, Sarge,' said Private White, who had spent a term at the University of the East Midlands (formerly the Brummigen Poly) before being sent down for sobriety at the Freshers' Ball, and fancied himself as a linguist.

'Triage!' screamed Sgt Stripe. 'You don't know the difference between triage and a pensioner's arse.' Sgt Stripe was not going to admit that he didn't know what triage was. 'You'd better explain, for the benefit of Private Smith 'ere.'

'Triage, Sarge...'

'You're not a fucking poet. Get on with it!'

'Triage is the process of sorting out those killed in battle into those who are going to survive and those who aren't. No point in wasting resources on those who aren't. Just a quick dose of the Last Rites, if that is they're left footed, and on to the next. And we didn't...'

'Just a minute,' interrupted Cpl Snodgrass, eager to justify his stripes. 'If you hadn't sorted them, they'd all be killed? But we didn't, and they wasn't. QED, eh, Sarge?'

Sgt Stripe's brain was beginning to hurt. It was time to bring the discussion to a close. 'That's right,' he said. 'QED. Quite Easy Darling. Now back to the boats, and I'll give you thirty minutes to parade at Base for your evening lecture on the threat from the Far East. Platoon 'shun! By the right, quick march!'

Despite the fact that North Uist and Benbecula had been joined these hundred years by a causeway, Sgt Stripe had insisted that the men travel by landing craft. You never knew when maritime skills might come in handy, particularly when faced with an enemy which had fought its way across the Pacific. And what his three ancient vessels lacked in technological sophistication they made up in romance. LC329 had served on the victorious retreat from Dunkirk. LC581 had been on the Normandy Beaches. And LC697 had done sterling service delivering spiritual support – mainly whisky – to the garrisons of Shetland. But their past glories were nothing in contrast with Sgt Stripe's vision of their future. In his mind's eye Sgt Stripe saw himself, armed to his false teeth, leaping from the bows of LC329 to liberate the Barra Aerodrome (aka the Cockle Strand) from a brigade of Japanese paratroopers, so that the 767s of US Air could once again land there in peace. In his imagination he saw the Japanese Emperor stepping aboard LC581 to hand him his sword as a gesture of surrender. In his dreams he saw himself marching off LC697 before a cheering crowd at the Tower of London, to receive his Victoria Cross from a grateful monarch. He shifted into nautical mode.

'Abaft, me 'earties. Splice the mainbrace, shiver the timbers, and untether the warps.' His lack of a Dartmouth education had been overcome through a detailed study of Treasure Island in the World Comics edition. His platoon, which had not benefited from such research, looked puzzled.

'Wot, Sarge?' ventured Cpl Snodgrass.

'Untie the bleeding boats and get the fuck back to barracks!'

The voyage to Benbecula was relatively uneventful. LC329 snagged its propeller on some lobster pots, but the crew resourcefully extemporised a tow rope out of the warps of the marker buoys. Cpl Snodgrass hit his head on stanchions of the bridge as they passed under the road that joined the two islands, damaging still further his limited intellectual powers. Lance Cpl Brown misjudged the leading marks to the beach and parked LC697 on the only rock in half a mile of sand. But they arrived without loss of life.

The Benbecula Barracks was not built during a good period for military architecture. No Vauban had designed its curtain walls. No

Wade had constructed its palisades. No Marlborough had laid out its parade grounds. Instead of porticoes there were Nissan huts. Instead of a vast parade ground there was a tiny square of weedy gravel. Instead of trophies of war there were one or two rusty field guns. But the mess silver was indeed a mess; and to Sgt Stripe the barracks was home.

The Lecture Room, or Seminar Suite as Sgt Stripe insisted on calling it, was a Nissan hut wedged between the Officers' and the Sergeants' Mess. Formerly the Chapel, it had been elaborately decorated by Italian prisoners of was during World War II. Not even the ceiling of the Sistine Chapel could rival its elaborate murals of the fall of man, the ascension of Christ, and the apotheosis of the Blessed Virgin Mary. But a change of policy in the MOD had rendered the Chapel redundant: henceforth, all religious observation on MOD property was banned because it might offend the atheist, humanist and agnostic minorities and stimulate the Buddhists to a holy war. Most chapels had been converted to NAAFIs and had fruit machines on the altars and bars in the vestry. But St Wellington's Chapel, Benbecula had been commandeered by Sgt Stripe for educational purposes.

He had made a good job of the conversion. Maps of the Japanese archipelago were pinned over the reredos, so that a naked Eve held out an apple to Hokkaido and Gabriel pointed an accusing finger at the new Osaka International Airport. The serpent's tail merged effortlessly with the track of the Bullet Train. The statue of the Madonna and Child was clothed tastefully in a kimono and sash; and the font, with very little modification, had been transformed into a sumo wrestler.

'Right lads,' Sgt Stripe was saying as his Platoon sat compliantly to attention in the former nave. 'What's the greatest current threat to world peace?'

'Football hooliganism, Sarge,' said Private Krunt, who was still nursing a black eye from a recent clash at Old Trafford.

'Wrong,' said Sgt Stripe. 'Any other suggestions?'

'Highland Games,' said Private Leask, who had been recruited only a month before and had received his first taste of action that afternoon.

'Wrong again,' said Sgt Stripe. Remember, the sooner you come up with sensible answers, the sooner you can get back to your billets to clean your kit for tomorrow's parade.' He gestured at the sumo wrestler with the billiard cue that he was using as a pointer. 'What's that, O'Donnell?'

'A font, Sarge,' said O'Donnell, who had been brought up as a Catholic. 'And if you're suggesting that Mother Theresa is a threat to world peace I have to demur.'

'Incorrect,' said Sgt Stripe. 'That, as anyone can see, is a sumo wrestler. What's a sumo wrestler, Brown?'

Donald and Lucinda MacDonald, meantime, were dining next door in the Officers' Mess with the Commanding Officer of the Base, Major the Honourable Cecil Prendergast, and Mrs Prendergast.

The message which Donald had received at the North Uist Hydro Hotel after he had finished sending his faxes had been terse in the extreme: *'Dinner. Eight. Both. Prendergast.'* Donald was eager for an early visit to Benbecula. He arranged for Miriam Katzenellenbogen to look after the twins – it would help take her mind off the search for Mary Lou Krantz – and had accepted the invitation with a rotundity of phrase which balanced Prendergast's terseness. Unfortunately the duty NCO to whom Donald had dictated his acceptance was not distinguished at scrabble. *'Mister and Missis Donald MacDonald of Macdonald hav grate pleshure in indickating there gratefull ackseptanse of Madger Perndegast's kynd invitashun to diner this eevnin at ate owclok,'* he had written.

Major Prendergast, who had the quickness of wit characteristic of our older regiments of foot guards, assumed that the orthography as well as the sentiment was that of his guest. Over the pre-dinner drinks – whisky and soda for himself and Donald, dry sherry for Lady Lucinda, and Babycham for Mrs Prendergast – he was wondering about the educational standards of the North British Office and trying to ascertain Donald's academic and social antecedents.

'Knew m'tutor at Eton?' he asked when the formalities had been completed. His father had made a pile in brass bolt manufacture during the war, and had the means to educate young Cecil at the most distinguished of England's ancient public schools. 'Excellent chap, what's 'is name. What *is* his name, Doris?'

Mrs Prendergast looked up from her Babycham, which she was stirring with a swizzle stick. 'The bubbles always make me sneeze,' she had explained to Lady Lucinda. 'Pratt, dear heart,' she replied.

'That's right, Pratt. D'you know him?'

'Can't say that I do,' replied Donald.

'Really? Thought you were at Eton. Harrow, was it?' Harrovians, in Major Prendergast's mind, had never been distinguished at spelling, or anything else for that matter.

'Winchester, actually.'

'Good God! Scientist, were you?'

'Classics. I went on to take a double First in Mods and Greats at New College.'

Major Prendergast was aghast. But he was distracted by a simultaneous sneeze from Doris Prendergast, whose actions with the swizzle stick had been inadequate to de-bubble her Babycham, and the appearance of Cook Sgt Carrier, who announced that dinner was served. His precise words, despite all Doris's attempts to teach him etiquette, were 'Plates on Table, Sah!'

'Won't you take my arm?' Major Prendergast offered his bar-propping elbow to Lady Lucinda and led the way through into the Officer's Banqueting Suite. Behind him, Doris Prendergast swallowed the remains of her Babycham and tried, unsuccessfully, to suppress a hiccough.

'Terrible place,' she said, grasping Donald's unproffered elbow. 'Awful climate, awful food, awful people. Thank God Cecil has to spend most of his time at MOD-OPS in London.'

Cook Sgt Carrier did not have Sgt Stripe's skill at interior decoration. The Nissan hut which had been converted into the Officers' Dining Suite had little of the elegance of the Seminar Suite. A stained table from which the walnut veneer was lifting held the mess silver – two candlesticks of doubtful provenance and an EPNS model of the first rocket which had been successfully fired from the Benbecula Range. On the wall, behind the obligatory portrait of Her Majesty by Annigoni, slightly stained by the damp, was a memorial to the fishermen who had died for their country when the rocket struck their boat. On the chipped sideboard were two bottles of Crimea Red lying in wicker baskets which Doris Prendergast had brought back from her last trip to Benindorm, and a bottle of Metaxa on whose label Major Prendergast had marked levels and dates in indelible pencil. The curtains were purple. While they clashed with the chairs, at least they toned in with Major Prendergast's complexion.

Major Prendergast took his seat at the head of the table, with Lady Lucinda on his right and Doris, now gently hiccoughing, at the foot. Donald took the chair to her right, in the draught from the cracked window. 'Good of you to invite us,' he said insincerely as Cook Cpl Roux entered with an immense iron saucepan from which he ladled large portions of an evil smelling broth.

'Pleasure to have company,' replied Major Prendergast. 'Tell you the truth, life's a bit dull here, what, Doris?'

Doris indicated assent with another hiccough, and Cook Cpl Roux poured out Soave into the brandy balloons.

'McTurk tells me you're on a secret mission for the government. Thought you bumph wallahs could spell though, what?'

Donald wondered who had told Major Prendergast about Dibbs' confusion with his name. He was torn between loyalty to the service and hatred of Dibbs. Loyalty, for once, got the better of him.

'It's easy enough to confuse a miniscule and a majuscule.'

Major Prendergast glanced at the Annigoni portrait. 'What the hell's her Majesty got to do with it?' he blustered.

'Nothing, so far as I'm aware. Though my letter of appointment did have "On Her Majesty's Service" on the envelope. There's nothing secret about my mission. I'm here to develop plans for the amalgamation of the Benbecula and North Uist Urban District Councils.'

'Amalgamation! Balderdash!' expostulated Major Prendergast. Amalgamation was, for him, the dirtiest word in the dictionary. Hadn't his own regiment, after so many victories, so many battle honours, finally suffered the ultimate humiliation of amalgamation with the Argyll and Sutherland Highlanders? Wasn't the European Union the product of amalgamation? Weren't all the economic ills of the country the fault of the Amalgamated Union of Printworkers, Leather Spiggot Weavers and Dockers? Hadn't he himself lost substantial sums on the amalgamation of his father's brass screw manufactory with the General Electricity Company? 'Amalgamation!'

Doris Prendergast noted the danger signals. 'Now, dear, don't excite yourself.' She removed her swizzle stick from her brandy balloon and waved it at her husband. 'We have strict rules in the

Mess,' she said to Lady Lucinda. 'No discussion of politics, religion, relationships, the monarchy, the European Union, children, grandchildren, the state of the economy, house prices, school fees or promotion prospects.'

'Good heavens,' said Lady Lucinda, breaking the interdiction on religion. 'What's left?'

There was a long silence. The wind whistled around the stove pipe and sent the occasional cloud of smoke down the stack. From the Seminar Suite next door came a muffled grunting, punctuated at intervals by someone shouting '*Hai*'. Major Prendergast examined his nails. Doris Prendergast took a little chrome-framed mirror from her handbag and adjusted her make-up. Donald MacDonald remembered dinners long ago with his Tutor on the High Table at New College. And Lady Lucinda looked aghast. Torpor overcame the Officers' Dining Suite.

Which at last was interrupted by the skirl of the Pipes. The door swung open, and Cook Sgt Carrier marched in playing 'Greensleeves' on a chanter, followed by Cook Cpl Roux, who carried what in the novels of Jeffrey Archer would have been called a groaning trencher, and Cook Private Floyd, who had an immense broadsword in his hand.

'The haggis!' exclaimed Doris, clapping her hands together like a little girl. 'The haggis,' groaned Major Prendergast, who had previous experience of Cook Sgt Carrier's experiments in the Scottish culinary arts.

The troop marched round the room, dislodging one or two pictures from the wall but, patriotically, leaving Annigoni's Queen undisturbed. Greensleeves came to an abrupt end in mid bar, and Cook Cpl Roux placed the trencher reverently on the sideboard and took the sword from Cook Private Floyd. He began to declaim, in the mellifluous dialect of Southern England –:

> *'I luv yer 'onnist, sun tanned faice*
> *Godfarver of the puddin raice*
> *Above them all yer taike yer plaice*
> *Guts, tripe or pies,*
> *Yer worvy of a bleedin graice*
> *Long as my thighs.'*

Donald MacDonald looked with horror at Major Prendergast. He was not a great admirer of Scotland's National Bard, preferring TS Eliot for raw emotion and Stevie Smith for intellectual challenge. But this was sacrilege.

'I had it translated into English,' whispered Major Prendergast proudly. 'No one understands the Scotch these days, least of all the Scotch.' Cook Cpl Roux continued –

'The groanin pla'er there you fill
Yer bu'ocks like a distant 'ill
Yer skewer would 'elp ter mend a mill
    In time of need,
While through yer pores greases distill
    Like amber bead.'

'You know,' said Lady Lucinda, 'this is the first time I've ever made head or tail of this so-called poem. Congratulations, Cecil, if I may call you that.' Major Prendergast smiled his pleasure, and Cook Cpl Roux raised the sword above his head and concluded in a roar –

' 'is chiv see manual labour grab
And cut you up wiv ready jab
Carving your gushing guts and flab
    Like down the pub
And then, O wot a sight so fab
    Like syllabub!'

He stabbed the blade into the steaming mess of entrails with all the skill gained from a long apprenticeship in the Mile End Road. At once a disgusting smell of rotting fish filled the room. 'What on earth?' screamed Lady Lucinda.

'Traditional 'aggis recipe from the He-brides,' said Cook Sgt Carrier.

'They're too fond of sheep here as personal pets and that sort of thing,' explained Major Prendergast, 'so they use cormorants. There's no need to eat much, but the Cooks will be offended if you don't have a little.' He filled an immense quaich with London Gin and handed it

Cook Cpl Roux as reward for his culinary and poetical efforts. Cook Private Floyd circled the Table, doling out vast portions of evil smelling pulp to each of the guests with a mighty ladle. Finally, Cook Sgt Carrier raised his chanter to his lips, and the cooking detail marched smartly out to the strains of *Men of Harlech*.

Silence fell. The clock ticked slowly on the wall. Lady Lucinda raised an empty fork to her lips, hoping that no one would notice. Major Prendergast lifted his glass and drank deeply of Soave. Donald removed a feather from his plate and wondered about Food Safety Regulations. And Doris Prendergast shut her eyes and thought of England – or to be more precise the cosy little semi-detached house in Esher where she hoped to retire. No one ate.

Next door in the Seminar Suite, Sgt Stripe had almost reached the climax of his lecture. He had covered Japanese history, culture, art, science, geo-political ambitions and fashion, and was turning his attention to sport.

'Now your average Japanese,' he said, 'is a little fellow, and little fellows ain't no good at competitive sports.'

'Beggin' your pardon, Sarge,' interrupted Lance Cpl Brown, 'What about featherweight boxers?'

'Me very point,' said Sgt Stripe. 'They ain't no good at competitive sports, so they has to compete against each other. You put a fevverweight boxer up against Mike Tyson and what do you get? Rape. Now your Japanese equivalent to your fevverweight boxer is your sumo wrestler. 'e starts off tiny, and 'e eats and eats until 'e's half the size of an elephant.'

'So how's he a featherweight, Sarge,' asked Private White.

' 'e's a fevverweight inside. Now, if we're going to understand the Japanese mind, we've got to understand 'is sport. So you lads are going to become the Benbecula and North Uist sumo wrestling stable. I want you to watch this video.'

Sgt Stripe dimmed the lights and switched on the TV. The screen flickered and revealed the Tokyo Sumo Stadium. A little man dressed in traditional Japanese dress held a fan and nodded at the two competitors. Their huge bellies bulged over their loin-cloths and they stared at each other and made animal grunts. After a minute or two the contestants turned away from each other, took a handful of salt each, and threw it into the ring. They resumed eye contact, grunted, then lumbered into the ring and caught each other in a bear hug. It was all over in seconds. The smaller of the two gave a flip of his buttock, and the larger found himself thrown out of the ring.

Sgt Stripe switched off the TV and turned to his men. 'White and Krunt, you pick up the font. Snodgrass and Brown, take that Madonna by the door and wrap a loin cloth around its waist. Now the object is to barge your opponent out of the ring, which is marked by this circle wot I 'ave drawn in chalk on the floor. I want you to imagine that the font and the Madonna are sumo wrestlers, and you're going to help them bash each other out of the circle. I'm the referee.'

'Where's the salt, Sarge,' asked Snodgrass.

'Forget the salt. That's lesson two.' Sgt Stripe plucked a fan from its place in an alcove and held it before his face. 'When I drop the fan,' he said indistinctly, 'you start.'

The two pairs of troopers lifted their mannequins and glared at each other across the chalk circle. Sgt Stripe muttered a few words in Japanese and dropped his fan. White and Krunt lifted the font and charged into the ring. Snodgrass and Brown, with an agility that owed more to Rugby League than to sumo wrestling, lifted the Madonna sideways, and the font was propelled out of the ring and against the flimsy plasterboard wall of the Seminar Suite.

Which collapsed in a cloud of white dust, allowing the font to crash through the wall into the room next door.

Where Major Cecil Prendergast and his guests were sitting, silent as on a peak in Darien, contemplating with a wild surmise their reeking plates of Cormorant Haggis.

* * *

CHAPTER 14

In which the Vatican becomes involved.

Donald Macdonald opened his eyelids gingerly and wished that he hadn't. The harsh Japanese light bored into his retinas like a high speed drill probing a particularly sensitive root canal without benefit of anaesthetic. The harsh Japanese air conditioning rasped on his lungs like the fumes of Mount Etna. The harsh Japanese telephone at his bedside table warbled incessantly like the dawn chorus on the Day of Judgement. Donald squeezed his eyes shut and lifted the handset.

'Yes,' he croaked when his parched mouth could produce sufficient saliva to lubricate his vocal chords.

'Stuart MacLellan,' said a voice which Donald vaguely recognised.

Donald opened his eyes and peered around the room. 'Not here,' he grunted. 'There's nobody here.'

'I'm Stuart MacLellan,' said the voice.

It gradually came back to Donald. He had been with MacLellan the previous evening. MacLellan was on his staff. They had eaten a traditional meal, each course more raw than the last, and each washed down with copious quantities of warm sake. Then they had repaired to a bar where they had drunk something called shochu mixed with hot water or cold tea. He had done his imitation of Sir Terence Mould singing *'I'll do it my way'* to the accompaniment of a Karaoke machine and many jeers. There had been some kind of argument.

'Why didn't you say so,' he said at last flatly, thereby omitting the question mark at the end of the sentence.

There was an exasperated gasp from the handset, then Stuart said: 'We have a meeting at the embassy at nine thirty. Then we are due at

Omeiwaku's Corporate Head Office at eleven. I'll meet you at the gate of the Embassy at nine o'clock sharp.' The line went dead.

Four Paracetamols, a cold shower, and a breakfast of mango juice from the mini bar in his room did something to restore Donald's health. The whirlpool in his stomach had calmed to a mild churning, like Corrievreckan at high water springs in a Force 9 gale. The pain round his cranium had retreated from the roots to the tips of his hair. He could open one or other of his eyes without flinching; both at once allowed too much brightness to echo around the reverberating cavity of his skull. He could almost think without mixing metaphors. He climbed his way into his second best suit, like a rock climber on a difficult pitch, pitched his pyjamas into the corner of the room, and tripped over the fax from Donald MacDonald, which had been slipped under his door while he was asleep. The fax confirmed the support of the North Uist Chamber of Commerce for the location of the Feelgood Project in North Uist, and said they would offer every assistance to make their potential visit a success. Thrusting it into his pocket for further consideration, he set his watch to Tokyo time, his face to magnetic north, and his steps towards the elevator and the taxi rank.

Her Britannic Majesty's Ambassador to the Chrysanthemum Throne and the Court of the Imperial House of Japan occupies, after the Emperor, the primest property in the most expensive city in the world. A vast Homes and Gardens house of silver granite sits amid gracious lawns hard by the Imperial Palace. Here and there, hidden among the rhododendrons and azaleas, the tennis courts and swimming pools, the squash racquets courts and croquet lawns, was a house in which a diplomatist's wife might entertain other diplomatic wives to tea. There was even the occasional office in which eager British consular staff queued up to stamp visas into the passports of Japanese businessmen. Many a near bankrupt Chancellor had cast envious eyes on the property; if it could be sold he could (depending on Party) reduce income tax to 10p in the £, or re-house all the Labour voters of Westminster in Sheffield, or renationalise British Telecom, or re-house all the Conservative voters of Sheffield in Westminster. But when the embassy was established the then Foreign Secretary, using all the negotiating skills which had subsequently lost Britain the Empire, had failed to persuade the Japanese government that he should be sold the Freehold: all he had managed to secure was a permanent lease at a peppercorn rent, the number of peppercorns to be determined by shifts in the value of the Yen. Generations of Chancellors had cursed him; and generations of diplomatists and pepper farmers had benefited from the deal.

Sir Jimmy Bloggs stood under the granite portico of Number One House (the Ambassador's Residence) rubbing his hands together. 'C'm on in, lads, and park yer bums on a seat,' he said. 'We've a lot to get through, and I've got to see the Papal Nancy Boy at ten.'

Sir Jimmy was not your typical diplomat. He had received his early education not at the Dragon School and Westminster, but at the Mafeking Road Elementary School in Rochdale. Instead of Kings College Cambridge he had graced the Army Interpreters' School at Catterick. But a facility for oriental languages – he spoke eight fluently and had a nodding acquaintance with another six – a razor sharp mind, and a rare willingness to call a fleshy spike of flowers a spadex and a broad based digging instrument a shovel, had propelled him to the highest reaches of the Diplomatic service.

He ushered them into his drawing room – a large sunny salon overlooking the lawns, furnished with the elegance of a Chatsworth or a Hatfield House. On the pale green walls were paintings of the Norwich School – Crome, Cotman, Bonnington – though to Donald, who preferred the Monarch of the Glen School, they might have been invisible. A Second Empire clock ticked on the mantle shelf. And, sitting on a fragile chair by the French windows, was Dwight Dildenschneider.

'Wayell, if it ain't my old friends Stuart MacLellan and Donald Macdonald,' he said, lumbering to his feet. 'How ya doin', boys?'

Stuart looked at him with undisguised contempt. 'What are you doing here?' he snapped.

'Breakfast meeting with mah old friend Ambassador Bloggs. We westerners must stick together, even if we are further west and you are going west! I guess the Ambassador will want to brief you boys on inward investment from Japan, so I'll be on my way. Wouldn't want any of my secrets to slip out by mistake!'

Dildenschneider puffed out his chest, putting dangerous pressure on the buttons of his shirt. 'Just bear in mind mah advice,' he said to Ambassador Bloggs, prodding the Ambassador's chest with a nicotine stained finger. 'Mah President aiyn't amused by every goddam European getting into bed with every goddam Japanese. And mah President will be specifically, and ah mean specifically, not amused if you boys clinch the Omeiwaku deal. So I suggest you leave Omeiwaku to your big brother, and go play with your marbles. Otherwise, I can't answer to the consequences for our two great countries.'

'Go fuck yourself,' said Ambassador Bloggs amiably. Dildenschneider inclined his head and went, though whether indeed to perform such an act history does not relate.

'Untrustworthy son of a bitch,' said Bloggs. 'If 'e thinks I think 'e's got the authority to speak for the US President , 'e's got another think coming. Fact is, 'e's got to win the Feelgood Project or they'll post him to Taipei. A bloke of 'is grotesque dimensions would never stand the 'umidity. And since I want 'im off my patch I'll make bloody sure that the UK wins it. If not, I'll eat Dildenschneider's ten gallon hat in a quarter pounder 'amburger bun. I don't give a fuck, though, if it's you or the Welsh who get it.'

'The Welsh?' asked Stuart, a note of alarm in his voice.

'They're 'ere too. I thought Donald might 'ave met them in the 'plane, though come to think of it they usually travel First Class. Very attractive lady leads the Welsh delegation, if you're a fan of Rembrandt. Megan Morgan Thomas. You can't miss 'er – always wears a Welsh Bonnet and buckled shoes. Now this is 'ow I suggest you approach the project.'

Ambassador Bloggs gave them a brief but incisive analysis of the Omeiwaku Corporation and its top management. The company had been founded in the Edo period by Jitakabi Omeiwaku, an itinerant sword sharpener who had noticed that the Chinese were keen to buy as many Japanese swords as they could lay their hands on. Unlike most swords of the time, Japanese swords were both flexible and razor-sharp, a combination achieved through repeated heating and hammering. Omeiwakusan had borrowed from his father-in-law and established a small manufactory to mass produce inferior swords to sell to the Chinese. The Chinese had fallen for the ruse, and when five years later they had invaded, they were cut to ribbons as their razor sharp but brittle swords snapped in their hands. Omeiwakusan was honoured by a grateful Emperor, and his son, who had been introduced to gunpowder by one of his Chinese trading partners, began to take an interest in cannons. He hired a Dutch sailor to steal one for him from a man-of-war anchored off Kobe. The Dutch sailor was flogged within an inch of his life, but Omeiwaku Junior enhanced the technology by a process of incremental improvement later to be employed with such success in Omeiwaku's electronics factories. Within three years he had produced enough guns to blast the fleets of Western merchants out of Japanese waters. He, too, was honoured, this time by a grateful Shogun.

The company had prospered and grown during the years of isolation, diversifying into boat building, ornamental ironwork, fan making, doll making, pharmaceuticals and drugs. When Lieutenant Pinkerton, with his passion for lepidoptery, had once more opened the country to outside influence, Omeiwaku Inc was well placed for the great leap forward. It sent emissaries all over the globe, clad in dark suits, bowler hats and white spats, in search of new technologies to beg, borrow or steal. In its armaments division it returned to its roots and prepared Japan for both World Wars. It established a toy factory in a little known suburb of Narita called England; plastic toys stamped 'Made in England' became sought after by little boys throughout the civilised world. Its shipbuilding division took on and defeated the mighty Clyde: as the steam hammers and rivet guns fell silent in Govan and Greenock, the welders of Osaka sweltered by day under an oriental sun and by night over an oriental mama-san.

But its joy and pride was its electronics division – Omeiwaku Denki. When a little known and soon to be forgotten Italian called Marconi had transmitted wireless telegraphy signals across the Atlantic, its men in white spats had been listening. When John Logie Baird had projected moving images across the ether, its men in white spats had been watching. And when Alan Turing had developed his model for a universal calculating machine, its men in white spats had thrown away their abacuses and started counting with electrons.

Omeiwaku Denki now owned factories across the globe, producing televisions, hi-fi, micro-computers, macro-computers, main frames, servers, multi-media home entertainment machines, and silicon chips. What did it care if most of the calculations done on its computers had the effect of undermining traditional values, and if much of the entertainment shown through its multi media machines did the same to traditional culture. It was into the hardware, not the software; and in any case Corporations do not have a conscience. And Hiro Yamamoto, its eighty four year old President, did not permit ethics to interfere with the vital search for diversification without which Omeiwaku Denki would wither and die. He had hit on a new project – and the Governments of the Western world were falling over themselves to support it.

Despite his great age, and perhaps because of his new young wife, Hiro Yamamoto had not failed to notice the twin forces of women's liberation and sexual permissiveness which were raging through the USA and Western Europe. And these forces, his still agile mind told him, had given birth to a new market opportunity which had a perfect fit with Omeiwaku Denki's existing technologies, and with a lot of other things besides. To be specific, a new improved remotely controlled variable speed electronic vibrator.

Initially his project – the Feelgood Project, or FGP as he came to call it – had not received the full support of his Board. Indeed some of the younger members, those in their sixties and seventies, had opposed it on the grounds that it would open Omeiwaku Denki up to ridicule and themselves up to charges that they were unable to satisfy their wives. Fujisawasan had even worried that it would damage his chances of a political career when he took early retirement at the age of seventy four. But Yamamotosan had pressed ahead with all the determination of a Kamikaze pilot on his fifth mission. Objections had been over-ruled. Opponents had been worn down. And by a process of decision making which owed more to Stalin's Supreme Soviet than to corporate governance in any Western sense, consensus had been achieved. It had taken two years, and Mrs Yamamoto was more in need of a successful outcome than ever.

Yamamotosan set some of the finest brains of the Omeiwaku Research Laboratories to work. Young idealists were removed at a moment's notice from their work on the design of nuclear triggers and range finding devices and set to devising new and more sensitive control mechanisms. Three Professors of Anatomy at the Tokyo University Medical School were put to work, one a specialist in the relevant male parts, one a specialist in the relevant female parts, and one a specialist in putting the one into the other. Several software engineers were recruited and fired when their programs were found to have insufficient stiffness; when he learnt of this, Yamamotosan decreed that the programming should be hard wired onto the chips. After a certain amount of experimentation, the consequent firmware was considered to be sufficiently firm, and the Chief Engineer of Omeiwaku Shipyards Corporation, a man more accustomed to building supertankers, was instructed to assemble a prototype. The marketing men did their market research, and the advertising experts came up – if that is the *mot juste* – with the brand name Feelgood ToyBoy™, and recommended that the scientists should come up with a complementary version, the Feelgood PlayMate^PMT^. Three weeks later Mrs Yamamoto appeared at her calligraphy class with a smile on her face.

All that remained was to find a suitable location for manufacture and to put the ToyBoy™ into production. But here again there was dissension on the Board. Fujisawasan, having decided that the bonus in jobs would far outweigh any moral outrage at the product, wanted the plant located in his prospective constituency. The younger members of the Board, worried at the strong Yen and mindful of golfing trips abroad, favoured other parts of SE Asia – Korea, perhaps, or better still Thailand. But Yamamotosan wanted the plant located close to its principal markets, in Europe or the United States. The fact that substantial government grants were available in both places to attract Japanese investment had clinched the matter; and Omeiwaku Denki had let it be known that they had in prospect a major project, promising substantial numbers of jobs, if the package of government support was right.

'So you see, boys, we've got a challenge,' concluded Ambassador Bloggs. 'The Yanks are determined to win the project for California – as if they've not got enough jobs in Silicon Valley already. The French 'ave offered illegal amounts of State aid to attract it to Dijon. Even the Irish have forgotten their 'ail Marys and are trying to persuade Yamamotosan to put it in Cork. And the British bloody Treasury has reduced the amount of grant we can offer and suggested that we can win the project on merit, whatever that is. It'll require charm, wit, courage, and a few white lies. Try to persuade Yamamoto to visit. That way we can get to work with the golf, the fishing and the Scotch. The old bugger's an autocratic sod, and no one responds to flattery more. So, whatever you do, suck up to 'im.'

Donald wondered about the propriety of sucking up to the inventor of the ToyBoy™. But his thoughts were interrupted by the entrance of a white coated Japanese servant. The Japanese bowed low before Ambassador Bloggs. 'His Very Reverend Excellency the Papal Nuncio is waiting, your Excellency, Sir,' he whispered.

'Bloody 'ell, I forgot all about 'im,' muttered Bloggs.' 'E's come to tell us to 'ave nowt to do with the Feelgood Project on the grounds that it'll make his flock less interested in the mass than masturbation. You might as well stay and 'elp me out.'

The Papal Nuncio was ushered in. He was a copious man who was sweating copiously under his cope. It was said that he was destined for the highest reaches of the Curia; but he knew well that if the Feelgood Project went ahead his vocation was as parish priest of a small mountain village in Umbria.

'Monsignor Carelli,' said Bloggs, clasping his hand warmly in his. 'What a pleasure to see you. I trust your children are well – 'as little Lucia started nursery school yet? Let me introduce my colleagues Stuart MacLellan and Donald Macdonald.'

Carelli shook hands limply with a damp paw, and heaved his bulk into a chintz sofa.

'These are a-difficult times, Ambassador,' he said. 'And I am here on a difficult a-mission.'

'Never 'ad difficulties with emission myself,' said Bloggs. 'But we're paid to 'andle difficulties, even if my reward comes a bit sooner than yours. If you'd find it easier, we can 'old our discussions in Latin. I'm sure Macdonald 'ere is fluent, and I used to be quite good at the old *amo amas amat*.'

'That won't-a be necessary,' said Carelli, who secretly yearned for the return of the Tridentine Mass and thought that Latin should be reserved for sacred uses. 'I would not a-wish to sully the language of Virgil, Livy, Cicero and, er, Sully with what I have to say, which concerns a matter of almost indelicate delicacy.'

'You mean you're prepared to sully the language of Shakespeare, Milton, Dryden, PG Wodehouse and Pope on such a matter? If so my Government will protest in the strongest possible terms.' Ambassador Bloggs believed that the essential art of diplomacy consisted in avoiding the point and wasting the maximum possible time on side issues.

'The Pope speaks Polish, a language where even angels fear to tread,' responded Carelli. 'But yes, I must sully the language of DH Lawrence, William Burroughs, Jackie Collins, Barbara Cartland and Irvine Welsh. It concerns the Feelgood Project of the Omeiwaku Corporation.'

'I'm not sure I know what you're talking about. You'll 'ave to be more specific.' Ambassador Bloggs believed that the essential art of diplomacy consisted of deviousness.

'The Feelgood Project must not-a be allowed to go ahead,' said Carelli, wringing his hands as though the project would make them redundant. 'It will corrupt the young, it will bring shame to the old, it will cause mothers to disown their daughters and sons their grandmothers, it will destroy the economy, and it will bring the wrath of God onto the land.'

'On the contrary,' said Ambassador Bloggs, 'it will bring delight to the young, it will bring comfort to the old, and it will bring jobs to the people. My economists 'ave calculated that it 'as an employment multiplier of 5.2. That is quite extraordinarily high.'

'But-a the whole point of the project is that it avoids multiplication,' expostulated Carelli. 'The Good Lord did not say to our parents in the garden, 'Go forth and vibrate', or 'go forth and feel good'. That is why it is so sinful, and why his Holiness the Pope will oppose it to the end.'

'How many Divisions has the Pope?' interjected Donald, who remembered the quotation but not its source. Bloggs affected to be horrified. 'We're talking of multiplication, not division,' he said, attempting to divert attention from politics to arithmetic. But the damage was done. Carelli heaved himself to his feet.

'I am not a-remaining here to be threatened with military intervention,' he said. 'I shall a-report back immediately to the Vatican. Your government shall 'ear more of this.'

And he gathered his cassock about his ample buttocks and flowed out of the room.

'Well done, lads,' said Bloggs as the door slammed shut behind him. 'That's put 'im in 'is place. Think they can run the country like in the days of Mary Tudor, they do. Never even 'eard of the Church of England and the Bishop of Durham. Now get you off to Omeiwaku Denki, and do your damnedest.'

CHAPTER 15

In which one of our heroes acts like a gentleman.

Torquil MacCorquodale, Wee Free Minister of North Uist, was a fundamentalist. That is to say, he took the Bible to be literally true down to the smallest detail, and read it accordingly. He did not covet his neighbour's wife, who was curiously mis-shapen, nor his neighbour's manservant, since he was not that way inclined. In accordance with Deuteronomy Chapter 14, he desisted from eating the camel, the osprey and the vulture. Had he been walking along a road in Samaria he would have been the first to cross to the other side to help a wounded traveller. But Mary Lou Krantz was not a wounded traveller lying by the side of a road in Samaria. So it was that, when at 11 pm his work on his five hour sermon on the sins of the flesh was interrupted by a frenzied rapping on his window, he turned the other cheek and drew the blinds.

Mary Lou Krantz was in no fit state to be turned away. Since fleeing in panic from the Highland Games she had wandered lost, through peat bogs and over rocky hillocks, in search of help. She had followed will o' the wisps down sheep tracks which even the sheep had forgotten. She had tracked footprints on the weedy shore, only to discover that they were her own. She had waded across lochans and fallen into streams. Once, as the light faded from the northern sky, she had caught sight of a lamp in a cottage window, but the plaster ducks which she saw when she peered in had sent her screaming from the scene. Her kilt hung wetly below her knees; cold draughts assaulted her naked nether regions (how she cursed Miriam Katzenellenbogen's dress code); her nails were broken; her arms were scratched and bleeding from gorse bushes. She was not at her best.

How she longed for the green lawns and wide shopping malls of home, the smart bungalows, each with their three cars in the driveway, the neat wooden fences, the basket-ball nets attached like exclamation marks to garage doors. She would never come to Europe again.

Sergeant McPloud of the North Uist Constabulary was also wishing that he were elsewhere. The telephone call to the crowded Public Bar of the North Uist Hydro Hotel had interrupted what promised to be a most enjoyable game of darts. His two off duty constables were already well gone in drink, and did not appreciate being recalled to the colours. The pensioner whose lack of agility had destroyed the Terrier Race and devastated the North Uist and Pabbay Highland Games was appeasing his conscience by buying drinks all round. But McTurk was insistent.

'I will not be having missing persons wandering all over the Island as though they owned the place,' he had said. 'Mistress Krantz hass been lost for six hours now; and Mistress Katzenellenbogen is beside herself with worry and iss convinced that she hass been kidnapped. If Donald MacDonald thinks that we cannot find a missing person on an island no bigger than Hyde Park, we've no chance of keeping our independence. I want road blocks on all the roads, look-outs at all the airports, extra watchers at the harbour, and black-house to black-house enquiries made. And put out an MP report on *Radio nan Eilean.*'

'But Sir Hector's at Westminster,' retorted McPloud, alluding to the island's courteous but generally absentee Member of Parliament.

'Missing Person, McPloud, you eediot. Iss it a wonder that you had to bribe the examiners to pass your Sercheant's examinations!'

So with a heavy stomach, McPloud had gathered his men in the car park outside the bar. 'There iss an American lady hass gone missing, presumed kidnapped for a great ransom,' he had elaborated. 'We are to find her; happen there will be a reward.' And they had gone forth into the night.

Mary Lou Krantz had, meantime, stumbled upon something familiar. She staggered out of a lochan, climbed a peat hag, and reached a flat piece of land which reminded her of the parking lot outside the Big Mick Drive-in Diner and Speedy Eatery back home.

She sat down for a moment, puzzled. Then she realised what it was – a road. Wearily she hauled herself to her feet and, sniffing the wind as she had been taught as a girl scout, began to plod in what she judged was a north-easterly direction. In fact, she was walking south, along the causeway that led to Benbecula.

Where, five miles away, Donald MacDonald and Lady Lucinda were taking their leave of Major and Mrs Prendergast. Their evening had not been a success. Major Prendergast had sought to obliterate the experience of being assaulted with Cormorant Haggis and ecclesiastical sumo wrestlers by plying his guests with excessive amounts of alcohol. But not even large draughts of Crimea Red 1999 could overcome the horrors of Cook Sgt Carrier's *Lapin Locale à la Sauce de Scotch Whisky*, semolina pudding and local ram's milk cheese. By the time the ladies withdrew to partake of cherry brandy and nescafé in the drawing-hut, leaving the menfolk to circulate the British port-style wine, Donald was too far gone to learn anything useful about Benbecula and its inhabitants. It was with relief mingled with apprehension that he rose to leave.

'Shure you won't shtay the night, old man?' asked Prendergast. 'The road around here can be pretty treacherous, and the beggars won't install street lights.'

'Must get back to the twins,' muttered Donald. Much as he disliked the company of Alsace and Lorraine, the prospect of having to breakfast with Major and Mrs Prendergast was even worse. The island porridge with a sea-weed garnish could not, in all decency, be washed down with alcohol.

'Then I'll order Sgt Stripe to drive you,' offered Major Prendergast.

'No, no, couldn't think of it. Quite fit to drive,' said Donald. He relished even less the prospect of spending more time with a deranged sergeant nursing outlandish geo-political theories.

'Well, drive carefully,' said Prendergast. 'And if you hit a sheep, make sure it doesn't fall into the hands of Cook Sgt Carrier. We normally eat frozen food from the co-op.'

'I'll do that willingly,' replied Donald. 'At least there are unlikely to be any police around.'

He steered Lady Lucinda into the passenger seat, engaged the gears of the hired 1965 Ford Cortina, and drove northwards into the night at a steady eight miles an hour. The single working headlamp lit up a desolate scene of windswept moorland, ice cold lochans, barren rocks. Here and there the eyes of animals gleamed in the dark and were gone. From across the machair came the angry roar of the sea. All was bleak, barren, bare.

'Donald, slow down! What's that?' Lady Lucinda peered into the gloom, to where a forlorn figure could be made out sitting on the parapet of the causeway.

Mary Lou Krantz's wanderings through the island had not improved her appearance. Her once white ankle socks were black with peat; her kilt was besmirched with mud; her hair hung in wet streaks from beneath her Glengarry.

'Another of Sgt Stripe's monsters – probably on sentry duty.' Donald pressed on the accelerator and brought the forward motion of the car up to 12 mph.

'No, no, it's singing Shenandoah!' shouted Lady Lucinda. For Mary Lou Krantz, as instructed by the Girl Scouts, was keeping up her spirits by singing songs of her childhood. When she saw the lights of the car, she doubled her volume and waved feebly, but in time to the music.

Reluctantly, Donald drew the car to a halt. 'Say, can you take me to a motel?' said Mary Lou Krantz.

* * *

CHAPTER 16

In which there is confusion.

The headquarters of Omeiwaku Denki is a glass and steel tower looming over the business district of Tokyo. Its earthquake proof foundations sink eight stories into the subsoil; its lifts and air conditioning plant consume more electricity than a small town; and it employs more window cleaners than Winchester. Everything, from the granite portico and the three storey marble faced atrium to the platinum flagstaff by the helipad forty-eight storeys above, is designed to show opulence and financial solidity.

A board by the entrance proclaimed *Omeiwaku Denki Corporation welcomes: Stuart MacRerran and Donard Makdonard.* Stuart strode past to the walnut veneered reception desk and gave his business card to a blue uniformed girl.

'*Ah so,*' she said, bowing low. 'You have appointment?'

'Yes,' said Stuart. 'With President Yamamoto. At eleven o'clock.'

'*Ah so,*' said the receptionist, bowing again and smiling behind her hand. 'One moment please.' She looked at a large sheaf of paper before her, then tapped into her computer.

'Sorry, no record,' she said after a moment. 'You certain meeting with President Yamamoto is today?'

'Of course,' said Stuart. 'Our names are on your welcome board.'

The young lady looked at the board. 'Oh no,' she said, 'You are mistaken. That say Mr Macrerran. You are Mr MacLellan.' She had done a postgraduate year at the University of Texas, and was proud of her mastery of English pronunciation.

'I am Mr Macrerran,' said Stuart slowly. 'And this is Mr

Makdonard. Give her your card, Donald.'

She inspected Donald's card carefully. 'Oh no,' she said, 'it is quite lucid. You are Mr Macdonald.'

Donald had visions of losing the Omeiwaku Project because of confusion between an 'l' and an 'r'. Little did he suspect that he had only been given the chance to win it because of confusion between a 'd' and a 'D'. He took a deep breath.

'We are Scottish, right,' he said slowly. 'In Scottish, the 'l' and the 'r' are interchangeable.'

' *Ah so*, interchangeable. Or intelchangeabre, no?' The girl giggled behind her hand.

'Precisely so. So I can be referred to as either Donald Macdonald or Donard Macdonard.'

'Ah, I see. But should it not be a capital 'D'?'

Fifteen minutes later they had resolved the finer points of English orthography and endured the vertiginous ascent in the High Speed Presidential Lift to find themselves on the 39th floor of the Omeiwaku Tower. It was a vast chamber modelled on, or rather taken from, a Venetian Palazzo. The oak panelling was hung with old masters: Titians, Giorgiones, an exquisite still life of flowers and butterflies by Peter Breugel the Elder. Suits of armour lined the walls, mostly European, but one, incongruously, from the Shogunate. Ancient moth-eaten battle standards hung from the ceiling, and in the centre of the room, standing on a silken Turkey carpet, an Omeiwaku electronic harpsichord played Purcell aires by itself, its keys rising and falling as if moved by the invisible hand of Adam Smith. Over all hung the heady scent of pot pourri and log fires.

At the foot of a broad staircase which curved into the heights stood an exquisite Japanese. She smiled and bowed low. 'Please, come this way. President Yamamoto is awaiting you.'

The meeting room into which they were led could not have been a greater contrast. A wide picture window over looked Tokyo harbour and the new bridge which had contributed so much to down town congestion. The furniture was of steel, chrome and glass. The glaring white walls were adorned with late impressionists and a late early Picasso, when blue was just beginning to shade into pink like a badly made Tequila Sunrise. Behind the table was an alcove in which sat a ming vase, a Japanese scroll and a single orchid.

The Japanese girl ushered them into seats in front of the alcove, and bowed again. 'President Yamamoto will join you shortly,' she said. She glided from the room as though on casters.

Donald looked round the room with awe, and Stuart with familiarity. 'Now don't forget what I told you about business etiquette,' he whispered. 'You are senior to me, so you must lead off the meeting. Exchange business cards with both hands, place them face up on the table, and whatever you do don't scribble on them. Don't blow your nose, even if you are itching for a sneeze; and always defer to Yamamoto.'

Donald remembered the advice of Dwight Dildenschneider, who had recommended an altogether more robust form of business etiquette. But was Dildenschneider to be trusted? The ambassador thought not; and his keenness to win the project for California cast doubt on his advice. On the other hand, he seemed a nice enough guy; and Donald had to assert his superiority over Stuart. Bosses should not slavishly follow the recommendations of their subordinates; otherwise there would be no point in being a boss. Donald decided to average their advice: he would follow Stuart's counsel on business cards, and Dildenschneider's on bowing and straight talking.

At this point the door opened and a diminutive Japanese, well advanced into old age, entered the room, bowing and rubbing his hands. He grinned, revealing crooked and nicotine stained teeth. 'Welcome to Omeiwaku Denki Corporation,' he said.

Donald stood up and resisted the temptation to bow. 'President Yamamoto, I am very pleased to meet you.'

The old man giggled. 'Oh, no,' he said, 'Yamamotosan not me. I am Hirosiguchi, personal assistant, Yamamotosan's aide. Plesident will join us shortly.' He reached into the pocket of his dark blue business suit and took out a leather wallet from which he extracted a business card. He handed this face up to Donald, holding it in both hands.

Donald fumbled in his own pocket for his card, thrust it towards Hirosiguchi, and dropped Hirosiguchi's card onto the floor.

Hirosiguchi studied Donald's card carefully as Donald scrabbled for Hirosiguchi's. '*Ah so* Mr Dildenschneider,' he said at last. ' I was expecting, ah, someone else. But this is a happy accident. President

Yamamoto has gleat admilation for your President Crinton, and many questions about possibility of trade war with Japan. Also project to discuss.'

Donald frowned. How could he be mistaken for a six foot two, eighteen stone Yank who chewed gum and brewed his coffee in a ten gallon hat. Stuart hissed in his ear: 'You've given him the wrong card, for Christ's sake.' He spoke in rapid and fluent Japanese to Hirosiguchi, who handed him Dildenschneider's card and looked questioningly at Donald. Donald reached into his pocket and, by a happy accident, produced his own.

The door opened again and three other Japanese entered. All wore identical dark blue suits, identical white shirts and striped ties, identical steel framed spectacles, identical clips in their buttonholes with the Omeiwaku Denki logo, and identical smiles. Introductions were effected; cards were exchanged. They were identified as the Project Team for the Feelgood Project.

Finally, and with due ceremony, President Yamamoto arrived. Despite his 84 years and his young wife, he was surprisingly unwrinkled. There was not a grey hair in his patent leather head; and his teeth had been expensively capped at considerable cost to his stockholders. Long afternoons at the golf club had preserved the firmness of his handshake; and while not even long afternoons in the Ginza could bring back the firm convictions of his youth, he was convinced that he had the answer in the FGP.

After the ritual exchange of business cards, he settled into the chair opposite Donald and looked him straight in the eye.

'Tell me about Wales,' he said.

* * *

CHAPTER 17

In which an American lady becomes an accessory.

Constable Gurk McGurk was blessed with a literal mind. This had helped his career in the police force to the extent that he could be relied upon to carry out his orders to the letter. But the consequent requirement for absolute precision in instructions had driven more than one of his sergeants to drink; and not even a string of successful convictions for speeding against miscreants who had confessed to being perhaps one or two over the limit had won him promotion.

But he was determined to prove himself. Sergeant McPloud had instructed him to find a kidnapped American lady who was being held for a large ransom, and he was determined to find her. Sergeant McPloud had instructed him to guard the causeway to Benbecula and not to let a living creature pass; he would follow those orders assiduously. Sergeant McPloud had instructed him to guard his post until morning, so he had taken a torch and the station's copy of the *Daily Sport* with him.

Not that he could find time to read it. It was not easy preventing animals passing. The sheep were relatively docile; but he had been compelled to take three dogs into custody and had tied them to the fence where they snapped at each other's heels and howled for their masters. And more than one rabbit had escaped him. With luck, though, Sergeant McPloud wouldn't find out – Benbecula rabbits looked very like North Uist rabbits, particularly at night.

He was at first so preoccupied in preventing the dogs from fighting amongst themselves that he did not notice the car on the causeway. Its single headlamp had dimmed to a glimmer, and at seven miles an hour its engine sound was barely audible above the sound of the surf. It was the noise of singing which first attracted his attention. Mary Lou Krantz, installed in the back of Donald's hired car, had exhausted Shenandoah and was singing a slave song of the old south to keep her spirits up and the driver awake–

> *'Ah'm a prisoner here on this lonesome road*
> *And ah wear mah pride in chains*
> *And ah think of the freedom that ah hoad*
> *And the cotton fields on the plains,'*

she sang at the top of her voice. Constable McGurk pricked up his ears and peered into the darkness.

> *'They took me away from mah dear old farm*
> *Where the river runs down to the sea*
> *And they shackled mah feet and they shackled mah arms*
> *An they don't give a fig for me.'*

Constable McGurk could now make out the car's headlamp and some of the words sung by Mary Lou Krantz. 'Prisoner', 'shackled', and 'chains' particularly struck him. He left the dogs to fight unhindered and stepped out into the road. Mary Lou Krantz was nearing the climax of her song–

> *'And here ah sit in this north-bound truck*
> *With mah head held high in pride*
> *Bound by captors who don't give a......'*

'Halt!' shouted Constable McGurk. 'What iss the meaning of this?'

Donald MacDonald stamped on the brakes, and the Ford Cortina slewed to a halt.

> *'A prisoner, captive, slave!'*

concluded Mary Lou Krantz.

'What in heffen's name iss the meaning of this?' repeated Constable McGurk.

'I might ask you the same,' responded Donald. 'Is there a problem?'

'We are hearing reports of a kidnap,' said McGurk. 'An American lady. And if I am not mistaken chust, that is an American lady in the back of your car who is claiming to have been kidnapped.'

'But this is preposterous,' said Lady Lucinda, who could articulate slightly more clearly than Donald. 'We found her on the road, and are taking her back to her hotel.'

'A likely story,' said McGurk. 'She iss shouting that she iss a captive. Iss that not right, Mistress?'

'Prisoner, captive, slave,' repeated Mary Lou Krantz, who was finding the constable's English difficult to follow. 'That's the last line. Moving, ain't it?'

'There!' exclaimed McGurk triumphantly. 'A clear accusation at all, at all. Since when has a prisoner been free?'

'But she's not a prisoner,' expostulated Donald. 'She's a hitch hiker.'

'I don't care how you hitched her to your car – she hass said quite clearly that she's a slave. Could you repeat what you said, Mistress?'

Mary Lou Krantz sang her song again – she was proud of her voice and sang pianissimo this time, and with more feeling. Indeed, she put so much emotion into her singing that she broke down after the last line and burst into tears.

Constable McGurk listened carefully, transcribing key words into his Notebook with a blunt pencil. 'I think that you had all better come down to the station,' he said when he had finished. 'But I should warn you that anything you say or sing will be taken down in writing in my Notebook and may be used in evidence against you in the Sheriff Court in Lochmaddy. You drive,' he said to Donald, 'so that I can write down what you say. And drive slowly, so that the bumps in the road do not render my handwriting illiterate.'

Donald put the car in gear and breathed deeply. 'A kidnapper I'm certainly not,' he articulated slowly. 'From the North British Office, here on duty.'

'Thank you,' said McGurk, 'that iss a most helpful admission, and should serve to reduce your sentence. "A kidnapper I'm certainly," ' he repeated, writing the words laboriously in his Notebook. ' "Not from the North British Office here on duty".' He found it difficult to follow the syntactical structure of the second sentence, but the man had obviously been drinking.

From the back of the car Mary Lou Krantz began to sing again. She had given up the struggle to make sense of events. All she wanted was a hot shower and a warm bed, and it looked as though the car would take her to a place where they could be found.

'*O give me mah freedom*,' she sang, '*unshackle mah chains*.'

'Don't worry, Mistress,' said Constable McGurk. 'You're in safe hands now.'

Sergeant Jock Greene, Desk Sergeant at the North Uist Police Station, had been fully briefed on the disappearance and possible kidnapping of Mary Lou Krantz. So when Constable McGurk arrived with his cargo of miscreants he was in no doubt as to what to do.

'You,' he said to Donald, 'will be charged with kidnapping, false imprisonment, driving a car on the public road in a state of intoxication, impersonation of a government official, and receipt of stolen goods. Your hire car was stolen six months ago from Thomas Macgillivray.'

'Phone McTurk,' shouted Donald. 'He'll explain everything.'

'It iss more that my life is worth to disturb him at this time of night. I will not hear of such a thing.'

'Then phone the hotel,' said Lady Lucinda in a more placatory tone. 'Miriam Katzenellenbogen knows the score.'

'Be quiet, you,' shouted Sergeant Greene. 'You will be charged with the same offences, apart from driving under the influence. And in the interest of logic it will be impersonating a government official's wife.'

'What about me?' said Mary Lou Krantz. 'Can I go now?'

'On the contrary. You will be charged with being an accessory to the crime. Without you there would have been no kidnapping and no false imprisonment. To be an accessory is regarded as a very serious matter in Scots law, and carries the same sentence as the original crime. I would imagine that you will all go to prison for a very long time indeed. Lock them in the cells, Constable McGurk, and well done.'

* * *

CHAPTER 18

In which the remarkable properties of the racoon are discussed.

'Tell me about Wales,' President Yamamoto repeated. 'I have always wanted to know your country's case.'

Donald looked at him perplexed. He had read the briefing most carefully, and, if one thing was clear, it was that he was to win the Feelgood Project for Scotland. But now the old bugger wanted him to bat for Wales – a country about which he knew nothing and cared less. He looked at Yamamoto's colleagues, but they offered no help. One, indeed, appeared to have gone to sleep.

But Stuart was not so slow off the mark. 'If I may,' he said, 'I will handle this.' Horiguchisan muttered into Yamamoto's ear; and Yamamoto smiled and nodded. 'Please,' he said.

'Wales,' said Stuart, 'is a land plagued by rain and bad roads. The workers are idle; transport is bad; and the people speak a language which it is impossible to translate into Japanese since they put the verb at the very beginning of the sentence, while you put it at the very end.'

Hashimotosan, the senior vice president in charge of the Feelgood Project, whispered into Yamamoto's ear. It was Yamamoto's turn to look perplexed. 'No,' he said. 'h-whales. I want to know why your country opposes Omeiwaku Industry's traditional activities in the hunting of the whale. Then we can talk about the attractions of Scotland from the point of view of inward investment. Tell me – have you read Moby Dick?'

Donald remembered that, in polite Japanese society, one never says 'no'; the correct formulation was, of course, 'of course'. 'Of course,' he said.

'And what do you think of Captain Ishmael?' said Yamamoto.

'I, er,' stuttered Donald; but the senior vice president rescued him. 'I think' he said, 'we should talk first of Scotland.'

'*Ah so*, perhaps,' said Yamamoto. 'Rand of the mountain and the frud. Why should Omeiwaku Denki rocate the Feelgood Project in Scotland? Will we not be troubled by frud?'

'Not if you place your factory on a mountain,' interjected Stuart before Donald had worked out what exactly was a frud and could do more damage. 'And we have many of those in our country. Also excellent government grants to help with your investment.'

'*Ah so*,' said Yamamoto. 'Government grants.' He turned towards Hirosiguchi. 'Write that down.'

'And a workforce well adapted to Japanese requirements, moreover.'

'*Ah so*, moreover. Moreover is key requirement for project. Write that down.'

'And an excellent supply chain,' continued Stuart, ignoring Yamamoto's interjections.

'*Ah so*, chain,' said Yamamoto. 'Chain no good for Feelgood Project. Not into bondage. No write down chain. Tell me about rocation.'

'Rocation?' queried Donald, still confused by Yamamoto's Janglish, but determined to seize the initiative from his subordinate.

'Yes, rocation, prace where ToyBoy assembled.'

'We have researched a number of locations,' said Stuart, wresting the ball from Donald. 'The most favourable is in Livingston, a new town on the motorway network, about 20 minutes from Edinburgh International Airport.'

'Livingston no good,' said Yamamoto. 'Livingston lost in Africa jungle, and has too many loundabouts. Livingston no good for Feelgood Project .'

'We have a place called Stanley,' said Stuart. 'About 20 miles from Perth.'

'Stanley no good,' said Yamamoto. 'Too close to Livingston.'

Donald decided to throw his trump card onto the table. 'There's a place called North...'

'Perhaps, then, you could outline your own locational requirements,' interrupted Stuart. He was not going to let Donald

Macdonald ruin their chances of winning the project, boss or no. 'I'm sure we can match them.'

Yamamoto whispered in the ear of the senior vice president, who opened a slim portfolio and removed a slim brochure. On the cover was a photograph of a sandy beach, with a blue sea stretching out to the horizon, spangled with rocks and islets, and a green lawn beneath an improbably blue sky. On the lawn stood a clean shaven man in breeches, clasping a golf club, and a bearded man in a kilt, clutching a bottle. Beneath the picture was the caption: 'Omeiwaku Strong English Vodka – the True Spirit of the Isles'.

'There,' said Yamamoto. 'That is where I wish to rocate Feelgood Project. Find rocation like that, and let me have details at noon tomorrow. But now, I have other meeting. Show our distinguished guests to the lifts, Mr Hirosiguchi.'

And with a low bow he swept from the room, followed by his entourage

'What now?' said Stuart as he helped himself to another raw shrimp in the Suchi Bar of the Origami Intercontinental Hotel. If you had to have a boss like Donald Macdonald, you might as well make him work.

'What do you mean, what now? I should have thought it pretty obvious.'

'All we need is a piece of flat land in an area of outstanding natural beauty, close to a white beach and backed with an 18 hole golf course, not to mention a 25 megawatt power supply and ready access to the motorway network and an international airport, where the Planning Authority will permit us to build a 25,000 square foot factory. Oh, and no loundabouts.'

'No loundabouts?'

'You heard the man.' Stuart bit the head off another shrimp and spat it expertly into the ashtray. 'I suggest we send a fax to Glasgow and have them do a run on available sites. There must be somewhere.'

Waste of time, thought Donald. He knew of the perfect site, and would fax Donald MacDonald for further details and photographs. But there was no harm in letting Stuart chase his tail; it would make his own contribution to winning the Feelgood Project look even more impressive. 'Good idea,' he said. 'I shall expect a full proposal by eight o'clock. I'm dining with Yamamoto and the project team this evening and I shall wish to discuss it with them then.'

'Dining with Yamamoto? Since when? '

'Hirosiguchisan asked me when I was leaving. Said they'd asked the Welsh and Californians along as well, to make up a party.'

'But...'

'By eight o'clock.'

The fax which Stuart received following his query to Glasgow was not particularly helpful. In fact it was not helpful at all. *'There are no sites meeting the specified criteria,'* it said. *'Your job is to attract investment to places like Glasgow, where they need the jobs. Please find attached list of brown field sites in Central Scotland. Suggest you try for Ravenscraig, where there is plenty of land and a ready made workforce of ex steel workers.'*

Donald, meantime, was sending a fax to his namesake in North Uist. *'Many thanks for your fax about investment in North Uist. I think that I have a suitable project and can persuade the company to visit. Please send me photographs of beaches and leisure facilities, together with a note on site availability and details of the workforce. Kind regards, Donald.'*

'Well it's not good enough,' said Donald, 'even if they did have to get up at six thirty in the morning to send it.' They were sitting in the bar waiting for Donald's lift to his dinner date with Omeiwaku Denki, and Stuart had just shown him the reply from Glasgow.

'It's a disappointment, but you cannot magic up sites from nowhere,' said Stuart. 'What if someone wanted to build a factory on a five thousand foot mountain? We don't have any!'

'Then we'd build one – it would improve Glasgow no end. But are you telling me there are no beaches and golf courses in Scotland? You must have been away for a hell of a time!'

'There are none which are suitable.'

'Well you can tell your friends in Glasgow to think again. Sir Terence Mould wants this project and I'm determined to win it for him.'

'Very well. But if you want my opinion they'll choose

California. Sun, sand, surf and sex is what they're looking for, and you don't find much of those commodities in Scotland.'

Donald knew precisely where they could find the majority of those commodities, even if the sun was somewhat fitful and the sex somewhat woolly. But he was damned if he was going to help Stuart. The longer Stuart was chasing will o' the wisps, the better it would be for his career. 'You must change their frame of reference, he said, 'Get them to associate the ToyBoy™ with mist, rain, slagheaps and Winciette nighties.'

'Fat chance, 'said Stuart.

Nothing which Donald had experienced in the Fish Bars of the Byres Road and the Curry Houses of Leith had prepared him for dinner in a Geisha House in Tokyo. There were six of them – Yamamoto, Hirosiguchi, his personal assistant, and Hashimoto, the senior vice president in charge of the project, together with Dildenschneider, Megan Morgan Thomas from the Office for the Urbanisation of Rural Wales, who was every bit as formidable as Ambassador Bloggs had warned, and Donald himself. They had travelled to the Geisha House in two limousines – one white, for the President, Dildenschneider and Hashimoto, and one black, for Hirosiguchi, Megan Morgan Thomas and Donald. Donald had tried to travel with Hashimoto so that he could begin to warm him up on the attractions of North Uist, but had been outmanoeuvred by Dildenschneider who, despite his bulk, was surprisingly nimble on his feet.

'So, Ms. Morgan Thomas, your first time in Tokyo?' asked Hirosiguchisan as they crawled through the traffic.

'Certainly not,' she responded in a rich baritone. 'I did a year's postgraduate study at Tokyo University.'

'Then you know much about Japanese culture perhaps? You know about Tanuki?'

'Of course. But I don't think that's a proper subject for discussion.'

'Why not? If Mr Macdonald is to understand Japan, he must understand Tanuki. Every lestaraunt has one outside for success. *Ah so*, here is Tanuki of Geisha House where we eat.'

Hirosiguchi pointed a wrinkled hand at a large ceramic model of a racoon, which stood in a place of honour by a pair of elegant gate posts. There was a knowing smirk on its face, a large jug of sake in each fore-paw, and, under a grotesquely protruding belly, an inflated scrotum brushing the ground. The tanuki was in a clear state of sexual excitement.

'Very pretty, no?' said Hirosiguchi, patting Ms. Morgan Thomas's knee. 'And much legend about Tanuki. Tanuki can change into handsome young man, like myself. But Tanuki love sake, so when he try to seduce beautiful young girl like yourself and she offers him drink, his tail rises up under his happy coat and she spots the trick. I more successful!'

Ms. Morgan Thomas removed Hirosiguchi's hand and looked primly out of the window. 'Really!' she exclaimed, with all the scorn of a primary school mistress confiscating condoms from an eleven year old boy.

'Yes, really,' replied Hirosiguchi, much encouraged, 'although my scrotum not as big as Tanuki's. Tanuki's scrotum cover area of six tatami mats.'

This promising line of conversation was cut short by their arrival at the entrance of the geisha house. The chauffeur leapt to open their doors, his teeth and gloves gleaming in the light of bamboo lanterns. An ancient woman dressed in a blue kimono was bowing by the doorway. Hirosiguchi bowed back.

'She owner of restaurant,' he said to Donald. 'Retired geisha. Very good in her time. Now too old.'

Donald stepped forward into the Geisha House, brushing his head on a banner which hung in the door. The retired Geisha gave vent to a torrent of high pitched language.

Ms. Morgan Thomas grabbed Donald by the arm. 'No no, look you,' she hissed. 'You must remove your shoes before you walk on the tatami.'

Donald had a particular aversion to being bossed about by women, and particularly by large Welsh women who were trying to steal his project. 'I'm damned if I will. I'm not putting my bare feet where a Tanuki's scrotum's been.'

'Don't be silly, they give you slippers. And you should remove your jacket also – they will give you a happy-coat to wear.'

'Happy-coat?'

'Short jacket made of cotton, ' Hirosiguchi interjected. 'Worn by Japanese when they make jigga jigga.' He leered at Ms. Morgan Thomas. 'You too will need happy coat. Then we shall see...'

Attired in their new finery, they shuffled along a wooden corridor and were ushered into a low room. Pale tatami mats covered the floor. Pale wooden screens served as walls. A pale paper lantern cast a pale light on a low table, around which Yamamoto, Hashimoto and Dildenschneider were already squatting. Six pale geishas, with salmon pink kimonos, white faces and red lips, stood bowing at the far end of the room. Pale lilies drooped in an alcove. This is beyond the pale, thought Donald.

With a grace of movement that belied her size, Ms Morgan Thomas slid to the floor and sat cross-legged before the Table, her skirt riding up above her knees and straining at her thighs. Donald averted his eyes. Hirosiguchi did not.

'Please, make yourselves comfortable,' said Yamamoto.

Donald hadn't sat cross-legged on the floor since he was in Primary I. He lowered himself slowly to the tatami and tried to bend his knees. How did Dildenschneider do it – he was sitting with all the serenity of a Buddha. Finally Donald resorted to sticking his legs straight out in front of him beneath the table. There was an ominous crack from his left knee, and an uncomfortable twinge in his lumbar regions. What one did for one's country, right or wrong!

'Good,' said Yamamoto, 'Now we can eat. Then after, perhaps, we talk of Feelgood Project.'

'Or have plactical demonstration,' said Hirosiguchi, shifting his buttocks on the tatami in the direction of Ms Morgan Thomas.

Yamamoto clapped his hands, and the six pale geishas glided into action. Glasses were filled with warm sake and cold beer. Plates were placed before them. Food was placed on plates. Forked wooden sticks wrapped in rice paper were laid beside the plates.

Donald looked at his plate with distaste. On it was a number of objects consisting of rice and uncooked fish, wrapped in dark brown leaves. Suchi, he thought. He picked up the forked wooden stick, removed the paper cover, and stabbed at one of the objects.

'No, no, spluttered Hirosiguchi. 'You must break chopsticks in two before eating. See, Ms Morgan Thomas has right idea. Breaking apart of two legs of chopsticks is symbolic of woman surrendering herself to man.'

Ms Morgan Thomas, who had been eating with gusto, placed her chopsticks hurriedly on the table and looked for a fork. Dildenschneider had emptied his plate and was eyeing Donald's greedily. Yamamoto and Hashimoto were delicately toying with their suchi, their eyes half closed as if in a state of contemplation. Hirosiguchi was gazing at Ms Morgan Thomas' thighs. Donald leaned forward and exchanged his plate for Dildenschneider's.

'Great God,' said Hirosiguchi, 'you eat fast. Now you must drink. Campai!' He swallowed his beer, and Donald followed suit. The glass was immediately refilled.

Course followed course, and drink followed drink. There were prawns fried in batter, which Donald did not eat. There was marbled Kobe beef, its delicate texture achieved through feeding the cattle with beer and massaging their flanks twice a day, which Donald did not eat. There was kaiso, harvested from the polluted waters of Tokyo bay, which Donald did not eat. There were exotic fruits, which Donald did not eat. And finally, there were bowls of rice which Donald, trained in the Chinese restaurants of the Byres Road, did attempt to eat, although more fell off his chopsticks onto his happy coat than reached his mouth.

Yamato looked at him and grinned crookedly. 'You no like Japanese food?' he asked. 'You prefer to have a bifubugger?'

'Bifubugger?'

'*Hai*, bifubugger. Flom Makudonarudo. Amelicans very fond of bifubuggers. Me not – fear of mad cow disease. Hirosiguchisan, he like, but he mad already. But now we talk of project rocation.'

He clapped his hands, and the geishas removed the bowls of rice and replaced them with bowls of green tea, which Donald did not drink. 'Now,' he said, 'I favour Scotland. But Hirosiguchi here favours Wales, and Mr Hashimoto favours California. Omeiwaku Denki is democlatic company, so we have ploblem. It's up to each of you to plesent your case.'

'Well,' said Donald, Dildenschneider and Ms Morgan Thomas in unison.

* * *

CHAPTER 19

In which the Great and the Good become involved.

'Not fucking guilty,' said Donald MacDonald in a wavering voice. He had had a bad night. Half a bottle of Major Prendergast's British port-style wine on top of the Crimea Red 1999 had not done much for his cerebellum. And a hard plank bench with no blankets had severely damaged his spine. He was in no mood for conciliation.

'It iss not the time yet for you to be pleading,' said Sergeant McPloud. 'That will come when the Sheriff from Inverness visits on Monday sevennight. In the meantime, I haff to decide whether you can be let out on police bail until the Procurator Fiscal considers your case.'

Lady Lucinda fluttered her eyelids at the Sergeant. She knew her husband, and she knew that without her intervention they would remain in police custody for a very long time. 'I'm sure that none of us is a threat, Sergeant,' she sighed. 'And I do have to look after the children.'

Mary Lou Krantz, meantime, was dabbing her eyes with a handkerchief on which was embroidered the Confederate flag. She, being sober, had passed the worst night of all. Her cell was cold and lit only by the flickering yellow light of Lochmaddy's one street lamp. Her tranquillisers were in her handbag at Mrs McTurk's black-house ; she was in need of her HRT pills; and she longed for a shower. 'Ah demand to see the US Consul,' she said.

Sergeant McPloud scratched his head. Nothing in his police career had prepared him for such responsibility. Dogs worrying sheep and out of date licence disks were one thing. But dealing with irate senior officials from the central government, the daughters of peers, and deranged American ladies from the Deep South, was quite another.

' I warn you,' shouted Donald. 'If I am not out of here in two minutes, your career will come to a rapid termination.'

'My children!' wept Lady Lucinda, wringing her hands and contriving to look like Dame Edith Evans playing Lady Macbeth.

'The Consul General will crunch your nuts and ah shall sue the British Government to the last bar of your gold reserves,' threatened Mary Lou Krantz, stamping her foot and contriving to look like Judy Garland arguing with the Tin Man.

Sergeant McPloud scratched his head again. What was that he'd been taught at the Police College about compromise? Very well, he'd compromise.

'You,' he said, turning to Lady Lucinda. 'You will be granted police bail in the sum of £5, chust so, so that you can care for your children. You,' he turned to Donald, 'will be granted police bail in the sum of £50, so that you can continue your important official work. But I shall haff to make an immediate report to the Chief Constable. And you,' he turned to Mary Lou Krantz, 'will remain in police custody, since without your partiship there would have been no crime, and I cannot be assured that you will not be kidnapped again.'

'Thank you, Sergeant,' simpered Lady Lucinda.

'You'll be hearing more of this,' snarled Donald.

And Mary Lou Krantz burst into tears.

The Chief Constable poured himself another coffee and cursed again at the fax from Lochmaddy Police Station. Nothing in his police career had prepared him for such responsibility. He buzzed the intercom and asked his administrative assistant to come in with shorthand pad at the ready.

The AA entered, gave the Chief Constable the kind of smile which had projected Paris across the Adriatic, Eiffel Tower in hand, to capture Helen, and advanced across the Turkey carpet with a motion of the hips which could have tempted St Simon the Stylite. If only his wife had as much charm and as much allure, thought the Chief Constable. The AA sank into the chair opposite the Chief Constable's desk, knees a little too far apart for the Chief Constable's peace of mind, and, licking the point of the little gold propelling pencil with the provocative tip of a pink tongue, prepared to take down the Chief

Constable's every word. If only his wife were as compliant, thought the Chief Constable. But he had work to do.

'Take a fax to the Permanent Secretary of the North British Office,' said the Chief Constable.

'Right, guv,' said the AA, crossing one elegantly trousered leg over the other and scratching his moustache. If only the Chief Constable would not look at him like that. It made him feel quite uncomfortable...

Sir Terence Mould, by contrast, had never felt more comfortable. He had spent a sleepless night brooding on how to suppress the Report from Donald MacDonald on the incompetence of the North Uist Urban District Council without putting his own career at risk. The fax from the Chief Constable of North Uist had given him just the ammunition that he needed. Donald MacDonald was in hot water and given enough rope would burn to ashes both himself and the Minister's plans for amalgamating the North Uist and Benbecula Urban District Councils. He reached for the Platignum fountain pen which his Aunty Gladys had given him for passing the scholarship examination to the Royal High School, and which he used to pen all his most important submissions. So swift ran his thoughts, and so pleased was he at the news he had to impart, that he had reached the foot of page two before he noticed that the pen was out of ink.

'No, a thousand times no,' said the Minister, crossing his legs.

'Millipede,' said the private secretary.

'What do you mean, millipede?' The Minister stared at the private secretary with goggle eyes.

'It was the millipede who said "No, a thousand times no, crossing its legs",' said the private secretary. 'Ministers simply dissent from the advice respectfully tendered to them by their permanent officials.'

'Well, you can tell Sir Terence Mould from me that I do not agree with the pusillanimous lily livered advice which the bloody man has given me on the question of withdrawing Donald MacDonald from North Uist; that I will not, repeat not, fucking, repeat fucking, have him taken off his duties which I regard as of the highest importance; that if Donald is prosecuted for what is clearly nothing but youthful high spirits I shall personally see to it that the Chief Constable spends the rest of his useless career doling out parking tickets in the pedestrian section of Sauchiehall Street; and that I shall expect fully worked up proposals for amalgamation of the two Councils within a week. Have you got that?'

'Yes, Minister.'

The private secretary retired to the cubby hole beside the Minister's office, which was dignified with the title of Private Office. The term Private Office, the private secretary reflected, was both etymologically and physically related to the term private parts, the Private Office being an organ of government where shameful but necessary deeds were done. He picked up his Dictaphone, stared at the photograph of Loch Lomond in a fog which adorned the opposite wall, and began to dictate a response to the Permanent Secretary. He had long since learned that Ministers, even Ministers of the North British Office are transient beings, departing at the unforeseen whim of a Prime Minister or the unfortunately seen unzipping of a fly, while Permanent Secretaries were, well, permanent.

'The Minister has noted with thanks your submission of 14 July on the question of the official examination into the possible amalgamation of Urban District Councils in the Outer Hebrides,' he began. 'He has asked me to say that he has every confidence in the work which is currently being undertaken; that he would regard it as inappropriate for the official charged with that work to be charged in relation to his activities in the region; and that he expects to see fully worked up proposals for the amalgamation by close of play on 21 July.' That should do it, he thought: this was as clear an expression of the Minister's wishes as anyone could want. Particularly the Permanent Secretary.

Some of the fog detached itself from the photograph of Loch Lomond and wound itself around the dictating machine.

Fog, too, had descended on the Lochmaddy Hotel. Miriam Katzenellenbogen, too, had spent an anxious evening. When she was not worrying herself sick at the fate of Mary Lou Krantz, she was driven to the end of her tether by the Sisyphean task of keeping Alsace and Lorraine apart. Since she spoke neither French nor German, and the twins on principle refused to speak English to Americans, she found her job more frustrating than that of a linguaphone salesman before the construction of the Tower of Babel.

At last she discovered, by trial and error, that the twins were prepared to speak Latin, a language which she had studied briefly at the Spartanburg Junior High School. *'Horus est, puellis lavatis, lectus intratus est,'* she said.

Mrs McTurk, who had come to the hotel to help out, looked up from her knitting. 'Vat is it that you are calling a whore?' she asked. 'Such language is not approved of in North Uist, and especially not in the presence of babes and sucklings.'

Miriam Katzenellenbogen looked as blank as the unwelcoming walls of the lounge bar, where she had taken the children to avoid the unseemly racket of the public. 'The hour is at hand when the bed, the girls having been washed, is to be entered,' she translated.

It was Mrs McTurk's turn to look blank. Her education, broad though it had been at the University of Hajduboszormeny, had not extended to the ablative absolute and the gerundive. Nor, apparently, had Alsace's or Lorraine's. Ignoring Ms Katzenellenbogen's clear instructions they began shouting in their respective foster-mother tongues and throwing ice cubes at each other from a bowl on the bar.

'Hot diggedy, Ah have never seen the like of such children,' said Ms Katzenellenbogen. 'In South Carolina, children know their place. Give them a bag of popcorn and the latest Steven King video and they will sit quiet for hours.'

Mrs McTurk glared at the girls with grandmotherly affection. Alsace was now astride Lorraine's chest, compressing her Miss Nuform pre-pubertal bra and stuffing ice cubes down her throat while screaming, in demotic French, for the return of the Rhineland. Mrs McTurk filled her lungs until the varicose veins stood out on her legs like the mould on a slice of Roquefort cheese. *'Vite, komm schnell,'* she screamed, *'Ouste, ich habe jetzt genug, au lit, ins Bett mit euch!'*

Miriam Katzenellenbogen stared in amazement as the twins meekly raised themselves from the floor, kissed Mrs McTurk on her cheeks (one each, so they did not cross contaminate each other with their germs) and slunk off to bed. Mrs McTurk saw the distress on her face. If anyone needed comfort it was she.

'Now, now dear,' she said to Miriam. 'Ve can have a nice little chat about Mary Lou. Don't fret yourself – I don't myself think zat she has been kidnapped: zere is not a man on the island sober enough tonight to do such a thing. It is far more likely, to my mind, zat she has wandered into a bog and been drowned. Or perhaps she has fallen over a cliff and broken her neck. Or she may have hanged herself at the Rowan tree out of shame at showing her private parts to ze Benbecula tug of war team when she fell over. It is shameful, shameful.'

Miriam Katzenellenbogen put her head in her hands and burst into uncontrollable sobbing.

Things were no better by morning. There had been no news of Mary Lou Krantz; and the children's parents had disappeared, as Mrs McTurk put it, like snow off a dike. Miriam Katzenellenbogen was too distressed to wonder for more than a moment why cocaine should vanish from a lesbian, and what could cause Mrs McTurk to use such a phrase.

A telephone call to Major Prendergast had elicited the information that Donald and Lucinda had left sometime after midnight to return to the hotel; they were, as the Major explained, in a state of considerable refreshment. The Radio Highland News had been more interested in the prospects for Inverness Caledonian Thistle in the Scottish Cup; and Miriam Katzenellenbogen had failed to find Radio Free Europe on the ancient valve wireless in her room. As they ate their way through a hearty breakfast of porridge and kippers, the twins planned a state funeral with full civil service honours – bowler hats and furled umbrellas on the coffins – for their parents, and interment in an unmarked grave in unconsecrated ground for Mary Lou Krantz, in recognition of the fact that she came of a nation which had no proper parentage.

So imagine their disappointment when the door of the dining room burst open to reveal Lady Lucinda and Donald. Alsace burst into tears of rage – this was even worse than the time the circus had been cancelled. Lorraine glared at her father and wondered, not for the first time, about her own parentage.

'Oh my darlings,' breathed Lady Lucinda, gathering the twins to her bosom with an expression of maternal solicitude.

'Where's McTurk?' shouted Donald, showing all the signs of paternal indifference.

'Where is Mary Lou Krantz?' whimpered Miriam Katzenellenbogen, in a tone of sisterly hysteria.

'In the chokey, charged with being an accessory to kidnapping,' shouted Donald. 'And if I have my way, she'll stay there for the rest of her natural. Now where the hell is McTurk – I've a thing or three to say to him about his bloody police force and his bloody Council, and it won't wait.'

The Consulate General of the United States of America sits in an imposing Georgian terraced house in an elegant terrace in Edinburgh's New Town. The Stars and Stripes droop lazily from the flagstaff attached to its wrought iron balcony. Behind its tall astragalled windows are elegant rooms, hung with reproduction portraits of dead white American Presidents and notices warning would be visitors to the US of A of the penalties for smuggling drugs or apples into the world's one remaining super-power. At his large empty desk in his first floor office, the Consul General scratched his chin and contemplated closure. For Congress had cut the State Department's budget, and the State Department had decided to economise by rightsizing the consular corps.

Henry J Klassinger III did not like the idea of closure. Edinburgh was as attractive a posting as an official of his meagre talents was likely to find. Neither too hot in summer, nor too cold in winter, nor too arid in spring, nor too humid in autumn, its climate compared favourably with Brasilia, or Taiwan, or Bogota, or Helsinki. Sure it rained in August: but that kept the English away, an objective with which Henry J Klassinger III, as the son of a Daughter of the American Revolution, heartily concurred. Sure the east wind sometimes blew sleet straight from the steppes of Siberia in June: but that kept the midges at bay. And since Congress, in its wisdom, had opened the US borders to visa-less citizens of the European Union, Henry J Klassinger III had had very little work to do, which suited someone of his temperament and competence very nicely.

But there was the rub. Without work, his campaign against closure would fail and he would be transferred to Brasilia or Taiwan. With work, he himself would demonstrate his lack of competence, and he would be transferred to Bogota or Helsinki. What he needed was a stunning diplomatic success, something which would create headlines in *USA Today* and the *Daily News* and be covered by CNN. Then Congress would campaign on his behalf, the Consulate General would be saved, and he could remain in his agreeable state of torpor. But how on earth could he orchestrate such a diplomatic success?

'Excuse me, Consul General.' So deep was he in his reverie that he had not noticed the Assistant Consul, a bright young thing from Vassar awaiting her first posting to Paris or Beijing, opening the door of his office.

'Yeah, what is it? Can't you see that I'm busy?'

'I guess I'm right sorry to disturb you, Sir, but there's a dame from South Carolina on the line says she's got a friend who's been copped on a kidnapping rap and needs our help.'

'How can I help some dame in South Carolina on a kidnapping rap? Tell her to get on to the DA!'

'She's not *in* South Carolina, she's *from* South Carolina. She's *in* North Uist.'

'South Carolina, North Uist, sounds like a police matter to me. Tell her we can't help.'

'But it's our job to help US nationals who get into trouble with the British authorities.'

Henry J Klassinger III steepled his hands beneath his chin and glared at the Assistant Consul. 'Why didn't you say so?' he said. Put her through.'

And so it was that thirty minutes later the Consul General's long suffering personal secretary was wrestling to find him a place on the first available flight to the Outer Hebrides. And that the Assistant Consul was speaking earnestly to a young lady at the News Desk of the London Office of CNN.

'*A Dhia, a Dhia,*' muttered Hamish McTurk, invoking the deity in his native Gaelic. 'What the hell can go wrong next?'

He had spent an uncomfortable morning in his panelled office in the Lochmaddy Municipal Buildings and Leisure Centre, taking a succession of calls from the Chief Constable, the Minister's private secretary, the Permanent Secretary of the North British Office, Donald MacDonald, Miriam Katzenellenbogen, the Assistant American Consul in Edinburgh, and a female reporter from the London Office of CNN who threatened to sue him for sexual harassment when he addressed her as 'my dear'.

The Chief Constable had made it clear that the law must take its course, and that Mary Lou Krantz would stay in custody at least until the Procurator Fiscal, who was taking his annual golfing holiday in Florida in company with his opposite number the District Attorney of Staten Island, had reviewed the case.

The Permanent Secretary had told him that he would strangle him personally if Donald MacDonald was not immediately returned to custody and did not go down for a ten year stretch in Barlinnie. The Minister's private secretary, by contrast, had told him to give every assistance to MacDonald; the Minister would strangle him personally if MacDonald spent so much as another half hour in police custody.

Donald MacDonald had told him that he was at that moment composing a further Memorandum to the Minister recommending (i) the amalgamation of the North Uist and Benbecula Urban District Councils, and the transfer of the Municipal Offices and Leisure Centre to Benbecula, brick by brick if necessary; and (ii) the abolition of McTurk's own post. He had made it clear as Edinburgh Crystal that McTurk would require to come up with some pretty convincing arguments, including the dropping of all charges against himself and Lady Lucinda, if he were to be persuaded to change his mind. And, by the way, he might start the process of rehabilitating himself by making preparation for a visit of Japanese industrialists, who were considering an important industrial development in North Uist.

Miriam Katzenellenbogen had been the easiest. She had telephoned, weeping into her mobile like that bird in the bible who had wept among the alien corncrakes, and pleaded for the release of her friend in the interests of international friendship, failing which the South Carolina Ladies' Highland Dancing troupe would never again return to the British Isles. McTurk had responded that the law must take its course; that he was not in the slightest bit interested in international friendship; and that nothing would give him greater pleasure than the continued and permanent absence of the South Carolina Ladies' Highland Dancing troupe from the shores of Europe, let alone North Uist. He sat back in his black leather executive swivel chair, feeling the first glimmers of pleasure at a job well done. As far as he was concerned Ms Katzenellenbogen could weep amid the alien corncrakes until the crack of doom.

But his satisfaction was not to last long. The US Assistant Consul had phoned to notify him of the prospective arrival of her boss, and threatened a global embargo on companies which traded with North Uist if Mary Lou Krantz was not released by the time that the Consul General arrived. And that bloody woman from CNN was planning to fly into Benbecula by private jet to cover the story live.

'*A Dhia*,' McTurk muttered again as the phone rang on his desk. It was his mother. 'Hamish, dear,' she said, 'I know zat you will be vanting a quiet day after the excitement of the Highland Games, but I vonder if you could run down to ze pier to beg a couple of mackerel for my tea?'

Donald, meantime, was working on his revenge. To his list of targets he had added the entire North Uist Constabulary for giving him one of the most uncomfortable nights of his life, Major and Mrs Prendergast, for their appalling taste in wine, and Hamish McTurk, for orchestrating the chaos from which he was trying to extricate himself. But top of the list remained Donald Macdonald, now no doubt enjoying the high life in Tokyo.

When he returned to his hotel room, Donald found the fax from Tokyo awaiting him. His reply was brief and to the point. '*Can offer 25,000 square foot factory, ready access to motorways and airports, highly trained workforce of ex crofters, 18 hole course, and many other leisure opportunities. Photos of leisure facilities and beaches appended.*'

He attached a postcard of the beach borrowed from the receptionist and asked her to fax it at once to Donald Macdonald at the Origami Intercontinental Hotel Tokyo, marked for his immediate attention. Then he picked up the telephone and spoke at length to Sgt Stripe.

* * *

CHAPTER 20

In which A loves B, who is vowed to eternal chastity, at least so far as A is concerned.

'*Ho*, you want temporary wife?'

The same unnaturally tall Japanese was standing at the same corner of the Ginza, plying his or her trade.

'Well...' said Donald, who reckoned that losing his virginity might just about recover what had been a disastrous evening.

'Bugger off,' said Hirosiguchi. 'We go to bar to talk business.'

The discussions with the senior management at Omeiwaku Denki about the potential location for the Feelgood Project had not, from Donald's point of view, been a success. Dildenschneider had spoken eloquently of California – its superb climate, its beautiful landscapes and beaches, its accommodating girls and boys, its ready access to the largest and most hedonistic market the world had ever known, its freeway and airline links, its serviced industrial sites, and the possibility of huge grants from the Californian state administration to help with Omeiwaku's set up costs. Hashimoto was mightily impressed.

Megan Morgan Thomas had made a similar, though somewhat less impressive, pitch for the Rhondda Valley. Hirosiguchi was moderately impressed, and invited Megan to discuss the matter further with him after the meal.

Donald, however, had eaten too little and drunk too much to marshal his arguments, and he was still awaiting details from Donald MacDonald. North Uist, he stammered, was a nice place with a nice beach. He thought that it might have a golf course, although he did not know if it had nine or eighteen holes. On balance it was likely to have several hundred, most of them dug by rabbits. There was a nice hotel where you could almost certainly drink nice whisky, although he did not know whether you could get Suntory Malt. There was excellent fishing; until the Spanish fishing fleet had been allowed into the Minch by the European Commission, Lochmaddy had been one of the nicest fishing ports in Scotland.

'But tell me about fly fishing,' Yamamoto had asked. 'That kind of fishing I like.'

'I don't know,' said Donald. 'But there are bound to be plenty of flies.'

Yamamoto was not impressed, and asked Donald to provide further details in the morning. 'We meet again at noon tomollow,' he said. 'Meanwhile, you go and keep eye on Hirosiguchisan and Megan Morgan Thomas-san. We don't want project decision distorted by panky-hanky.'

The bar which Hirosiguchi took them to in the Ginza was on the fifth floor of an apartment block, served by a narrow lift. Donald found himself squashed uncomfortably against Megan Morgan Thomas's thighs and DD cups, as she sought to avoid contact with Hirosiguchi, who found himself squashed comfortably against the same. At each floor the lift opened, and they were faced with a garish neon notice in English and Katakana.

'Pussycat Klub' announced the first, reinforcing its message with a neon portrait of a scantily dressed female of Eurasian extraction and a poodle. 'Doggybag Klub' said the next, showing the same female minus some of her clothes and caressing a long-haired Burmese cat. 'Penguin Klub' was the next, showing the same female, now minus most of her clothes and caressing a giraffe wearing a dinner jacket and with an unnaturally short neck.

' Good, *so des ne*?' said Hirosiguchi, gesturing at the giraffe.' You go inside, and neck get to proper length.'

Megan Morgan Thomas pressed herself even more closely into Donald, though whether from embarrassment stemming from her upbringing in the Primitive Methodist Chapels of Blaenau Ffestinniog, or sexual excitement at the thought of what would happen to the giraffe's neck inside the club, Donald couldn't tell. 'You

Japanese are obsessed with animals,' he said.

'We love animals, *hai*,' said Hirosiguchi. 'But not obsessed. Look!'

They had arrived at the fifth floor. The lift doors opened to reveal a garish neon picture of an Anglican bishop in full episcopal purple, and the master of a Cambridge college in the robes of a doctor of divinity. At their feet lay the female of Eurasian extraction, dressed, as the bishop might have put it, in the entrancing robes of our mother Eve before the fall. 'Athanaeum Klub' read the sign.

'Hirosiguchisan, what a pleasure!' The mama-san advanced from behind her narrow bar like a galleon in full sail. 'You have been ignoring your Mama-san, and your whisky bottle is still almost full.'

Hirosiguchi sank his head in shame. 'Abload on business,' he ejaculated. 'I bling foreign colleagues with me tonight to celibate a hopeful deal. Tomorrow we shall finalise details. But tonight we dlink.'

Hirosiguchi, thought Donald, was in no fit state to celibate anything – particularly Megan Morgan Thomas. And his ejaculation was, to say the least, premature. But no doubt this was how things were done in Japan.

'Please.' The Mama-san gestured at a low table against the wall and clapped her hands. Two girls of Eurasian extraction appeared as if from nowhere. 'This is Sammy, and this is Doreen,' said the Mama-san.

Each was wearing a salmon pink dress cut low at the bosom and split to the upper thigh. Their lustrous black hair was pinned up, and on it one of them wore a mortar board and one a mitre. The professor was holding a tray on which were glasses full of ice, and the bishop an almost full bottle of Old Parr whisky. They slid onto the banquettes beside Hirosiguchi and Donald, and poured whisky into the glasses.

Donald took a deep pull. He was aware of a hand on each of his thighs – one cool and slim and with long fingers and elegantly manicured nails; the other hot and clammy, with short podgy fingers and ragged nails bitten to the quick.

'I'm Sammy. You want me make Tokyo even more preasent for you?' asked the owner of the mitre and the elegantly manicured hand, doing something exquisite to the inside of his thigh with her nails.

'You've got to get me away from Hirosiguchi,' muttered Megan

Morgan Thomas, squeezing his left knee at the reflex point so that his foot jerked up and made contact with Sammy's. She smiled at him with white regular teeth and crossed her legs so that even more thigh was revealed.

'I'll sell a lot to win this project for the Principality, but not my body,' continued Megan.

' I'd sell a lot, including my body, to win it for Scotland,' thought Donald. 'Quite right,' he replied. And, for the first time in his life, he said a gentlemanly thing: 'I'll take you back to your hotel when its time to go.'

Sammy, meantime, was continuing to file her finger nails on Donald's trousers, having shifted her centre of operations to the region around his fly, where the cloth was presumably rougher and more suited to her purpose. Donald swallowed, then realised that swallowing with an empty mouth has its drawbacks and took another large gulp of whisky. Hirosiguchi reached over and filled his glass. It would be touch and go, Donald thought, whether his deeds would match his gentlemanly words. One more touch of Sammy and he might find himself coming rather than going.

'You like whisky?' asked Hirosiguchi.

'Aye,' said Donald. 'But with so much ice it's difficult to tell how much you're drinking.'

Donald remembered little of the subsequent events. Hirosiguchi had lain siege to Megan Morgan Thomas's knees and been rebuffed. Megan Morgan Thomas had pleaded for Donald's assistance and been reassured. Doreen had taken herself off to entertain other clients. Ice had tinkled in glasses, and the Mama-san had produced another bottle of whisky. Sammy had completed the manicure of her left hand, and had started work on her right. The Karaoki machine had been switched on and Hirosiguchi had entertained them with renditions of Loch Lomond and Annie Lollie. Sammy had crossed and recrossed her legs, giving new piquancy to the words of the old hymn 'When I Behold The Wondrous Cross'. Donald had staggered to the Karaoki machine and got through half of *I'll do it my way* before doing just that and falling over. Finally, they had found themselves in a taxi. Megan Morgan Thomas, despite Hirosiguchi's attempts to drag her into the back, had got in beside the driver; and Donald shared the back seat with Hirosiguchi and Sammy, who was still demonstrating an overpowering obsession with her nails.

'Origami Intercontinental Hotel,' said Hirosiguchi.

Donald rolled over in his king size Origami Intercontinental bed and was aware of warm flesh beside him. His loins stirred as he remembered slim hands with long red finger nails, long legs, white thighs, mysterious shadows.

'I don't know how to thank you enough,' said Megan Morgan Thomas, planting a wet kiss on Donald's mouth and reaching down with her short fat hands with their bitten nails. 'But perhaps I can try. You were too far gone last night, but it would be a pity to let our rivalry over the Feelgood Project interfere with a beautiful relationship.' She hoisted her massive bulk on top of Donald so that he was quite unable to move and her breasts encircled his nose like parentheses around a particularly irrelevant aside. He gasped for breath as he tried to remember events after they had left the taxi. Surely he couldn't have mistaken Megan Morgan Thomas for the slim lissom Japanese with her small firm breasts and thrilling finger nails?

Megan, unlike Donald, began to move. She had clearly taken his gasps for passion. 'Take me,' she said. 'I am yours, look you.'

Donald was in no fit state to look at anything. Megan Morgan Thomas's breasts had moved upwards to deprive him of sight, one engorged nipple pressing against each eyeball. In his frequent fantasies about the loss of his virginity he had planned to prolong his pleasure by reciting Keats's Ode on a Grecian Urn backwards. But Megan Morgan Thomas was clearly no unravished bride of quietness; and when that long anticipated event occurred he would simply have to relive this experience.

Megan Morgan Thomas reached down again to search for the source of mutual pleasure, and Donald freed one eyeball long enough to see that the light on his bedside telephone which signified *Message Waiting* was flashing urgently by the electronic clock, which read 5.45 am.

'Wait,' he gasped. 'There's a message. I can't concentrate if I don't clear it.'

'Ah,' said Megan Morgan Thomas. 'You could not love me so much, loved you not honour more. I respect that.' She rolled off him and sat cross legged on the bed, chewing her nails, as he lifted the telephone.

'*Hai*, Mistah Macdonurandu? Urgent fax for you from Scotland. You want me send it up straightway?'

'No, no,' said Donald. 'I shall come to collect it.'

'No sir. Please not! No ploblem to deliver.'

'But I should prefer to collect.'

'But Origami Intercontinental Hotel plide itself on service.'

'And in Britain we pride ourselves on self service.'

Megan Morgan Thomas listened to Donald's side of this conversation with a petulant frown. It was clear that she did not wish him to leave. And it was clear that she did not approve of self service. She shifted her bulk to reveal that part of her anatomy which, on the Adult Channel of the in-house televisual entertainment experience, was blocked out with little migraine inducing flashing squares.

Donald averted his eyes and reached for his trousers.

* * *

CHAPTER 21

In which the benefits of a well disciplined army, new technology and effective local government services are demonstrated.

'Platoon, shun!' shouted Sgt Stripe in his best parade ground voice. 'By the right, quick march! Left, left, left right left!' He was about to pull off the biggest coup of his career, and promotion beckoned. And then, who knows: transfer to the Life Guards? Regimental Sergeant Major at Sandhurst? Military Attaché at the Washington embassy?

The phone call from Donald MacDonald had been quite specific. A small and highly dangerous group of crack Japanese troops would shortly be arriving on the islands disguised as businessmen. Ostensibly they would be considering the potential of the islands for a major electronics factory. Covertly, they would be preparing for their capture and use as a launching pad for an assault on the European Union. The consequences if they were successful were too horrible to contemplate: the collapse of economic and monetary union, the destruction of the Euro, the abolition of the European Parliament, the removal of e-numbers from food labels, the devastation of the Common Fisheries Policy, the reintroduction of the imperial system of weights and measures. It had fallen to Sgt Stripe to foil their dastardly plans. And foil them he would.

He pulled himself out of his reverie in time to see his platoon march off the hard surface of the parade ground and onto the soft and squelchy surface of the surrounding peat bog. 'Mark time!' he screamed. Thirty soldiers stopped their forward movement and marched heavily on the spot. Black mud splashed up over their immaculate gaiters and sullied their perfectly creased trousers. Some of the men in the front ranks began to sink into the bog and break step.

'Keep time, you 'orrible little men!' he yelled. ' 'Ow are you going to win the third world war against the bleeding Japs if you can't even fucking march on the spot? Left, left...'

The platoon redoubled their efforts and sank further into the bog.

'Platoon, halt!' shouted Sgt Stripe. 'At ease! Fall out!'

Several of the platoon misinterpreted his final order and fell in. The rest squelched their way back onto dry gravel and stood in a muddy and disconsolate group. 'Help, help!' shouted those who were left.

'Carry on, Corporal Snodgrass!' said Sgt Stripe, who had spotted Major Prendergast emerging from the Officer's Mess. 'Get the men fell in for inspection.' He marched smartly over to the Major and saluted. 'Platoon almost ready for inspection, Sah!' he roared.

Major Prendergast flinched. If anything, he had drunk even more than Donald MacDonald the previous evening, and the light was doing something unpleasant to his eyeballs. He peered over the parade ground, to where Cpl Snodgrass was lining up the Platoon. They didn't look as well turned out as usual, but the Major put that down to the spots swimming before his eyes.

'I think we can take the inspection as read this morning, Sergeant,' he said. 'Jolly fine show; keep it up!' And he strolled back to the Officers' Mess to partake of a large black coffee and the Telegraph Crossword. He needed something to prepare him for his discussion with Doris about her planned visit to her sister in Bournemouth.

'Right, you lot!' yelled Sgt Stripe when Cpl Snodgrass had restored some semblance of order into the ranks. 'I've never seen a bigger bloody shower! 'Ow the 'ell are you going to win the third world war when you can't even march in a straight line?'

'Please, Sarge,' said Lance Cpl Brown, who had fallen into the deepest part of the bog and whose condition fully justified his name. 'It ain't possible to march on that.'

'Shut up, you 'orrible little man! Did you clean your kit last night?'

'Yes, Sarge, till it shone like Major Prendergast's nose.'

'Well, it don't bleeding look like it. You're on a charge! Now listen, you lot, I've got news for you.'

Meanwhile, seven miles across the machair in his austere 1950's Council office, Dudley Scrope was preparing for the visit by Donald MacDonald. Dudley Scrope was as modern as Hamish McTurk was old fashioned. A product of Keele University and the London Business School, he had entered local government because of a burning mission to help his fellow man – and woman, because he was a new man. He had taken the post of Chief Executive of the Benbecula Urban District Council because he wanted early experience of leadership. No other council would have appointed as Chief Executive a 24 year old with lank brown hair, the remnants of acne on the back of his neck, and a shiny forehead. But Dudley Scrope had taken every opportunity to shine.

He had computerised the office, so that council tax payers received their bills the year before they were due and council minutes were produced, without the aid of pen and ink, the week before the relevant meeting. He had achieved the Council's recycling targets by turning it into the only paperless local government office in the Outer Hebrides – and indeed the Western World. He had improved the environment by designating the island as a smoke free zone. He had been awarded a massive grant from Brussels to research the development of smoke-less fuel from peat, and employed 15 crofters in a fruitless search for the Holy Grail of a carbon neutral peat fire. In the meantime he had negotiated additional social security benefits for the former employees of the salmon smoke house. He had made friends with the local Greens by proposing the relocation of the rocket range to North Uist, and with the local Tories by arguing equally forcibly for its retention in Benbecula. He was every inch a modern local government official.

But he had a dilemma. Hamish McTurk had told him that the Minister did not trust Donald MacDonald, and reversed his every recommendation. But was Hamish McTurk to be trusted? Dudley Scrope's best interest would be served by the amalgamation of the two Councils, with himself as chief executive. Conversely, his worst interest would be served by amalgamation under McTurk. Neither he nor McTurk would win if the councils remained independent, but neither would they lose.

Dudley Scrope scratched the boil on the back of his neck. It was a classic problem in game theory, such as he had wrestled with on many a dreary afternoon at the London Business School. And Dudley Scrope knew how to find the answer. He reached across his desk, switched on his computer, and called up the relevant program.

The computer crashed.

Dudley Scrope had a logical mind. He knew that using his computer could help him solve a difficult problem. On the other hand, Donald MacDonald was due at his office in 10 minute's time. He could not afford to be seen fiddling with a bit of hardware, still less teasing a bit of software, when MacDonald arrived. It was a classic problem in game theory.

Dudley Scrope began to sweat. His lank brown hair hung lankly over his pockmarked brow. He could hear his heartbeat thumping in his ear-drum. His eyelids flickered. He recognized the classic symptoms of stress.

Ah, he thought, this is a classic problem in stress management, such as he had contemplated on many a stress free afternoon at the London Business School. He turned to the bookshelf where he kept his rows of business books.

The books were arranged in alphabetical order by both author and title, according to a scheme of Dudley Scrope's own devising. He had realized that he often forgot either the title or the author of the book he was seeking, but that he could generally recall one or the other. The trouble was that he had no means of knowing which he would remember. The solution, which he was trying to patent, had come to him in a flash, and like all the best inventions was simplicity itself. By the straightforward stratagem of buying two copies of each of the books he required and placing them on his shelves in alphabetical order by author *and* title he would never lose a book again.

Stress Management should be on the shelf between *Screwing The Competition* by Lee Harvey Jones and *Successful Sales For The Super Salesman* by Alan K Sugar Jnr. It wasn't.

Dudley Scrope racked his brain. If he remembered correctly, the volume he sought was authored by a well known psychologist. He searched the shelves for Freud, but could find only his early and now forgotten work *Harnessing the Sex Drive for Business Success*. Jung offered up *Archetypal Patterns in Business Management*. Anthony Storr's seminal work on *Psychoanalytical Techniques and Management Development* was there, as was Claire Rayner's *How to*

Tell your Wife that you will be Late Home from Work (a book now sadly neglected because of its alleged sexism). But of a book on stress management there was no sign.

'Fucking fuck,' muttered Dudley Scrope under his breath. (He had learnt at the London Business School never to show his emotions.) He turned to the computer and thumped it hard. The computer whirred into life.

Dudley Scrope looked at his watch. He had three minutes before Donald MacDonald was due to arrive. He punched in some figures and waited for the results.

The computer scratched its head and thought. Finally it came up with the answer: 'YOU HAVE AN EQUAL CHANCE OF A POSITIVE OUTCOME WHATEVER THE INPUT.'

There was a knock at Dudley Scrope's office door. His secretary appeared, followed by a short stout man with ginger hair. 'Mr MacDonald from the North British Office,' she said.

'My dear chap,' said Donald MacDonald, taking in at a glance the computer, still with its enigmatic message, and the shelves of business books. 'What a pleasure to see a modern office in such an out of the way place.'

'We do our best,' said Dudley Scrope, rubbing his hands together. 'You should have seen the place when I arrived. Not a single piece of hardware around, dog-eared papers all over the place, and the most awful pictures of dead deer and dying fishes on the walls. Very similar, in fact, to the North Uist Council Offices!' Dudley Scrope paused. The computer had been quite clear - he had better equivocate. He rapidly changed tack.

'Of course,' he said, 'my predecessor was one of the most effective local government officials of his era. Not only was he President of the Convention of Scottish Urban District Councils, but he introduced the abacus into local government accounting throughout the United Kingdom. Before him, they had to use tally sticks.'

'Impressive,' said Donald. 'And I am particularly impressed by the way in which you bring together the old and the new. For example, the concept of the Urban District Council went out with the ark. But you have succeeded in bringing to it the whole machinery of modern government.'

Dudley Scrope preened himself. The interview was going well.

But was it? If Macdonald recommended his appointment to a unified authority, the Minister might well veto both unification and his appointment. If the Minister was indeed likely to overturn MacDonald's recommendations, he should encourage him to recommend against amalgamation, and that McTurk should be appointed to the unified council if, notwithstanding that, amalgamation went ahead. But if the Minister trusted MacDonald, MacDonald should be encouraged to recommend in favour of amalgamation and Scrope. Dudley Scrope's brain began to hurt.

Donald MacDonald's brain was hurting too. Crimea Red and English port-type wine did not suit his delicate constitution, and still less did the treatment he had received at the hands of the North Uist constabulary. He needed some fresh air.

'McTurk said that you would arrange for me to visit the school and the old peoples' home,' he said. 'I have a tight timetable, and I'd appreciate it if we could do that now.'

'Certainly,' said Scrope. A visit to the school and the old peoples' home would suit his tactics very well. The school, according to a recent report by SCOFFSTED (the Scottish equivalent of the Office for Standards in Education), was one of the worst in the country. The old peoples' home, by contrast, was according to SWAG (the Social Work Advisory Group), one of the best. But he did not want MacDonald to see the official Jaguar XK150. 'I suggest that we should walk,' he said.

'Nothing would please me more,' said Donald.

Private Smith, aka Hirohito, crouched in a burrow behind a peat hag. The wind had fallen. A soft rain trickled down his neck. A cloud of Kamikaze midges swarmed around his head. Every now and again, a squadron landed on the back of his hand and inserted their probosces into his skin before being sent to the great mosquito swamp in the sky with a splat. Four clegs circled his beret waiting their opportunity. Private Smith was not a happy man.

Sgt Stripe had harangued his platoon for ten minutes on the subject of the imminent invasion of the islands by a corps of crack Japanese troops disguised as businessmen. The platoon had listened impassively; they had heard it all before, and Sgt Stripe would no doubt use his fantasies to impose on them yet further discomfort and humiliation. What would it be this time – more sumo wrestling to get them inside the body of the enemy; an hour of Zen meditation to get inside their minds? Finally Sgt Stripe had put them out of their misery.

'I want two volunteers,' he said, 'to masquerade as Japanese troops disguised as Japanese businessmen 'iding in the 'eather. The rest of you will sweep the island and bring them in for interrogation.'

'Please Sergeant, we ain't got no brooms,' whined Private Parts.

'You will use your hands,' said Sgt Stripe. 'Now, who will volunteer? You, you and you.'

'Please, Sergeant, that's three,' said Private Smith, who had a degree in astro-physics and vague pretensions to numeracy.

Sgt Stripe glared. 'I know it's fucking there,' he shouted. 'I want two volunteers out of the three. Which is it to be?'

'Me Sarge,' said all three, reckoning that to hide would be cushier that to seek.

'I said two,' snarled Sgt Stripe. 'Can't you fucking count?'

'Yes, Sarge. But we all want to go,' said Private Parts.

'Well you'll have to fucking choose,' said Sgt Stripe. 'How do you choose in today's modern army?'

'Toss a coin, Sarge?'

'What do you think this is, a fucking casino?'

'Draw straws, Sarge?'

'We're not at a fucking kid's party!'

'Dib dib dib, dob dob dob, Sarge?'

'Who do you think I am, fucking Brown Owl?'

'Set up a super computer to generate electronic random numbers at the press of a key?'

'In fucking Benbecula?'

'Go Eenie Meenie Miney Mo, Sarge?'

'That's right. We use the EMMM drill, as set out on page 102 of the War Book. You've practiced it before, so let's see if you remember it. By numbers, one!'

'Eeenie!' shouted the platoon, more or less in unison.

'By numbers, two!'

'Meenie!' shouted the platoon.

'By numbers, three!'

It was when they got to 'by numbers, six,' that disaster struck. A third of the platoon used the traditional but politically incorrect form. A third used the variant 'rigger', as taught in the schools of Aberdeenshire. And a third used the variant 'politician', thus destroying both the sense and the rhythm of the rhyme.

'How the fuck are you to choose if you don't even know the drill?' shouted Sgt Stripe. 'You, Smith and you, Krunt, will volunteer. Put on these kimonos and get the hell out of here. The rest of you – ten minutes smoko, and then get the hell after them!'

Private Smith drew his kimono over his ears and peered over the peat hag. Of the searchers there was no sign. Around him, peat bog and heather stretched featureless to the horizon, empty apart from myriad biting insects. He imagined himself as the English Patient, staggering across the desert in search of help for his wounded lover. He imagined himself as Lawrence of Arabia, lying about the time it took him to cross Sinai with the Bedouin. He imagined himself being stung to death by bees. One of the clegs landed delicately on his cheek and bit hard. He had to get out of here.

He scanned the horizon, looking for a place of sanctuary. And there, half hidden in a hollow, not more than 200 yards distant, he saw the chimney of the Benbecula and District Secondary School and Community Resource Centre. He stuffed his kimono into his knapsack and set off at the double.

Private Krunt, meantime, drew his kimono over his ears and peered over the peat hag behind which he was cowering. Of the searchers there was no sign. Around him, peat bog and heather stretched featureless to the horizon, empty apart from myriad biting insects. If it had been a dark and stormy night, and if, like Private Smith, he had been of a literary bent, this narrative might have continued in a similar vein for another paragraph or two. As it was, he decided that he had to get the fuck out of here.

He scanned the horizon, looking for a place of sanctuary. There, half hidden in a hollow, not more than 200 yards distant, he saw the chimney of the Benbecula Old People's Home and Retirement Day Care Resource Centre. He set off at the double.

'My dear Finch, we were expecting you yesterday. Why is it that student teachers always turn up late?'

The Headmaster polished his spectacles on the sleeve of his gown and ushered Private Smith into his study. He rebalanced them on his red and bulbous nose and peered at Private Smith's uniform. 'Didn't they tell you that the Combined Cadet Corps parades only on Wednesdays?'

Private Smith was an opportunist. If the Headmaster of the Benbecula and District Secondary School and Community Resource Centre, who had found him skulking in the playground, thought he was a student teacher, then a student teacher he would be. It was lucky that he had hidden his kimono in his knapsack.

' I'm sorry, Sir,' he responded. 'The train was late due to the wrong kind of sheep on the line, and I missed the connection at Inverness and the ferry at Uig. But I'm ready to start straight away.' He wondered what subject he was supposed to teach. English and astro-physics would be OK; anything else would be a disaster.

His luck held. 'You're timetabled to take poor Blenkinsop's classes in physics. He broke out of the clinic in Peebles and had a serious relapse in the Two Bells. He'll be away for another three months at least. Not that I blame him – Class 4D would be enough to drive an Ayatollah to drink. They're waiting for you now.'

The Headmaster ushered Private Smith out of his study and led him along a sick green corridor lit on both sides with clear glass windows. On one side was a quadrangle in which a few sick green blades of grass struggled for survival against a sea of chip-wrappings, pizza packages, hamburger cartons, lager cans, alcopop bottles and the odd French letter. On the other was a succession of sick green classrooms, each holding a regulation 30 adolescents, buzzing with ignorance and hormones, and a single teacher, variously shouting, weeping or wringing his or her hands. As they progressed from the younger classes to the older, the noise of swearing, shouting and screaming grew louder, until at last they reached a sick green door bearing the legend *Mr Blenkinsop B Sc: Physics.*

The Headmaster paused with his hands on the door handle. 'Here we are,' he said unnecessarily. 'I think that you'll find them an interesting bunch.'

Private Smith glanced through the clear glass windows of the classroom. The pupils were obviously enthusiastic students of the laws of physics. Some were studying the trajectories of moving objects by hurling pieces of chalk of varying mass at their fellow pupils. Others were researching aerodynamics with the help of paper airplanes, their noses dipped in black ink the better to track their landing point. Still others were proving the third law of thermodynamics by overturning desks and tipping their contents onto the floor. Others were enquiring into the electrical conductivity of the human body with the aid of a 12-volt battery and one of the prettier girls. And some were exploring the effect of gravity on fluids with the help of a bottle of red ink and Mr. Blankinsop's lab coat.

The Headmaster threw open the door and made his own contribution to scientific research by hurling the blackboard duster at the largest of the boys. 'Silence!' he shouted. 'I want you to meet Mr. Finch, who will be replacing Mr. Blenkinsop for the next few weeks.' He retreated before the third law of thermodynamics could reassert itself.

In the temporary lull caused by the paralysis of the largest boy, Private Smith looked round the class. 'Now you lot,' he said firmly. 'Settle down and I'll teach you how to make an atomic bomb.'

Dudley Scrope led Donald MacDonald along the single track road which meandered the two miles from the council offices to the secondary school. Every now and then they had to leap into the ditch to permit a speeding Dutch or Belgian motorist towing a 30 foot mobile home to pass. Once they stopped to give directions to an earnest German student driving a Trabant. They spoke little. Donald was nursing his hangover. Dudley Scrope was considering how to give Donald the worst possible impression of what was indisputably the worst school in the country, if not in Europe.

The teachers were universally incompetent and were particularly hopeless in the matter of discipline. But even the second most hopeless, faced with a visitor, would make some effort to restore order – or rather, like God on the first day, to create order out of chaos, since to restore order implied that order had been there in the first place. (Despite his liberal upbringing and his education at Keele, Scrope had absorbed some theological ideas from Mgr McCavity, the island's priest.) It followed that surprise was essential, and that he should seek to surprise the most incompetent teacher of all. Without a doubt that man was Blenkinsop, the physics teacher.

Scrope led MacDonald to the back of the school, where a special door had been constructed to permit the installation of a cyclotron. Putting his fingers to his lips and bracing himself for an assault of pieces of chalk, dead frogs, and worse, he pushed open the door and led Donald inside.

All was calm, order, quiet. The class sat at their benches taking copious notes in their jotters. In front of them, a young man wearing a slightly grubby battle dress was covering the white board with neat equations, among which Scrope recognized $e=mc^2$. Christ! he thought, forgetting Mgr McCavity's exhortations against blasphemy. What the hell's going on here? He strode to the front of the class and rapped on a test tube for attention.

'Now boys and girls,' he announced, knowing that nothing was guaranteed to enrage a bunch of Benbecula adolescents more than being addressed as boys and girls. If they weren't rioting when he arrived, at least he could provoke a riot in the course of his visit.

The class looked up, still silent but with some encouraging signs of irritation.

'Boys and girls,' he repeated, 'I want to introduce Mr. Donald MacDonald, who is visiting us from the North British Office.'

A pustular youth at the back of the class put up his hands and rose politely to his feet.

'Well, boy, what is it?'

'Please Sir, would you mind terribly if you didn't interrupt our lesson. It is crucial to our future that we get good grades in our Highers, and we wish to profit to the full from Mr. Finch's presence among us.'

One of the girls raised her hand, emphasizing the womanly swell beneath her blouse.

'Please Sir,' she said, 'it is customary for visitors to the Benbecula High School to sit quietly at the back of the classroom, observing the excellence of the teaching which we are privileged to receive from our elders and betters. We'd be frightfully grateful if you and Mr. MacDonald, whom we are charmed to meet, would adopt the same procedure.'

'Damn,' thought Scrope. Frightful was the last thing this class was likely to be. He took Donald MacDonald meekly to the back of the lab and sat meekly on the hard bench.

Private Krunt peered carefully through the almost closed blinds of the Benbecula Old Peoples Home and Retirement Day Care Resource Centre. In the corner of the day care room a television set flickered bluely. Around the walls, dozing in high backed chairs, sat the ancients of the island, the men dressed in neat tweed suits, the womenfolk in flowered dresses. A matron in a spotless blue uniform wandered around the room, rearranging pillows and offering those who were awake refreshing cups of herbal tea.

Private Krunt pulled off his battle dress and hid it beneath a rose bush. He'd not pass for one of the old men in his uniform, and if the platoon caught up with him it would be curtains. But with his beret pulled down over his ears to hide his razor cut, and his kimono wrapped around his lean frame, he had a fighting chance of passing for one of the old women. It was a pity that he had forgotten to shave that morning, but it was dark in the day care room, and in any case most of the old women had beards.

He lurked outside until the matron left to replenish her pot of herbal tea, then climbed quickly through the window and installed himself in a vacant chair opposite the television set.

Half a mile away across the peat bog, Sgt Stripe rallied his men. 'It is time,' he said, 'to introduce you to our secret weapon against the Japanese. Rover.'

''Rover?' interrupted Lance Cpl Brown, 'wot you mean, Rover?'

'Your Jap is a cunning sod,' said Sgt Stripe, 'and when attacked he is likely to go to ground. It will be essential to find him and root him out. And 'ow to find him in these godforsaken parts? With a bloodhound, of course.'

'But there ain't no bloodhound 'ere,' objected Lance Cpl Brown.

'Precisely. So I 'ave trained a sheep dog to perform as a virtual bloodhound. Watch!'

Sgt Stripe gave a piercing whistle, and a black and white collie appeared from nowhere. It jumped up at Sgt Stripe and licked his hands. Sgt Stripe patted it affectionately, then pulled a piece of cloth from his haversack and held it beneath the dog's nose. The dog sniffed noisily, barked twice and streaked off across the bog.

'I am most impressed,' said Donald MacDonald. 'Such polite pupils, such keenness for their subject, such inspired teaching. Now tell me about the Old Peoples Home. I am so much looking forward to visiting it.'

Dudley Scrope swelled with pride. Perhaps McTurk had misled him and the Minister would take MacDonald's advice after all. The Old Peoples Home would reinforce the rosy view which MacDonald was forming of his competence, efficiency, keenness, intelligence, nous, ability and all round suitability to become Chief Executive of the Benbecula and North Uist District Metropolitan Council. He led Donald MacDonald rapidly along the road to the Home.

Private Krunt pulled his beret further down over his eyebrows and sank further back into his seat. A chair opposite the TV set had seemed a good idea at the time: all eyes would be on it, and none on him. How was he to know that he had installed himself beside Priapic McTavish, Benbecula's living proof that some urges never die? In Priapic McTavish's case, thanks to a healthy outdoor life amongst the sheep, they had not even faded.

'New here, are you, at all, at all?' McTavish cackled through toothless gums. 'It iss not often that the Benbecula Palace welcomes a new resident, and rarely one of chust such charm as yourself, chust so.'

Private Krunt, as he had been instructed by Sgt Stripe, rapidly assessed the options. Murder was not on; he had no weapon, and strangulation would be bound to attract the attention of at least one of the ancients mumbling by the walls. Seduction was not on; even someone as aged as his new neighbour was bound to discover sooner or later that he was two mammaries short of a starlet. He decided on the Altzheimer opening, and stared silently into space.

It was the worst possible strategy. Priapic McTavish had been cursed with a wife of legendary garrulosity, and that, coupled with his years amongst the sheep, had taught him that there was nothing more attractive in a female that silence. He reached over and put a bony claw on Private Krunt's knee.

Priapic McTavish had assisted at the parturition of many a healthy lamb, and had extraordinarily sensitive hands. He swelled with excitement at what he found.

'No stockings,' he cackled, 'I love a woman with no stockings. She's gone half way to meeting a man already, chust.'

Had Private Krunt been half a woman, he would have known to snap his thighs together and crush the bony fingers between his femurs. As it was, he continued to stare fixedly at the TV set, where Tom and Jerry chased each other endlessly around a steamroller.

The bony fingers made their way up his inner thigh and towards his regulation army issue khaki boxer shorts Mark V like a pair of ragged claws scuttling across the floors of silent seas. Private Krunt began to wish that he had worn his trousers rolled beneath his kimono. In the room the women were talking, but not of Michaelangelo. As it was, his neighbour was about to receive a nasty surprise.

When the door of the day care room was thrown open, filling the room with sunlight. The matron stepped briskly inside, ushering in two men in suits. 'Now, ladies and gentlemen, I should like you to meet...'

Through the open window streaked a black and white bundle of fur, which hurtled round the room overturning chairs, snapping at wrinkled stockings, knocking out false teeth, licking mucus from the noses of the old men, barking at the television set, where a cat was doing unconventional things to a mouse, pissing against the potted plants, smashing crockery, and attempting to herd those of the senior citizens who had stumbled to their feet into the corner of the room. Not since the day of the terrier race had the dog had so much fun. Finally, remembering its bloodhound role, it sniffed at each of the ancients in turn and leapt onto Private Krunt's lap, trapping Priapic McTavish's hand as it was about explore the hidden mysteries of his regulation army issue khaki boxer shorts Mark V.

An uneasy peace settled. The matron clapped her hands. 'Please, please, take your seats if you can and help your neighbour if you can't.' A little logical confusion was excusable in the circumstances.

The old people began to pick themselves up and dust themselves down, muttering through toothless gums. Private Krunt patted the dog's neck and persuaded it to sit at his feet. Priapic McTavish removed his hand from Private Krunt' regulation army issue khaki boxer shorts Mark V, still unenlightened about their contents, but puzzled as to why French knickers should be made of such a course and hairy material. The matron clapped her hands again.

'Now, when you're all sitting comfortably, we can begin our daily quiz.' She turned to Donald. 'It is so important to keep their minds active,' she said.

Order was restored. False teeth were replaced. Paper and pencils were issued. The old people sat expectant in their chairs, anticipating the excitement of the quiz and the prizes for the winners. Last week it had been a chocolate cake, cooked by Mgr McCavity's housekeeper, and the week before a bottle of Spanish alcohol free whisky presented by the local branch of Alcoholics Anonymous.

'Now then. From which army grouping did the first troops ashore in the Normandy landings come?'

The doors and windows burst open, and Sgt Stripe and his platoon leapt into the room, weapons at the ready.

Sgt Stripe let fly a burst of blank ammunition from his sten gun, dislodging a wally dog from its position on the mantle shelf and destroying the chandelier.

'Freeze!' he screamed.

* * *

CHAPTER 22

In which one of our heroes embarks on a philosophical journey,
leaving others to bring home the bacon.

Donald Macdonald sat gingerly in the coffee shop and examined the fax which he had picked up from Reception. It contained everything that he needed – a concise description of industrial facilities and transport links, a poetic evocation of leisure opportunities, even a photograph of a local beach on which seals competed for space like sun bathers on bank holiday Monday in Brighton. Surely this would be enough to persuade Omeiwaku Denki to visit.

Donald ordered a large black coffee and a croissant. There would be time enough to remind Megan Morgan Thomas of their meeting with Omeiwaku after he had restored some kind of equilibrium to his cerebellum; and the House phone would enable him to speak to her without further risk to his chastity. But why should he remind Megan of the meeting at all? Uncharitable thoughts began to course through his brain stem. What if he told everyone, Dildenschneider included, that the meeting had been postponed?

Donald had heard of the legendary psychic powers of the East, but he was not prepared for what happened next. The idea of asking for the House telephone had barely formed in his still tender brain when a waitress appeared bearing the said instrument in her hand.

'Terephone corr for Mistah Macdonurandu,' she said in her sing song voice. 'It is very virgin.'

'Virgin?' asked Donald. 'What do you mean, virgin?'

'Must be answered at once,' said the waitress. She handed the phone to Donald.

'Mr. Macdonald?' said the telephone. Despite the fact that it was a Japanese instrument made in a converted shipyard, it spoke with an American accent.

'Yes?' responded Donald.

'Thank God I've tracked you down,' said the telephone. 'It's Dildenschneider here. I've an urgent message from Hirosiguchisan.'

Donald forced his brain into gear. 'So have I,' he said. 'I was just about to call you. This morning's meeting has been postponed.'

'Well, ain't that the darndest thing,' said Dildenscheider. 'He asked me to call you and to give you the same message. The big boss has been called away to Kyoto, and we are all to meet him there this afternoon at the Shoren-in Temple. I've already told Megan – for some reason she was in your room at the Origami Intercontinental, nudge nudge wink wink, as you Brits say. Now listen carefully and I'll tell you how to get there.'

Donald spent 20 minutes trying to contact Stuart MacLellan. He was not at his apartment, nor at his office. The commercial section at the British embassy was closed, and Donald was defeated by the switchboard at Omeiwaku Denki's headquarters, where a fluent English speaker utterly failed to understand his Scots accent. Megan Morgan Thomas, meanwhile, had joined him in the coffee shop and was looking anxiously at her watch.

'Dildneschneider told me about the change of plan,' she said huskily. 'If we don't hurry, look you, we shall miss the 6.40 Shinkansen.'

'But I must track Stuart down.' Despite his overweening self confidence, Donald was beginning to think that it might be helpful to have an expert on tap, if only to give directions to the taxi driver.

'No point in finding him if it's too late to get to the meeting. That way Dildenschneider will win the project for the USA, and we go home empty handed. Anyway, you showed such skill in handling the Japanese at dinner last night that I would have thought that you were perfectly capable of landing the project by yourself. Provided of course that they don't want to come to Wales. But it's up to you. I'm going anyway.'

A rapid calculation suggested to Donald that it would be better for him to accompany Megan Morgan Thomas to the meeting and take the credit if Scotland won, than to let her go on her own.

Besides, he wanted to know the answer to a crucial question. What the hell was the Shinkansen?

The journey to the Shoren-in Temple should have been easy. Japanese trains run to the second, and Japanese taxi drivers are reasonably skilled at reading instructions written in Katakana – the script which adorns the headbands of sumo wrestlers. But it is a feature of human psychology, Japanese no less than European, that people hear what they expect to hear. So when Megan Morgan Thomas asked the concierge of the Origami Intercontinental to write the name of the Shoren-in Temple on a slip of paper, so that she could show it to the taxi driver when they reached Kyoto, the concierge wrote 'Golden Temple', which is where 95% of tourists visiting the former imperial capital wish to go. Megan thanked him profusely and set off to enjoy one of the great train journeys of the world, with Donald following obediently at her more than ample rear.

All went well until they reached Kyoto. The taxi from the hotel had deposited them in good time at Tokyo Central Station, and they had found tickets and seats without difficulty. It was somewhat surprising that Dildenschneider wasn't there, but he might have caught an earlier train. The Shinkansen, much to Megan's scorn, had left two seconds late, and before every station a sing song Japanese voice announced in English that the train was about to arrive, that the station was called such and such, that passengers who were leaving should remember to take all their luggage with them, and that passengers who were not leaving should not leave the train. A similar message was given in Japanese, although Donald surmised that, such was the cunning of his hosts, it could be exhorting them to work even harder to ensure that the economic miracle didn't grind to a halt.

Donald bought a breakfast box from one of the trolleys which joined the train at every station to sell regional specialities, and cricked his neck looking for Mount Fuji across the green tea plantations. Megan confined herself to reading her brief and casting the occasional lustful glance in Donald's direction.

But at Kyoto their luck changed. It had begun to rain the warm clammy rain of the sub-tropics, and there was an extensive queue for taxis. Their own driver didn't appear to have the robust intelligence you are accustomed to finding in London or New York. He gazed vaguely at the slip of paper which Megan handed him, on which the concierge had helpfully written the name of the Temple where they were to meet the President of Omeiwaku Denki, clashed his taxi into gear, and pulled out into the traffic.

'*Ah so,*' he said over his shoulder as they sped past a cyclist, narrowly avoiding a collision. 'Gorendenru Tempu. Many tourist go to Gorendenru Tempu. Vely beautiful.' He changed gear to overtake a tourist bus, and swerved to avoid an oncoming truck.

Donald glanced at Megan, who was gripping his thigh with the agonised concentration of one who was about to meet her maker. 'I thought the meeting was at the Shoren-in Temple .' He leant forward to the driver.

'The Shoren-in Temple ,' he enunciated slowly. 'We want to go to the Shoren-in Temple.'

'*Ah so.*' There was a squeal of brakes as the driver squeezed between a handcart piled high with straw hats and a forty ton truck. 'Vely beautiful. Best tempu's in world in Kyoto.' He accelerated away from the owner of the cart, who was making some very impolite gestures at him, and began to climb into the hills.

'Must be his pronunciation,' said Megan. 'He's got the concierge's slip, and surely there can't be much room for error.'

There was. Twenty minutes later they drew to a halt outside a large park. Through the trees they could make out a golden pagoda gleaming in the rain. A long queue of Japanese schoolchildren waited patiently outside, dressed in sailor suits and drinking from cans of cola. '*Hai,*' said the taxi driver, grinning round at them with uneven teeth, 'Kinkaku-ji! Gorendenru Tempu!' By the gate, indeed, was a notice in English. 'Golden Temple' it said.

The taxi driver gestured at the meter. 'Five thousand yen,' he said.

'But we want to go to the Shoren-in Temple,' expostulated Donald. 'This is the Golden Temple.'

'*Hai*, Gorendenru Tempu'. Most popular tourist spot in all Japan. Five thousand yen.'

Donald pointed at the slip of paper, which the driver had left on the passenger seat. 'That's where we want to go to.'

'*Ah so.* Gorendenru Tempu where all tourist want to see. Look, many Japanese – popular with us too. Enjoy!'

'There's no point, look you,' said Megan, looking at her watch. 'Let's get out of here and find another taxi. Otherwise we'll never get to the meeting on time.' And she retrieved the slip of paper from the driver and climbed from the taxi, leaving Donald to struggle in his wallet for the 5000 yen.

Megan found another taxi which was depositing a group of dispirited Americans at the gate, and showed the driver the slip. 'We want here,' she said pointing at the Japanese characters. 'Not here, look you,' pointing at the temple.

The driver looked puzzled. Kinkaku-ji said the slip, and Kinkaku-ji was the place. Everything which they said about foreign devils was true; they had no idea where they were. Then enlightenment dawned. '*Ah so,*' he said. 'Not Kinkaku-ji. Ginkaku-ji! Please, get in.'

Megan levered her bulk into the back and waved at Donald. 'I think its OK now,' she said. 'This one looks a good deal brighter than the other, and we've still got almost an hour.'

They screeched into the traffic, narrowly avoiding an ox cart, and set off at high speed. Twenty minutes later they pulled up outside another park. Through the trees they could make out a silver pagoda gleaming in the rain. The same long queue of Japanese schoolchildren waited patiently outside, dressed in sailor suits and drinking from cans of cola. Donald wondered how they had managed to get there in from the Golden Temple in advance of Megan and himself.

'*Hai,*' said the taxi driver, grinning round at them with uneven teeth, 'Ginkaku-ji! Silavaru Tempu!' By the gate was a notice in English. 'Silver Temple' it said.

Megan swore briefly but powerfully in Welsh. Then for Donald's benefit she translated. 'This is the fucking Silver Temple. We want the fucking Shoren-in Temple. You pay off the fucking driver, and I'll ask where the fuck we ought to be going.'

Donald searched in his wallet for the 2000 yen registered on the meter. He was rapidly running out of cash; and he didn't see why he should have to finance the activities of his Welsh competitors. But without Megan he was unlikely to get to the meeting at all. Damn Stuart MacLellan for failing to turn up that morning! He handed over the notes and rejoined Megan by the gate to the temple.

'No problem,' she said, smiling broadly for the first time since he had left her frustrated in his bed. 'It's a short walk down the Path of Philosophy. This helpful guide has given me detailed instructions.' She nodded at an old man who was holding out his hand. 'Give him a tip, Donald, there's a dear.'

The Path of Philosophy, Megan explained, was named after a philosopher who had walked it every day as part of his search for enlightenment. It ran besides a small stream which joined the Golden and Silver Temples, and was lined with other temples, some Buddhist, some Shinto, some lavish, some as simple as an English parish church. The Shoren-in Temple was a mere half mile away, and they had ample time to get there. 'We have to start in the grounds of the Silver Temple. Be a dear and get the tickets, would you?'

The Path of Philosophy lived up to its reputation. Shaded by trees and wandering by a gentle stream in which lazy trout and somnolent carp basked in deep pools, its peace was broken by nothing but the occasional swish of rollerbladers meditating on zen and the art of speed. Donald began to relax. Hiroshiguchi was hardly likely to be sympathetic to Megan Morgan Thomas after last night's fiasco, and Dildenschneider had obviously missed the train and might not make the meeting. He, Donald, had enough information to persuade Omeiwaku Denki to visit Scotland, and when they got there the Feelgood Project would be in the bag. Since Stuart had disappeared he would be able to claim all the credit. Promotion and honours danced before his eyes like the little flies glittering above the stream.

Megan caught his arm and pointed at a footbridge which crossed the stream to a small temple on the opposite bank. 'Look at that dear little temple, look you' she breathed repetitively. 'Let's go and pray for success!'

The temple had more in common with a Welsh country church than with St Paul's. True the alcohol was stored in vast barrels by the altar rather than in the pub next door, and there were scraps of paper covered in Japanese script tied to the bushes. But there were statues – not of the saints, but of squirrels and foxes who had no doubt very similar characters. And there was an ancient crone, dressed in a gown not unlike a cassock, who approached them with hands outstretched and spoke in a wheezy voice.

'Give her alms, Donald,' said Megan. 'The success of our mission depends on it.'

She struck a gong before the altar and bowed her head in prayer. Donald shook his head at the crone, who grasped his sleeve in a surprisingly firm grip and continued her wheezing. Donald pulled out his trouser pockets to show that he had no coins. The crone retained her grip and with her other hand pointed at the area of his jacket where westerners are known to keep their pocket books. Acknowledging defeat, Donald removed his wallet and handed his last 1000 yen note to the crone.

Another twenty minutes took them to the gates of the Shoren-in Temple, which were firmly shut. Megan pulled on the bellrope, and after a short wait the gate swung open. A monk clad in saffron robes ushered them inside.

'Welcome,' he said in perfect American English as the gate slammed behind them. 'Mr Macdonald and Miss Morgan Thomas, is it not? Dwight Dildenschneider told me to expect you. Welcome to our Temple, and to our week of silent meditation for beginners. I am sure that you will attain enlightenment.'

Back in Tokyo, Stuart MacLellan had given up a fruitless search for Donald Macdonald. Two hours in the sauna of his Health Club followed by a half hour massage delivered by a retired sumo wrestler had restored his body from the stresses of the previous day; and he felt almost fit for the meeting with Omeiwaku Denki. He felt fitter still after his hour's jog around the walls of the Imperial Palace. It was only when he returned to his apartment at 10 am that he realised that he had forgotten to switch on his answerphone – but after yesterday Donald was hardly likely to be trying to reach him at that time. Still, he had better make sure that Donald was up and ready for the noon meeting. He might be the most incompetent colleague that he had ever had the privilege of working for, but he was still the boss.

There was, however, no answer from Donald's room, and the normally helpful reception desk was unable to help him. 'Perhaps he in health club,' said the receptionist, 'or perhaps in coffee shop. We send bell boy to find him. Please hold...'

Stuart listened to a tinny recording of the first ten bars of the Goldberg Variations – surely the most irritating piece of music ever composed – interspersed with the occasional message: 'please hold: we are trying to connect you' – in English, Japanese, French German and Chinese. Then at last the receptionist got back to him. 'Very sorry. Mistah Macdonurandu not in hotel. He left in taxi about three and a half hours ago with very fat woman.'

Megan Morgan Thomas, thought Stuart, what the hell is she up to? He would have to go to the meeting on his own and hope that Donald caught up with him there. And if not, all well and good; he had far more chance of landing the project on his own than if Donald failed to turn up to draw attention to the superior merits of North Uist as against East Kilbride. He reached for his phone and called a taxi.

Omeiwaku Denki had put out the red carpet. On the flagpoles by the gates drooped the Union Jack, the dragon of Wales, the St Andrew's Cross, the Stars and Stripes, and incongruously the Confederate Flag. The board by the entrance had been amended: it now read *Omeiwaku Denki Corporation welcomes Stuart MacRerran, Donald Macdonard, Megan Molgan Thomas, and Dwight Dildosnooker*. It was clearly going to be a crunch meeting.

In Reception, Dwight Dildenschneider was leafing through a copy of *USA Today* and smoking a fat Havana cigar contrary to both US Trade policy and the 'No Smoking' sign above his head. He looked up at Stuart and heaved himself to his feet. 'Wayll, ain't that the darndest thing,' he said. 'I'd almost given you up for lost. Where's the boy and the fat lady – still enjoying the fruits of their illicit passion? The party ain't started until the fat lady clings!'

'I thought they might be with you,' replied Stuart. 'Didn't you take them back to the hotel last night?'

'I made an excuse and left,' said Dildenschneider. 'Megan looks big enough to cope with two, but a boy from a southern Baptist Sunday school can't handle that kind of thing. We'd better get this meeting started without them. I guess they're looking into the depths of their souls by now.'

Looking into the depths of their souls was precisely what Donald and Megan were doing, although less willingly than Dildenschneider had implied. When the gate of the Temple slammed shut behind them, the monk who had welcomed them put his fingers to his lips. 'There must be silence until the setting of the sun,' he whispered.

'Without such silence, the elusive gift of enlightenment is unattainable.'

'But we're here for a meeting with the President of Omeiwaku Denki,' expostulated Donald. 'The message was absolutely clear.'

'There are many roads to enlightenment,' whispered the monk, 'and our disciplines will help you find them for yourselves. For some, the way of the Denki is the clearest path. For others it is the path of nothingness. In your case, I suspect that that will be the more fruitful. Follow me, please.'

Donald turned back to the gate and pulled at the handle. It was firmly closed. He looked at Megan in exasperation.

'What the fuck's that bloody swine Dildenschneider been up to,' he hissed. 'And if the meeting's not here, where the hell is it.'

'Follow the monk,' said Megan. 'There must be a telephone somewhere in this building – after all, this is Japan. We can at least try phoning the Embassy.'

The monk led them silently through the wooden passages of the temple to a Zen garden shaded by the branches of an ancient cedar. On the ground, gravel was raked into strange patterns. Boulders of strange shapes and colours reared up at random; and water flowed darkly into a pool by the wall. The whole place had an uncanny atmosphere of tranquillity.

'Fuck,' shouted Donald. He could see the Omeiwaku project, his prospects of promotion, the OBE which was surely his by rights, going down the plughole to California. 'Fuck, fuck, fuck, fuck,' echoed the walls of the temple garden.

The monk turned to him, a pained expression on his previously impassive face. 'You will disturb the ancestors,' he intoned. 'Wait in this pavilion until sundown, and then we shall review progress. It is a great privilege to be here; this is the Abbot's Cherry Blossom Viewing Chamber.'

'But there isn't any cherry blossom,' shouted Donald, whose years in the Department of Agriculture, Fisheries and Training had not taught him about the seasons. 'Not even for polishing your fucking shoes.'

The monk looked down at his feet, which were bare. 'You will contemplate the cherry blossom of the mind,' he said. 'And remember: absolute silence. To remove the temptation to leave, I shall lock the door behind you.'

And he turned and slipped silently away.

'Gleetings, gentlemen. How you feeling today?'

Of Hirosiguchisan's excesses the previous night there was no sign. His skin was clear, his eyes were bright, his step was brisk, and his hair was polished into the patent leather sheen which only the most expensive Japanese hair lotion can produce. Nor did he have the disappointed look of someone whose subtle and erotic approaches had been brutally rejected. For like all Japanese raised in the fifties he knew that another Shinkansen was always along soon, timed to the second. He wasn't going to tell Dildenschneider and MacLellan that he'd returned to the Athenaeum Club after being humiliated by Megan Morgan Thomas, where he had taken his pleasure with the mama-san, who understood everything there was to know about consoling a disappointed lover. Dildenschneider could think he was in denial if he wanted to.

'So, you had enjoyable evening,' he said. 'Ginza many enjoyables, *so des ne*? But where Miss Morgan Thomas and Mr Macdonard? They too invited to meeting. President Yamamoto he no like be kept waiting.'

'I think,' said Dildenschneider, 'that we should go ahead without them. I am sure that Stuart here can handle the interests of the Brits, and I sure as hell can handle those of the Yanks.'

'Yes indeed,' said Stuart. 'I agree we should go ahead without them.'

They entered the executive lift and were rocketed as before to the Venetian Palazzo on the 39th floor. Hirosiguchisan left them at the foot of the stairway, and the same exquisite Japanese woman who had greeted them before bowed low, ushered them into the meeting room and invited them to sit before the alcove, in which the ming vase, the Japanese scroll and the single orchid had been replaced by an American flag. Dildenschneider looked at it approvingly. 'Wayall,' he said, smiling broadly, 'I guess you've got your answer, Stuart.'

If Stuart MacLellan had attained enlightenment, Donald Macdonald certainly hadn't. He paced up and down the Abbot's Cherry Blossom Viewing Room like a hamster in its cage, but unlike a hamster he was cursed with the power of speech. What little he knew of Zen meditation had taught him that adepts made a considerable use of mantras – phrases given in the utmost secrecy by your zen master which when repeated over and over again lost their meaning and allowed the mind to reach tranquillity. Well, he didn't need a zen master to give him a mantra – he had one of his own, though it was doing little to help him attain the promised state. 'Fucking Dildenschnieder,' he muttered again and again. 'Fucking Dildenschnieder!' And occasionally for variety, 'Fucking, fucking Dildenschnieder.'

'Why don't you shut up and try to get us out of here,' said Megan. She was becoming exasperated with Donald's cursing, and beginning to wonder how she could have found herself in bed with him. The glances that over cocktails had seemed so very sweet, did not seem quite so charming, erotically attractive, alluring, seductive or desirable now.

'Fucking Dildenschnieder,' continued Donald. 'How the fuck am I to get us out of here. The fucking monks won't speak to you, the fucking Abbot's Cherry Blossom Viewing Room is locked, and the fucking wall is about twelve feet high. Fucking Dildenschnieder. I hope he gets fucking fucked.'

President Yamamoto was led into the meeting room by his two acolytes and Hirosiguchi. He peered round the room through his thick spectacles and at last focussed on MacLellan and Dildenschnieder.

'*Ah so*,' he said, 'I am most preased to see you again. But shouldn't there be more? I was expecting also the large Welsh woman and the scrawny Scotsman.'

Hirosiguchi leant over and whispered in his ear.

'*Ah so* – unavoidably delayed by the panky hanky, so? Perhaps explerimenting with a prototype of the Feelgood Toy Boy™. No matter, we can do without. I have here fax from Sclotland.'

Hirosiguchi handed him a sheet of paper which he held up close to his eyes. 'Sent to Donard Macdonard from a place called North Oooshti, and copied to Commercial Section at Blitish Embassy, who wisely sent it on to Hirosiguchisan. Many fine fishing and gorf course. Also good tlansport links and fine workers. Plovided place meets plospectus, Feelgood Project will go there. Please arrange immediate visit.   That is my decision, and conglatulations, Mr MacRerran.'

'Well I'll be fucked,' snarled Dildenschneider.

Donald Macdonald's mantra had worked after all.

* * *

CHAPTER 23

In which it is better to travel fearfully than to arrive, and Sir Terence debates the Constitution.

Henry J Klassinger III, possibly Temporary Consul General of the United States of America, did not enjoy flying. And he particularly did not enjoy flying in anything smaller than a Boeing 767. But he calmed himself with several large glasses of Wild Turkey in the Executive Lounge at Glasgow Airport, and he settled into the bus which would take him and his fellow passengers to the aircraft with relative equanimity, knowing from past experience that the panic attack would not hit him until he clambered up the aircraft steps. It was only when the bus was halfway down the runway that he realised that it was about to take off.

Sweat broke out on his brow, and he gripped his arm rest in panic. 'Say, what is this?' he screamed at the passenger in the next seat, a florid gentleman in a hairy tweed suit. 'This crazy jerk trying to fly a bus to the Hebrides?'

His companion looked at him with alarm. 'The Short's Islander isn't the most elegant of aircraft, but it's the only plane which can get into the landing place at Barra.'

'This a fucking aircraft?' shouted Klassinger. 'It ain't big enough to handle the school run at Cohasset.'

'Any bigger and they'd have to fit it with floats. Now do calm down, my dear chap, and let a fellow do the Financial Times crossword in peace.'

The aircraft lurched into the air, and Henry J Klassinger III stared around him with wild eyes. The shuttle to Heathrow was bad enough, but this was intolerable. Sure, the cabin of the Islander was relatively high, but what it gained in cubic feet it lost in comfort. Rivets strained and rattled on the metal walls. The seats were of a design rejected by the makers of the Lada. The noise of the turbo prop engines hurt his ears and made thought almost impossible. But Henry J Klassinger had only one thought in his mind.

'What do you mean, they'd have to fit it with floats?'

His companion turned to him with irritation. The crossword was particularly challenging, and he was stuck on 15 Down: *'Protected Helen with the gloom of plonk (3 letters)'*.

'We land on the beach, and if the plane was any bigger we'd finish up in the sea.' Ah, that was it, 'sea' as in Homer's 'wine dark'. 'Thank you,' he said, 'you've solved a problem for me.'

'Land on the beach,' screamed Klassinger. 'You may not have a problem, but I sure have. I gotta get out of here.' He unstrapped his belt and stumbled to his feet.

'Now now,' whispered the stewardess, appearing at his elbow. 'What is all this?'

'I gotta get out of here,' repeated Klassinger. 'I got diplomatic immunity, and I ain't landing on no beach.'

'Sit down,' ordered the stewardess in accordance with Part I of the Training Manual for Handling Unruly Passengers. 'You're not going anywhere,'

Waves of panic began to break over Henry J Klassinger III. 'But how the hell can we land on a beach – what if the tide's up?' He began to flail his arms.

'We wait until the tide's out,' said the stewardess, gripping the Consul General's arms and forcing them to his sides. 'Now will you sit down – you're disturbing the trim of the aircraft.'

'Let me go...I have dipsomatic immunity,' shouted Klassinger.

The stewardess moved to part II of the Manual and kneed Henry J Klassinger III in the groin. He doubled up into his seat, and she whipped a handcuff from her shoulder-bag and locked his wrist to the armrest. 'Now will you keep quiet,' she said.

'The American President will get to hear of this,' screamed Henry J Klassinger III. 'If your tinpot airline has landing rights in the USA you can forget them. Kidnapping a representative of the world's greatest remaining superpower has led to war in the past.'

'Certainly Sir,' said the stewardess calmly. 'And I'm sure it will in the future. Now if you keep quiet, I'll fix you a drink'

The Johnny Walker and Coke which she handed him had enough tranquillisers in it to calm a Nuremberg Rally, and Henry J Klassinger III spent the rest of the flight staring fixedly ahead of himself muttering, 'Planes don't land on beaches,' over and over again.

No such problems were troubling the Lear Jet which was transporting the CNN crew from London City Airport to Benbecula. CNN had had no difficulty in persuading the Ministry of Defence to permit them to land on a military airstrip – they had too much dirt on the higher command to make refusal a possibility, and the Chiefs of Staff had no wish to see the worldwide broadcast of the Fudgy Tapes.

Ms Amaryllis Squaff, the presenter, gazed out of the window at the spectacularly boring British Lake District. She came from Boise, Idaho, and everything was too green and on too small a scale for her taste – they had bigger mounds in Legoland. She turned her attention to the brief which her researchers had prepared for her.

This was some story! American cultural mission harassed by tribal factions. Ongoing hostage situation. British government officials assisting the oppressors. Breaking of the historic links between Scotland and the USA. Possibility of retaliatory action by the USA through the banning of Caledonian Societies, the proscription of Burns, and the prohibition of exports of Scotch Whisky. American Carrier USS Enterprise ordered from the Gulf to the North Atlantic. Reserve troops on standby. If anything was going to drive the President's latest problems of overexposure off the screens, this was it. Amaryllis Squaff took her gold Waterman out of her executive briefcase and began to scribble notes in the margins.

'Ladies and Gentlemen,' announced the Captain of the Short's Islander. 'I regret to announce a short delay in our landing time. Jeannie McDougall has signalled that the tide is still too high, and we shall enter the holding pattern above Pabbay. I expect to land in about fifteen minutes, if all goes well. In the meantime, enjoy the remainder of your flight, and we hope that you will fly again soon with Scottish Island Airways.'

Sweat broke out on Henry J Klassinger III's brow. He raised his free arm and signalled the stewardess. 'Another of those drinks,' he panted, 'and for Chrissake get us down fast.'

'All in God's good time,' said the stewardess, and turned to add another tranquilliser to the whisky.

The aircraft made a number of steep turns, dipping its wings at the spectacular cliffs of Pabbay. Gulls and bonxies swept backwards past the windows. Waves dashed white against jagged rocks. A herd of feral goats scattered for cover. Henry J Klassinger III gulped his drink and held out the empty glass for another. The intercom crackled into life.

'This is your Captain speaking. I am pleased to tell you that the tide has now retreated sufficiently far for us to land. That is the good news. But the bad news is that a herd of sheep has wandered onto the runway, and Jeannie McDougall's dog is away courting Alastair MacKenzie's bitch at the other end of the island. Everything possible is being done to clear the runway, and we shall land you as soon as possible. We shall enter the holding pattern above Eriskay while the problem is resolved. In the meantime, enjoy the remainder of your flight, and we hope that you will fly again soon with Scottish Island Airways.'

Eriskay was less rugged than Pabbay, but the same seagulls and Bonxies flew backwards past the aircraft's windows and the same angry waves dashed themselves against the shore. The stewardess handed Henry J Klassinger III another drink without being asked.

'Kranzgate,' wrote Amaryllis Squaff in the margins of her brief. She looked at it for a moment or two, then crossed it out. It lacked resonance. She licked the nib of her Waterman, then tried again. 'Mary-Lougate.' No. 'Katzenellenbogengate.' Better, but still not right. She crossed that out too. 'MacDonaldgate,' she wrote at last. That was it. MacDonald was the limey official who had kidnapped Mary-Lou Krantz, sexually harassed her and was using his powers as an organ of the British State to have her held hostage until she agreed to drop not only any charges against him, but probably also her knickers as well. 'The MacDonaldgate Affair,' she wrote in capital letters, and underlined it three times.

The white beach was rushing towards the aircraft, dangerous worm casts promising instant destruction and the blue sea threatening barely less instant drowning. If it were a choice between death by fire and death by water, Henry J Klassinger III would choose retirement by a golf course in Florida. The engine roared to a new pitch, and he covered his ears with his hands. Henry J Klassinger III was not a happy man. He squeezed his eyes shut and muttered 'Planes don't land on beaches' over and over again.

But the plane did land, successfully if a little bumpily, on the beach. The stewardess unshackled the Consul General and he walked unsteadily to the entrance, focusing with difficulty on the stairway. He stumbled down the steps, noticing two policemen in full dress uniform waiting at the bottom. At last he was getting the honour he deserved as Consul General of the world's last remaining superpower. Despite his double vision and incipient headache, he began to feel almost better. He only wished that he had brought his cocked hat with ostrich feathers and his white ducks. His chest swelled with pride: he would sort out the problem of Mary Lou Kranz in the full blaze of the world media, and his career would be made.

He stumbled again as his feet hit the soft sand, and found himself face down on the beach. Spitting sand out of his mouth as he pulled himself to his feet, he was accosted by the welcoming party.

'Henry J Klassinger III,' said Sergeant McPloud in his most official voice. 'I am arresting you on a charge of causing an affray in an aircraft while in the high seas above Scotland. You are not obliged to say anything, but if you don't...'

'The Minister will see you now, Sir Terence.'

Sir Terence Mould had been kicking his heels in the Minister's Private Office for 25 seconds, and he didn't like to be kept waiting – particularly by a mere junior Minister of the North British Office who had peculiar views about local government reform. Still less did he like his weekly progress meetings with the Minister, because each had an entirely different agenda. The Minister, in keeping with his view of the Scottish constitution as established by the Declaration of Arbroath, the Treaty of Union, and the Scotland (Scotland) Act 1998, felt that his role was to initiate policy, to review progress, to take credit in parliament and the media for the successes of his Department, and to offload blame for the cockups of Ministers onto his officials. Sir Terence, in keeping with his view of the British constitution as interpreted by Bagehot, the Cabinet Office and the Committee of Permanent Secretaries, felt that the Minister's role was to agree to the Department's proposals, to defend them in the Scottish Parliament, to be economically truthful about them to the media, and to resign when officials really cocked things up. Each regarded the other as a potential sacrificial lamb; and each did his best to keep the other in the dark.

Sir Terence gathered up his papers and strode purposefully into the Minister's room. The Minister, whose literary references were extending into the realm of symbolism, was lighting up a Hamlet in contravention of the NBO's no smoking policy. Sir Terence glared at him.

'May I remind you, Minister, of the Department's policy in regard to smoking on the premises, and invite you, with the greatest respect, to extinguish that cigar.'

'You may and you may not,' said the Minister, causing a slight blurring in Sir Terence's normally crystal clear mind.

'I fear that I do not entirely follow you,' he said.

The Minister frowned. 'You may remind me of the Department's no smoking policy, if you must. But you may not invite me to extinguish my cigar. I trust that I make myself clear.'

'With respect, Minister...'

'And you may not, in particular, speak to me with respect.' The Minister was enjoying himself. 'For a civil servant to speak of speaking with respect to a Minister is to do precisely the reverse. And now, with respect Sir Terence, I should welcome a progress report on the Outer Isles. Have you brought the Romeo of North Uist and the Juliet of Benbecula to bed yet?'

'I shall come to that,' responded Sir Terence, deciding to leave the most gratifying item until last. 'But first I must insist on reverting to the government's no smoking policy. It is forbidden to smoke in the Office. And that policy applies to Ministers as well as to officials. May I remind you of the Government's commitments in the White Paper *Health of the Nation*.'

'You may not,' said the Minister. He was rather enjoying saying 'no' to Sir Terence. It reminded him who was boss. 'If you consult Bagehot,' he continued, 'you will find that it is Ministers who make policy, not mere officials. I do not recollect having made policy on this issue.'

'Ministers were fully consulted,' said Sir Terence. 'They fully endorsed the policy.'

'But I wasn't. If you consult Bagehot you will find that Ministers are not bound by the decisions of their predecessors.'

'I thinks that you will find that applies to Ministers of a different administration,' said Sir Terence. He was not having a whippersnapper with less experience of government than Monica Lewinski lecturing him on the niceties of the constitution.

The Minister inhaled deeply, contrary both to departmental policy and his doctor's advice. 'Nonsense,' he said. 'Verse than nonsense, as Edward Lear might have put it. And it certainly doesn't apply to Ministers of a different Executive, and responsible to a different Parliament. So tell me about progress in North Uist.'

Sir Terence gave up the tobacco ploy and tried another tack. 'There is another development which I should brief you on first,' he said. 'We are about to land a major investment from Japan, and you will get considerable political kudos if it comes here. You will recollect the Omeiwaku Project?'

The Minister racked his brains. His private secretary put so much paper into his red box and packed so many meetings into his crowded day that he often had difficulty remembering whether he took coffee or tea in the morning. 'The lottery application for the kung fu centre in Coatbridge?' he hazarded.

'No Minister. It's...'

'No, don't tell me, Sir Terence. It's the motorbike factory they want to build in Glen Feshie. Bloody good project, if you ask me. I can't think why all the eco freaks are up in arms about it.'

'No Minister. It's...'

'The new chain of office for the Lord Provost of Glasgow?'

'No Minister.' Sir Terence had decided to be unhelpful.

'The National Park and Natural Heritage Centre in Clydebank?'

'No Minister.'

The Minister was running out of patience. 'Then what the hell is it?' he asked.

Sir Terence recalled his Bagehot. When a Minister asked a direct question, it was incumbent upon a civil servant to give him a truthful response. But not necessarily a full one. 'It's a substantial inward investment opportunity,' he said, 'affording the potential for considerable amelioration of our deficit in the balance of trade relative to our partners elsewhere in the European Union and having the potential for the safeguarding or creation of up to a minimum of 2k job opportunities in both production and R&D in an area of significantly high unemployment in the health electronics sector.'

The Minister was not prepared to be bamboozled, with respect or without it. 'Health electronics? What in heaven and earth, Horatio, is that?'

Sir Terence decided the overlook the fact that the Minister appeared to have forgotten his name. 'The application of recent developments in micro electronics technology to the alleviation or cure of symptomatic disorders of the human physiology,'he said. He forebore from explaining that the project was involved with sex toys. Whatever Bagehot said, you didn't have to give the Minister the full story.

'Ah, I understand,' said the Minister, who didn't.

'We have been in Japan for the past week discussing terms with the company, the Omeiwaku Denki Corporation. I sent one of our most able young officers to deal with the matter personally, and I am glad to say that he has persuaded the Corporation to visit Scotland to look at sites and agree a package of incentives. Donald Macdonald. I don't know whether you have met him?'

'I remember him. But I instructed that he should be sent to North Uist to abolish the Urban District Council. I am waiting for his recommendations.'

'No Minister, that is another Donald MacDonald. He spells his name with a capital 'D' and is, I am sorry to say, by no means as able. But by strange coincidence, the Omeiwaku Corporation have decided that they wish to look at North Uist as the location for their project. It should give a significant boost to the economy of the island. I recommend that you should visit the Island to meet the Corporation. If nothing else, it will provide a splendid photo opportunity.'

'All the more important to amalgamate the Councils. We can't have the Japanese dealing with a bunch of hick provincials from the boondocks. You were about to report progress on the amalgamation. How is Donald MacDonald, whatever he is called, getting on?'

It was time to put the boot in. Sir Terence smiled unctuously and rubbed his hands. 'I am sorry to inform you, Minister, that he has found himself in serious trouble with the police. Since then he has been involved in an unseemly brawl in an Old Peoples' Home in Benbecula, and he has made no effort to submit his report. I am, I regret to say Minister, having serious doubts about your wisdom in selecting him for a task which I regret to say appears to be well beyond his capability. Most regrettable.'

The Minister asserted his authority. 'He was selected on your recommendation, Sir Terence. Be that as it may, I am expecting the Department to effect the abolition of the North Uist and Benbecula Urban District Councils at once, or at least by the end of next session. If Donald MacDonald isn't up to the job, then I suggest you find someone else. And fast.'

'Yes, Minister,' said Sir Terence.

Donald MacDonald, despite Sir Terence's attempts to blacken his character, was fully up to the job. He had restored order at the Benbecula Old Peoples Home and Retirement Centre and assured Dudley Scrope that the unfortunate incident with low flying dogs and Sgt Stripe's sinophobic platoon would not feature in his report to the Minister. He had paid a visit to the local presbytery, where Mgr McCavity had given him sweet tea and rock cakes and complained bitterly about the neglect of central government and the need to bring more economic activity to the islands for the benefit of his flock. He had called in at the primary school, where a ravishing young teacher called Flora Macdonald was teaching her charges computing through the medium of Gaelic, and coping admirably with Alsace's interruptions in French. And he had returned to the North Uist Hydro Hotel in high spirits to find a fax from Donald Macdonald to say that senior personnel from Omeiwaku Denki were on their way to North Uist.

He spent a relaxed evening playing tri-lingual scrabble with Alsace, Lorraine and Lady Lucinda, and resolved to spend the next morning finalising his Report to the Minister on the creation of the Benbecula and North Uist Metropolitan Council. Things were moving happily to their conclusion.

* * *

CHAPTER 24

In which the reader's credulity is at risk of being stretched and there is a surprising turn up for the book.

Donald Macdonald felt obliged to say something, but there was no-one to say it to but Megan Morgan Thomas and she had heard it all before. Eight hours of zen meditation and a night on a futon as soft as a block of granite had done nothing to soothe his temper. He was seeking enlightenment all right – but it wasn't the kind of enlightenment you were likely to find in a Zen Buddhist temple with weird stone patterns in the gardens and a cherry blossom viewing room. He wanted to know how to get out, how to find Dildenschneider, and how to kill him slowly and painfully, preferably but not essentially without being found out.

Megan Morgan Thomas had taken things more philosophically. True that her taste in oriental religions inclined more to Tantra than to Zen, and true that her attempts to seduce Donald were unlikely to be successful when he was in his present mood, but the peace of the Abbot's Cherry Blossom Viewing Room gradually seeped through her pores and into her endocrine system. She squatted cross-legged on the wooden floor, revealing a massive expanse of Welsh thigh, and gazed through the lattice windows at the bare trees which for three weeks in the year were decked in bridal blossom for the delectation of the Abbot and his senior monks. She was reminded of the slag heap above Blaenau Ffestinniog where she had sat as a girl viewing the blossoms of the may trees and dreaming of seduction.

Her reverie was interrupted by the reappearance of the monk who had led them to the Abbot's Cherry Blossom Viewing Room. He was wearing a blue robe and an apologetic smile, and in his hand he carried a sheet of paper which Donald took to be one of the ancient scrolls of the Temple. 'So,' he said in his perfect American English, 'Good morning to you. But I regret that I have bad news.'

'What do you mean, bad news?' snarled Donald.

'I have a fax here from Dwight Dildenschneider. He regrets that it is no longer feasible for you guys to stay for the week's course in enlightenment for beginners. Apparently there have been some developments in Tokyo, and you have to return immediately.'

Donald leapt to his feet. 'Give it here!' he shouted.

Dwight Dildenschneider's English was not as elegant as that of the monk, but it was clear enough. Donald read it out loud. ' "Sorry about change of plan. Omeiwaku Denki changed venue for meeting at last minute. Too late to inform you." '

'Lying bastard,' he interjected. 'If he thinks he can con us into thinking that he didn't set us up...'

'Get on with it, look you,' said Megan quietly. She was still half absorbed by the tranquillity of her meditations.

' "Regret also that you must return immediate priority to Tokyo. Developments here require your personal attention. Kindest personal regards, Dwight." I'll give the bastard kindest personal regards!'

'Come,' said the Monk. 'I have ordered a taxi for the station.'

Stuart MacLellan was at Tokyo Central Station to meet them. He was wearing a new suit and a look of smug satisfaction which did not at all please Donald.

'Welcome back to Tokyo,' he said smiling broadly. 'Though I fear you won't be staying for long. Events have moved on since your little unscheduled trip to the country. Dwight told me all about it; I think it was very altruistic of him to do so. But how the hell you could bugger off in the middle of a delicate negotiation to indulge your interest in zen meditation, if that's what it was, beggars belief.'

Donald's blood pressure began to rise to dangerous levels. He did not expect his staff to address him like that, and as for the idea that Dildenschneider had been altruistic... 'That bastard,' he spluttered, 'that bastard told us that the meeting had been rescheduled for Kyoto.'

'Yes, he told me you'd say that,' said Stuart. 'He said that after your night of unbridled passion you'd decided to leave the negotiations to me as an expert and to take the day off for some unbridled meditation, and that you would probably try to put the blame on him. Perceptive chap, Dwight, despite his origins.'

'I'll murder the bugger,' shouted Donald. 'I suppose he's met with Omeiwaku and persuaded them to go to Califuckingfornication. What the hell are we to tell the Minister?'

'I've already told the Minister, giving full recognition to your own personal contribution,' said Stuart quietly.

'You mean you've blamed me for the loss of the project? If you think that's the way to get promotion I'll get you transferred to the Bovine Offal Grants Branch.'

'On the contrary, I've given you full credit for your own contribution to our winning it. President Yamamoto was so impressed with my presentation that he's decided on a visit to North Uist. If that goes well, the project's in the bag for Scotland. We have to make a brief call on the Ambassador, and we leave on the late afternoon flight. Sorry, Megan, but the best team won.'

'That's all right by me,' said Megan. 'I'm thinking of moving to Scotland to live with Donald, aren't I my little leek.'

Oh God, thought Donald, that's all I need.

His Excellency Ambassador Sir Jimmy Bloggs was in excellent form. 'Well done, lads,' he said as he ushered them into the drawing room of Number One House, 'I'm sorry to see my old mate Dildenschneider shafted, but all's fair in war and love. Talking of which, I gather you've been consoling the Welsh, Donald. Seems to me that's taking duty too far, but *chacun à son gout*, eh?' Jimmy Bloggs had joined the diplomatic service when French was the language of diplomacy, and he still regarded it as such and peppered his conversation with the odd half remembered phrase. Donald opened his mouth to attempt a denial, but Jimmy Bloggs silenced him with a wave of his hand.

'Don't worry, lad. I might have done the same at your age, provided the lights were out. Though I'd have preferred a Feelgood Playmate[PMT] if they'd had such things then. Where is the lass? Keeping your bed warm at the Origami Intercontinental?'

Donald was spared the need to respond by the entrance of a private secretary bearing a crimson envelope embossed with a Cardinal's hat. 'Dispatch from the Papal Nuncio,' he intoned. 'The First Secretary says it's extremely urgent and recommends that you should read it at once.'

'Bloody Nancy boy's given me no peace since the Feelgood Project appeared on t'horison. What's his 'oliness griping about now?' Jimmy Bloggs tore open the envelope and scanned the missive.

'Bloody thing's in Latin. What the 'ells this – "*Ex parte Patris Sanctissimis in re bonorum sensorum proiectae*". I'll give 'im sensitive bones! Hasn't anybody told 'im the language of diplomacy's French.'

'The First Secretary has made a translation. He says he's prepared to make allowances for grammar school boys. It's attached to the back of the letter.'

Jimmy Bloggs turned the page and began to read. ' "*De la part du Saint Père en ce qui concerne le projet des bonnes sensations*." Who the hell does the First Secretary think I am – Maurice Chevalier?'

'I think, Ambassador, that you will find an English translation attached to the French Version.'

Jimmy Bloggs turned the page and found what he was looking for. He scanned it rapidly, then burst into peals of laughter. 'Bloody man says that the Vatican know about the visit and will do everything in their power to oppose the Feelgood Project going to North Uist. How the hell they know beats me – someone in the Commercial Section must have had a fit of conscience, and some papist priest must have breached the secrecy of the Confessional. But if they think that the Vatican can scupper the project for Scotland they've got another think coming. Have a drink, lads, and then get back home and do your worst!'

The British Overseas Airways flight from Narita to London was not crowded, and the Feelgood Project Task Group spread themselves out. In First Class were the representatives of Omeiwaku Denki: President Yamamoto, Hashimotosan, Hirosiguchisan, two Professors from Tokyo University who were to provide technical advice, Yamamotosan's golfing partner who was to advise on the suitability of local golf courses, and his mistress who was to advise on hotel beds. In Business Class were Donald Macdonald and Megan Morgan Thomas. In Economy were Stuart MacLellan and, wearing dark glasses and a red scarf to hide his dog collar, Brother Francisco Ignatio Loyola from the Papal Nuncio's Office. Brother Loyola had been despatched to Europe incognito by Mgr Carelli to liase with the Papal Authorities on Benbecula and to do what he could to scupper the Feelgood Project. Each was entertained according to their station in life.

In First Class they were pampered with a wide choice of gourmet dishes, including beluga caviar, smoked salmon (with a health warning that smoking damages your health), *pâté de foie gras* and beef *consommé* off the bone, T bone steak on the bone, a choice of French cheeses, and orange sorbet, all washed down with Krug Champagne, Chateau Yquem 1959, and Chateau Mouton Rothschild 1946 Premier Cru. In Business Class they were offered salmon pate, shepherds' pie and fruit salad with jelly (optional), washed down with a selection of very new wines from the New World. In Steerage they had ham sandwiches washed down with beer or cider.

Donald Macdonald ate sparingly and drank less. He was determined to get the credit for the Feelgood project, whatever Stuart MacLellan had done to land it, and that would require a clear head. Besides, Megan Morgan Thomas was sitting on his left, and in her present state of sexual excitement she might launch an attack on his virginity at any minute. It was one thing to aspire to join the Mile High Club, but Donald had no desire to join the Ton Up Club for Partners of Overweight Babes at the same time.

'Mind if I join you?'

Pussy Galore lowered herself into the vacant seat to Donald's right and adjusted her mini skirt. 'I'm in First, but a Japanese has been making lewd suggestions and I thought I'd come back to Business for a bit of peace and quiet. Or for a bit of Business, if I could find anyone nice. I saw you at the Airport having that argument with the Emigration control, and realised that you must be on the same flight.'

Donald did not wish to be reminded of his encounter with Emigration Control. No one had told him that he had to pay an airport tax on departure, and Megan had cleaned him out of his remaining Yen on the abortive trip to Kyoto. Stuart had gone through ahead of him, and were it not for a whip round by the Japanese Bridge Building War Veterans Association who were stuck in the queue behind him he would be in Narita still. 'Horiguchisan?' he asked, changing the subject.

'Horiguchisan?'

'The Japanese who was harassing you. He's noted for it – he tried it on Megan here the night before last.' Donald made the introductions, and the two women bristled at each other.

'Pleased to meet you, I'm sure,' said Megan, who wasn't. 'Likewise,' said Pussy, who wasn't either.

Donald dragged his mind back with difficulty to his last encounter with Pussy Galore. 'I though that you were staying in Japan for a year,' he said when he had connected the right neurones.

'I am,' she replied. 'But Daddy's been invited to a wedding in Scotland, and he wants me to accompany him. It's an outdated bourgeois institution of no interest to a post structuralist feminist, but he sent me the tickets and I thought it would give me another opportunity to join the Mile High Club. If, that is, I could meet the right person.' She shifted in her seat, revealing even more of her slim white thighs, as the lights dimmed.

By the time they reached European airspace both Pussy Galore and Megan Morgan Thomas were sleeping peacefully with blissful expressions on their faces. And Donald Macdonald had joined the Mile High Club. Twice.

* * *

CHAPTER 25

In which an American gentleman is discommoded.

Donald MacDonald awoke to a bright day. The sun, looking mildly bored, shone out of a clear blue sky. A fresh wind ruffled the sea and combed the manes of the white horses.

Below him, in the gardens, Alsace and Lorraine sat at a table playing three dimensional chess. Beyond them, Lady Lucinda was walking on the lawns with Miriam Katzenellenbogen and old Mrs McTurk. She was holding a parasol and wearing a fresh white dress which the strong north westerly wind moulded into her still charming figure. And, away over the sea, Donald Macdonald and his group of Japanese industrialists were on their way to meet their nemesis on the form of Sgt Stripe and his platoon of madmen. It would be the perfect revenge. God was in his or her heaven, and all was right with the world.

Donald lifted his eyes, and gazed out to the sea and the sky. To the south, a light aircraft was approaching the airstrip on Benbecula, and out at sea, buffeted by the waves, was a launch sporting the ensign of the North Uist Constabulary

Henry J Klassinger III was not best pleased. His dislike of aeroplanes was, if anything, exceeded by his fear of boats – a fear founded on infantile experiments in his bath when he had proved beyond any reasonable doubt that objects made of metal could not possible float. Even when he had turned to other experiments of a less infantile nature, in the bath and elsewhere, he had remembered his early experience, leading to a lifelong fear of water and women.

'Ah am not, positively not, going in that,' he screamed at Sergeant McPloud as he was frog marched down the Barra Quay. 'As the representative of the world's greatest superpower I insist that you release me at once and call a taxi to drive me over dry land to North Uist.'

Sergeant McPloud twisted the Consul General's arm even further up his back, as he had been taught in Part One of his Unarmed Combat course. If he twisted any further, Henry J Klassinger III would be unarmed indeed.

'Will you be calming yourself and quieten down, chust,' he murmured. The Instructor at his Unarmed Combat course had suffered from laryngitis, and had given his students the quite unjustified impression that to calm terrorists it was only necessary to whisper to them. 'If it iss overland that you are wishing to travel to North Uist, then it iss a submarine with wheels that you will be after needing.'

Henry J Klassinger III stopped struggling. If boats were bad, submarines were a thousand times worse. But he was not going to almost certain death without a shout. 'The President of the United States will hear of this,' he yelled as he was marched up the gangplank.

'Iss that so?' whispered Sergeant McPloud. 'I am told that there iss nothing between here and the United States of America but water, unless you count the whales. But you will have to shout a little louder, chust, with the wind in this quarter.'

Sure enough, the wind had freshened from the North West and was forcing Barra's single tree to prostrate itself towards Mecca. Henry J Klassinger III was pushed down heavily on a bench, and the crew laid aside their bottles of whisky and cast off.

Lost Memory Syndrome cast a veil over the events of the voyage. Henry J Klassinger III was vaguely aware of winds howling, spray spraying, spindrift spinning, seabirds screaming, ice cold water trickling and then rushing down his neck, and always the sickening lurch of the vessel as she plunged down the trough only to struggle up the next roller. But a blessed forgetfulness erased the memory of the helmsman letting go of the wheel to light his pipe, whereupon the boat slewed sideways and nearly foundered. And a sacred amnesia blotted out the sight of the crew swigging neat Scotch from their almost empty bottles as they speculated on Motherwell's chances in the premier league.

At last, after what seemed like hours and was in reality hours, Henry J Klassinger III felt the vessel's motion ease. He pulled his Stetson firmly on his head and opened his eyes. They were approaching a quay. They bumped alongside and, after some difficulty with the warps, were sufficiently moored to allow Sergeant McPloud and Constable McGurk, who was waiting for them on the quay, to escort Henry J Klassinger III ashore and up to the police station.

Amaryllis Squaff adjusted her mini skirt and made sure that the microphone was secure within her cleavage. She had taken up position outside the North Uist Police Station, and had placed the cameraman so that his lens took in the barred windows of Mary Lou Krantz's cell and, to the left, the municipal tip. Out of shot were the purple heather clad hills, the white beaches, and the golden sea sparkling with sunlight – but Amaryllis Squaff was not here to do a piece for the North Uist Tourist Board. No Siree! She was going to crucify these Hebredean barbarians, and when she'd finished Beirut and Chechnya would be featured above Scotland in the recommended holiday destinations of the American Association of Package Tour Operators.

Provost Farquhar Urquhart waited impatiently to be called. He hadn't been on the telebhisean before, and had initially refused to be 'squeezed into that accursed box'. But when Hamish McTurk had told him that he would be seen by his great nephews and nieces in Australia and Canada he had relented, even though he didn't relish the idea of travelling all the way to the Southern Hemisphere crammed into a box three feet by two.

He calmed his nerves and prepared for the voyage with several glasses of his favourite Chateau Margaux and Diet Coke. 'Now tell me, McTurk,' he asked as he combed his beard with his fingers and buttoned his tweed coat to the neck. 'What iss it that the young lady wishes to ask me?'

Amaryllis Squaff had been less than honest when she had asked McTurk to arrange for her to interview the Provost. 'She is doing a piece for the world telebhisean, chust,' replied McTurk in the time hallowed tradition of public servants making misleading and often dangerous comments on the basis of the best information available to them at the time. 'It iss about the traditions of the islands and the peauty of our peat bogs in summer. One of they naturist programmes, so it iss.'

Farquhar Urquhart looked alarmed. 'I am not after having to take my clothes off, McTurk?' he gasped.

'Whateffer could give you such an idea – of course not. But you must be careful to be concise when you are talking to the camera. Cameras have not the attention span of a Benbecula hen, and they like to have short statements, not the kind of rotund oratory that you use so well in meetings of the Urban District Council. These televisual machines like to have sound barks, so they do.'

'What in the name of Cheesus is a sound bark?' spluttered the Provost.

Hamish McTurk was relishing his role as a spin doctor, and didn't wish to admit ignorance.

'It iss like a dog bark, only shorter. And you must not snarl!'

'Och so,' said the Provost, adding some whisky to his Margaux and Coke. 'It is chust simple, this telebhisean thing. And to think that my own great nephews in Australia will be seeing me by the comfort of their own peat fires!'

Amaryllis Squaff clicked her fingers at the cameraman and beamed her 10,000 megawatt smile at CNN's 100 million viewers. But she didn't forget that her real audience was Joe Ordinary in Boise, Idaho. Keep it simple was her motto, and keep it simple had taken her to the pinnacle of her profession.

'This is Amaryllis Squaff,' she began, 'reporting from Lock Maddy in the island of North Oost in the Outer He-brides. An unlikely place to be the world's hottest trouble spot, but the Macdonaldgate Affair, as it has come to be known, could lead to war between the United States and its oldest ally the United Kingdom of North and South Britain. At the very least, it will seriously damage relations between our two countries.'

The cameraman zoomed in to the rusted bars of Mary Lou Krantz's prison. 'In a squalid cell in the jailhouse behind me,' continued Amaryllis Squaff, 'languishes Mary Lou Krantz from Spartanburg, South Carolina, accused by the British Authorities of being an accessory to her own kidnapping. The Captain of the City Police Force has released the kidnapper, Donald MacDonald, an official of the Scottish State Government; and the Government and City Hall are determined on a cover up.'

Amaryllis Squaff paused to flick a lock of immaculately highlighted hair from her sincere baby blue eyes so that she could look indignant and reflect the outrage of Joe Ordinary in Boise, Idaho. Then she strode over to the Provost. 'Farquhar Urquhart,' she said, 'is leader of the City Council, and has agreed to come out of his sumptuous office in City Hall to explain this outrage. Mayor Urquhart...'

'Provost!' barked Provost Urquhart. There was nothing that annoyed him more than being described as Mayor, and besides the woman's pronunciation of his Christian name left a lot to be desired. 'It iss the Provost that I am after being.' McTurk had told him to bark like a dog, and bark he would. 'A Mayor iss the leader of one of those tin pot places like New York or Chicago or London. Up here we have Provosts.'

Amaryllis Squaff was used to interviewing warlords and generals in danger zones throughout the world. She had intimidated South American politicians and Korean gangsters. She had questioned stone age tribes in the Amazon jungle and stoned hippies in the forests above Big Sur. But all of them spoke English more clearly than the Mayor. She tried again.

'Mayor Urquhart, if I may call you that for the benefit of our international audience.'

'You may not, young lady,' snarled the Provost, forgetting McTurk's advice, and simultaneously flattering Ms Squaff by his use of the epithet 'young' and offending her feminist sensibilities by his use of the substantive 'lady'. 'It iss the Provost that I am, and it iss Provost that I will be called. It iss time that you young things learnt some respect for your elders and petters. You would not like to be called Mrs when you are certainly a Miss.'

Off screen, Hamish McTurk put his head into his hands. This was no way to attract the tourists of the world to his beautiful island to swell the coffers of Mistress McTavish's Tea Room and the Lochmaddy Handloom Weavers Olde Factory Shoppe. But the Provost was in full flight. He tugged at his beard, rebalanced his pebble glasses on his bulbous and rubicund nose, and staggered up to the cameraman so he was peering into the lens from about six inches.

'Let me say this for the benefit of your international viewers, chust so. North Uist is a beautiful and tranquil island, so it iss. But it iss so because here the young show respect for their elders, the womenfolk show respect for their men and gather the peats whateffer the weather, and everyone shows respect for the Provost. And one more thing...'

The Provost paused to allow a flock of screaming gulls to pass on their way to the municipal tip. He grinned into the camera, revealing teeth blackened through decades of smoking Old Navy Shag tobacco in his vile pipe. Then he stepped back a pace and waved.

'Hullo, Ewan, Calum and Tonald in Queensland, Australia. This iss your Uncle, Provost Farqhuar Urquhart, speaking to you all the way from North Uist! I hope that you've enough peats for your fire, and your Aunty Urquhart has asked me to remind you to change your socks at least once a month and your underpants four times a year. Unless of course you are still wearing the kilt, in which case you shouldn't wear underpants at all, at all.' And with a final wave at his distant relations the Provost turned on his heel and stumbled towards McTurk.

'Well, McFirk, that was chust fine,' he barked, forgetting that he was no longer on screen. 'I could become one of those telebhisual personalities like Jeremy Packman or Anchela Rippoff, no pother at all.'

Amaryllis Squaff, meanwhile, was gesticulating angrily at the cameraman. He panned his camera rapidly towards her, catching a brief glimpse of two policemen escorting a fat man, drenched to his boxer shorts and sporting a dripping Stetson hat, across the machair. Amaryllis Squaff struggled hard to regain the initiative.

'So here we have it. Municipal indifference to the plight of an American citizen in distress. Deliberate attempts to avoid and cover up the issue by City Hall. Offensive expressions of outdated values which will cause offence to the vast majority of our viewers worldwide. And there have been...'

One of the gulls, returning from the municipal tip to the wide blue fishing grounds to hunt for Henry J Klasssinger III's breakfast, deposited a gob of bird lime on Amaryllis Squaff's immaculately quaffed hair. Its screams were interrupted by the shouts of the angry damp man in the Stetson hat, who had just come within range. 'I am

Henry J Klassinger III, the American Consul General, and I demand to be treated with the respect due to my position!'

'Will you be shutting your fat mouth,' yelled Sergeant McPloud, 'And get in there!' He tripped the Consul General into the police station, and the door slammed shut behind them.

The cameraman had caught it all. It was the scoop of a lifetime. Amaryllis Quaff, with the sang froid that had taken her safely round many a tight corner, ignored the sticky liquid trickling down her brow and addressed the viewers of the world, and particularly Joe Ordinary in Boise, Idaho.

'...yet further outrages against the citizens of the United States of America, including our Consul General. One thing is certain. The White House will not let these offences go unpunished. This is Amaryllis Squaff of CNN News reporting from Lock Maddy in the Outer He-brides.'

Mary Lou Krantz had heard the altercation outside the police station, and she had made out one or two of the words. 'Wayall, ain't I just glad to be seein a fellow American,' she said as Henry J Klassinger III was hurled into her cell. 'And the Consul General too – ain't that just dandy? Ah guess you'll soon hayave me out of here and way bayack hwome where ah belong.'

'It ain't as simple as that,' replied the Consul General. How could he explain to a fellow citizen that a man in his position was a prisoner too?

'Whayatt does you mean, ain't as simple?' Mary Lou Krantz was close to tears. 'You're the Consul General, and you've come at Miriam Katzenellenbogen's request to spring me out of this jailhouse, ain't you? Then we can all go home and far away from this danged awful place. What could be simpler than that?'

Henry K Klassinger III's dream of the Congressional Medal and a posting to Paris was fast fading before his eyes. A posting to Helsinki or Vladivostock was the best he could expect now. But he was nothing if not honest.

'It is not simple, because I too am a prisoner.'

A solitary tear trickled down Mary Lou Krantz's cheek, like the consequences of turning on a tap belonging to the South Western Water Company. Then she remembered her girl scout training and began to sing –

> *Ah'm a prisoner here in this lonesome jail*
> *And I wear mah chains with pride.'*

And the Consul General joined in, proud to be American –

> *'And ah eats bread and water and ah pisses in a pail,*
> *And ah'm proud to be inside.'*

* * *

CHAPTER 26

In which the threads of the plot are woven together, and the United States prepares for war.

In the Oval Office the President zipped up his fly and turned to matters of state. 'Send a telegram to the Captain of USS Enterprise,' he said to his intern. She put her handkerchief safely back in her handbag for subsequent forensic investigation, and reached for a pad. 'Yes Mr President?' she asked in her girlish voice.

'I'll give it to you orally. Take this down.'

The intern began to marvel at the President's powers of recovery, but the President continued speaking.

'Open quotes. Situation in North Uist has worsened period. Consul General comma Henry period J period Klassinger III comma now in custody period. Prepare to make landing of platoon of marines immediate repeat immediate on further orders to effect release period. Close quotes. Got that?'

'Yes, Mr President.' She had indeed. But why was the President so obsessed with periods?

Provost Farquhar Urquhart poured himself another glass of Margaux and Diet Coke and installed himself behind his desk. Donald MacDonald, who wished to keep a clear head for the denouement, was nursing a very small glass of Talisker. Hamish McTurk, who wished likewise but whose wish was further from the deed, was gulping from a very large tumbler of Glenfiddich.

'And so you see,' Donald was saying, 'the Japanese party will be arriving by helicopter on the Field of the Gathering of the Clans, accompanied by the Minister and Sir Terence Mould, Permanent

Secretary at the North British Office. It is vital that they get a good reception. The Japanese will be deciding on the location of their plant, and if you give them what they want, the Feelgood Project will be in the bag.'

'What iss it that you mean?' interjected the Provost. 'The Japanese wish to plant a plant in our bog? What kind of plant iss it that they are wanting to plant? You should know that nothing grows in the bogs of North Uist except bog asphodel and bog cotton and...'

'It iss a factory for the making of electronical goods,' interrupted McTurk. 'Two thousand jobs for the crofters of North Uist, and who knows the Minister may decide to save the Urban District Council ass well, isn't that right, MacDonald?'

Not if he could help it, thought Donald. 'Absolutely,' he said.

'And will the telebhisean people be there?' asked the Provost, thinking of his budding career as a television personality.

'They will indeed,' replied McTurk. 'And the *West Highland Free Press*, to report the story for the world's newspapers. It will be a great day for North Uist, so it will. And you will be at the centre of it.'

'Well, we must have a Piper to pipe in the helicopter machine. And he must be playing the piobaireachd – none of your Scotland the Brave rubbish, that iss only good for football hooligans at rugby matches. He shall play *Provost McFee's Return to the Isles,* so he shall.'

McTurk shook his grizzled head. 'Do you not think, Provost, that that iss a little long? It lasts 45 minutes without the repeats – and it would be an insult to your distinguished ancestor to leave them out – and another 25 if you add the grace notes.'

'That will be perfect,' said Donald quickly. The longer the Japanese were kept in the driving rain, the more time there would be to orchestrate an attack on them. 'Now, have you thought about a Guard of Honour?'

'That iss chust what we are wanting,' said the Provost. 'A Guard of Honour.'

'I am sure that Sgt Stripe's platoon from Benbecula would make a perfect Honour Guard, and impress the Japanese no end,' said Donald. 'If you wish I shall telephone Major Prendergast at once.'

McTurk shook his grizzled head once again. 'That will not be doing at all,' he said. 'They are aliens, from England and, what is worse, from Benbecula. Why do we not use Sergeant McPloud and the North Uist Constabulary?'

But already in the eye of the mind of the Provost was forming a vision of himself, Provost Farquhar Urquhart of the North Uist Urban District Council, being saluted by smart men dressed in khaki with their medals gleaming in the sun. 'I think the platoon from Benbecula will be chust fine.'

McTurk began to splutter, and Donald, drawing on his long years of civil service training, saw that a desperate compromise was required. 'Perhaps I could suggest a middle way,' he said. 'An Honour Guard formed of both policemen and soldiers. That will really impress.'

'Chust so,' said the Provost. 'Now how about inviting the Wee Free Minister, Mr MacCorquodale, to pray for God's blessing on the proceedings?'

'*In nomine patris, et filii, et spiritus sancti*' said Brother Francisco Ignatio Loyola, straightening his shades and pushing his hat to the back of his head.

Before him, in the little Catholic Chapel of St Priapticus the Fornicator in Barra, sat the Nuns of the Holy Order of the Immaculate Contraception. Beside him, in his monsignor's stall, sat Mgr McCavity. All were waiting intent on his words. He crossed his lips and surreptitiously removed the chewing gum from his mouth, sticking it beneath the lectern for later use.

'I have been sent here among you,' he began, 'by de Holy Father himself. All de way from Japan I have come, to do battle against de forces of evil and against a threat which could call into question de very existence of your Holy Order.'

Several of the nuns blanched. What could he mean? But he did not keep them long in suspense.

'Your Holy Order of the Immaculate Contraception was brought into being by de Blessed Mary Stopes, with de authority of de Holy Father Pope Pius XII himself, to preach de virtues of immaculate contraception through the rhythm method.'

The Mother Superior nodded in agreement. The nuns followed suit, so that soon the whole chapel was suffused by a rhythmical nodding of heads. 'Praise the Lord and Blessed Mary Stopes,' shouted one of the older nuns, who had been flirting too closely with the charismatic movement.

'And now de Japanese have developed a product which dey plan to make in North Uist in a feelgood factory, and which will make any form of contraceptive, immaculate or not, redundant.'

Brother Loyola proceeded to describe in graphic detail the nature, shape, colour and *modus operandi* of the Feelgood ToyBoy™. The nuns listened intently, and the Mother Superior resolved to purchase one at the earliest opportunity so that she could know her enemy.

'It is our task, given us by de Holy Father himself, to prevent de manufacture of dis evil object, and in particular to prevent its manufacture in North Uist. Mgr McCavity will now brief you on de plans of the Japanese company and what we shall do to secure de project's abortion.'

'*Raconte moi une histoire,*' shouted Alsace.
'*Erzähl mir eine Geschichte,*' screamed Lorraine.
They were gambolling across the machair with old Mrs McTurk. Behind them skulked the Pekinese dogs; and Lady Lucinda and Miriam Katzenellenbogen brought up the rear.

So, using the ingenious combination of French, German and Hungarian which she had developed for her conversations with the twins, and which in Italian restaurants throughout the land is known as macaronic, Mrs McTurk retold the story of the Man in the Iron Mask, unjustly imprisoned in the Bastille.

'*Mais, c'est horrible,*' said Alsace when she had finished. '*C'est la même histoire que celle de Mary Lou Krantz, emprisonée par les flics dans cette horrible cave.*'

'Say, what's that she's saying?' asked Miriam Katzenellenbogen. 'She's talking about my poor Mary Lou.'

'She's saying that she's imprisoned like the man in the iron mask,' said Lady Lucinda.

'Gee, have those cops put Mary Lou in an iron mask, like in the film by Alexander Doomas? This is just too awful. Ah only hope that the Consul General can get her released.'

'But haven't you heard?' said Mrs McTurk.
'Ain't I heard what?'

'The Consul General has been arrested. He's being held in the cells along with Mary Lou Krantz.'

The twins, forgetting that they wouldn't admit to speaking English, listened to this exchange with shocked attention. Their imaginations fired with stories of adventure and derring do, they cried with one voice, 'Then we must break them out...'

'Now listen, men,' said Major Prendergast. He thwacked his stagger stick on the lectern and glared round the seminar suite. 'I have been called back to Whitehall for urgent discussions with MOD OPS, and will be off base for at least two weeks.' There was no need to tell them that he was, in reality, spending a fortnight with Mrs Prendergast's sister Mabel in a caravan in Bournemouth. 'I am placing Sgt Stripe in supreme command. You will obey his orders without question, to the second and to the letter. Is that understood?'

The men stared glassily back at him. They didn't relish the prospect. It promised nothing but blood, sweat and tears, waiting on the beaches and the peat bogs for an enemy which never came while being eaten alive by mosquitoes and gnats and clegs and midges. But MOD OPS was MOD OPS; and the men were trained to blind obedience.

'Tomorrow morning,' continued Major Prendergast, 'you will have the first chance to prove yourselves. You are detailed to form a Guard of Honour, together with a detachment from the North Uist Constabulary, to welcome the Minister of State at the North British Office, who will be visiting North Uist with a group of highly important Japanese businessmen. Sgt Stripe will brief you fully on the details, but I don't need to emphasise the importance of the occasion to the honour of the Regiment. You will be smart, well turned out, punctual, and alert at all times. It is imperative that we do not permit a re-run of the North Uist Highland Games. Do I make myself clear?'

Major Prendergast's troops were trained to recognise a rhetorical question when they heard one. Not so much as a flicker stirred on their impassive faces.

'Very well then. Carry on Sergeant!'

Major Prendergast gave them one final glare, like a Gorgon turning Lot's wife into a pillar of Cerebos (the Major's grasp of mythology was, like Sir Terence's, somewhat tenuous), then turned and marched out of the room. A fortnight's holiday with his sister-in-law in a caravan in Bournemouth was not his idea of heaven; but at least Mabel's cooking was better than Cook Sgt Carrier's.

Sgt Stripe moved rapidly to the rostrum. 'Right lads, listen to me,' he said in a conspiratorial whisper. 'Reliable intelligence sources – and I mean reliable – 'ave confirmed that the Japanese visiting North Uist tomorrow along with the Minister ain't businessman at all. They're a crack troop of the Imperial Japanese Army, or Defence Corps as they insist in calling it to confuse the rest of us, aiming to take over North Uist as a prelude to world domination. It's our job to stop them. Now 'alf of you will be in the Guard of Honour along with the bunch of flatfeet from the North Uist Constabulary, and 'alf of you will be in the 'eather awaiting for my signal. This is what we're going to do...'

Amarylis Squaff squatted behind a peat hag and tried to swat the brown speckled insect which had alighted on her forearm. She had proposed that they should do some filming for local colour; but this did not seem such a good idea now. The only colour that they had filmed was brown – the brown of the sodden peat hags, the brown of the dying bracken, and brown of the ubiquitous heather – and none of the people whom they had met had been prepared to speak English. But she was on air live again tomorrow, when she was to cover the visit to the islands of the Minister and a group of Japanese businessmen; and she needed some background to supplement her exposure of the treatment of an innocent American citizen and the Consul General of the most powerful superpower on Earth by so called allies. At the very least, she should be able to make the Minister's visit hell.

She swept the representative of the Scottish Blood Transfusion Service angrily from her arm, and set off across the bog to film a cow. It was brown.

The Minister replaced his copy of *Childe Harold's Pilgrimage* in his desk drawer. He was sitting in Lady Caroline Mouton's room in Bute House, and he was deeply puzzled. The book, which had been recommended to him by Sir Terence, was nothing to do with mid-twentieth century politics, and nor did it have a single reference to pipe smoking and gannex raincoats. Besides, the lines on the page were cut up into the most irritating lengths; and the final words of the lines had an even more irritating tendency to rhyme with each other. So far as he knew, moreover, Harold Wilson had had nothing to do with the liberation of Venice from the Turks. But he had other, more important things to think about.

He rose to his feet as his private secretary ushered in President Yamamoto of Omeiwaku Denki. Yamamoto was accompanied by three Japanese in identical blue suits and white shirts, one of whom was leering at the private secretary. They were followed by Sir Terence Mould and a young official whom he had not yet met, who was clutching a bulging file of papers.

'*Igorishiro watawa shogunate arigatosan,*' intoned the Minister, clasping his hands together and bowing low.

'Please?' said Yamamoto.

Hirosiguchi stopped leering at the private secretary and exchanged rapid words with Yamamotosan. Then he turned to the Minister.

'Yamaotosan say he cannot understand Japanese of honourable Minister because Honourable Minister's Japanese is Japanese of Honourable Imperial Household and too elegant and refined for mere businessman like himself to follow. I cannot understand it also, because I am even humbler and more obedient than Honourable Yamamotosan. If you please, we will use English of Honourable Queen. I will act as humble interpreter.'

The Minister was momentarily annoyed. He had learnt the phrase, with great difficulty, at the Foreign Office Language School in order to impress his guests and make his own contribution to winning the Feelgood Project. But the key thing was to win the project; and he would claim the credit in any case. 'Please sit down,' he said, in the closest approximation to the Queen's English that he could manage.

The group ranged themselves around the Minister's conference table. Tea was served, introductions were effected, business cards were exchanged, the Department's offer of financial support was discussed, the proposed location was described and praised, and the Minister resolved once again to instruct Sir Terence to ban the uses of the passive voice in Departmental submissions. Why was it, he asked himself, that everything that they did was put into the passive voice, before realising that he had fallen into the trap himself.

He wrenched his attention back to the meeting. Donald Macdonald, the impressive young official who had negotiated the project and been so highly praised by Sir Terence, was speaking.

'...and so you will arrive in North Uist, by helicopter from Achnasheen, at 10 30 am tomorrow morning. The Minister, Sir Terence Mould, Stuart MacLellan and I will accompany you. We shall be shown round the site by the local officials, led by Provost Farquhar Urquhart of the North Uist Urban District Council, together with my colleague Donald MacDonald who has proved most helpful in identifying a suitable location. I am sure that you will find North Uist a most exciting prospect...'

How exciting, Donald Macdonald was shortly to discover.

* * *

CHAPTER 27

In which the protagonists prepare for battle.

'Light thickens,' said Sgt Stripe.

'It does indeed, Sarge,' replied Cpl Snodgrass.

'And the crow makes wing to the rooky wood.'

'Not exactly,' said Cpl Snodgrass.

'What do you mean, not exactly?'

'Ain't no woods in Benbecula, rooky or otherwise, though you got plenty of rookies in your platoon innit. More like "makes wing to the blasted heath" '

'Sure thing,' interjected Private Smith who, despite his degree in astrophysics, knew a fair bit about botany.

Sgt Stripe looked distinctly annoyed. The night before battle was a tense time at best, and he had taken it upon himself to visit the troops and bolster their morale. A little touch of Stripey in the night, he told himself, would do wonders for their performance on the morrow. Strictly speaking, this was a job for Major Prendergast; but the Major had important things to do with MOD OPS, and he, Sgt Stripe, stood to benefit from the Major's absence if all went well. A VC was within his grasp if his men didn't let him down.

Across the Sound, he could make out the lights of North Uist glimmering on the steely waters. Fire answered fire, and creeping murmur and the poring dark filled the wide vessel of the Hebrides. A cold wind sprang up, ruffling the waters. Somewhere an owl shrieked.

Sgt Stripe turned to his men. 'He that outlives this day...' he began.

Three miles across the machair, in the high tech offices of the Benbecula Urban District Council, the lights were burning late. Dudley Scrope sat before the flickering screen of his computer, examining the results of his calculations with care.

The graphs and charts, with their strange mixtures of angles and glyphs, were hard to follow. But the words were clear enough. 'Pluto conjunct Mercury', he read, 'signifies a period of change. Psychological pressures or external events may press you to a re-evaluation of priorities and could lead to a change of your world view.'

So far, so good. He clicked his mouse, and scrolled down the screen. 'Sun transiting the Tenth House,' he continued, 'signifies a period when you will enjoy great professional success.' Better still.

'Mercury in the Tenth House signifies a period when you should reflect seriously on your career. In addition, you will find it auspicious to propose new projects and will have success in persuading others to your views. Saturn transiting the Tenth House indicates, however, that you will take on a heavy burden of responsibility and will need to work hard to bring your ambitions to fruition.'

Dudley Scrope frowned. He was not averse to hard work, but he preferred things to come easily to him. But there was more. 'However, this transit also signifies a period of great success, especially with large projects. With Jupiter square Mars, you will achieve great things.'

Dudley Scrope exited the programme and leaned back in his chair. So that was it. The stars had spoken. He would take on a heavy burden of responsibility, but he was ready for that. All his ambitions were coming to fruition. Tomorrow he would confront the Minister with his proposals for information systems in the new Benbecula and North Uist Metropolitan Council and be rewarded with the post of Chief Executive. Nothing could go wrong now.

Provost Farquhar Urquhart poured himself another glass of Margaux and Diet Coke and added a generous splash of Bruichladdaich. The lights in his office were low, and the deer heads cast strange gothic shadows on his desk where the sixteen pages of his draft welcoming address lay scattered like leaves after the first gale of autumn. Should he begin in Gaelic, English or Japanese? Should he bow to his visitors, or maintain the rigid upright posture for which the island men were famed? Should he shorten or lengthen the passage on the preservation of the Urban District Council?

There was a knock at the door, and Hamish McTurk entered. 'I am after bringing you another bottle, Provost,' he said, 'to help your concentration. It will be a great day the morn's morn, so it will. Will you be joining me in a toast, Provost?'

He recharged the glasses and lifted his to the portrait of Provost McFee. 'Success to the North Uist Urban District Council, and damnation to our enemies' he said.

'Damnation,' echoed the Provost.

'Damnation,' muttered Brother Francisco Ignatio Loyola. He had repaired from the Presbytery to the chapel of St Priapticus the Fornicator, Barra, to consult his masters in Japan on how far he should press the demonstration against the Feelgood Project and his bookmaker in Brooklyn on the odds for the next World Welterweight championship, and his mobile phone was disobligingly refusing to give him a signal. He shook it angrily, and the battery fell off and clattered to the floor. The Chapel was lit only by the sanctuary lamp, and he had to break the habit of a lifetime and remove his shades to search for the means of communication with his gods.

He was prostrate before the statue of the Black Madonna of Sgeir na Laimhrige Moire, scrabbling for his battery in the dust and employing language a good deal more colourful than damnation, when the nuns of the Holy Order of the Immaculate Contraception entered in procession for their evening devotions. The Mother Superior raised her hand and brought the procession to a halt.

'What a holy man,' she whispered. 'It is of such devotion that saints are made.'

'Amen!' replied the sisters. 'This truly is a holy man.'

'But is he not holding a mobile telephone?' asked the nun who had been infected with the charismatic movement, and who did not approve of modern technology.

''Each of us has our own way to speak to the Almighty,' said the Mother Superior. 'Now, let us pray.'

Donald Macdonald stirred uneasily in his bed in the Station

Hotel, Achnasheen. The morning would see the culmination of his efforts – a successful visit to North Uist with the Omeiwaku Denki Corporation, the landing of the Feelgood Project in the presence of Sir Terence Mould and the Minister, and a massive boost to his reputation and career prospects. He began to dream of advancement.

His reverie was interrupted by the bedside telephone. He groped for the light, cranked the handle and picked up the handset.

'Yes?' he croaked.

'Donald,' said the Welsh voice. 'It is so good to be hearing your tender and eloquent voice. I wanted so much to tell you how much I am missing you and how I wish that you were here with me at this moment in my bed in Abergavenny.'

'Oh,' croaked Donald.

'It is a beautiful night here in Abergavenny. On such a night it was, indeed, that Dido stood with a willow in her hand upon the wild sea banks, and wished for her love to come again to Carthage. I am standing on the wild sea banks in Abergavenny wishing my love to come again. Do you feel like that, Donald, look you?'

'No,' croaked Donald. With Megan Morgan Thomas, to come once was enough.

Hull down, the USS Enterprise waited for dawn and for the order from the White House that would send it into battle. Admiral Schwartznegger had briefed Master Sergeant of Marines Capote at sundown. Now they had nothing to do but while away the hours. At eight bells, if all was well and the President could keep his mind focused sufficiently long on affairs of state, a heavily armoured platoon would be on its way to the low sandy shore of North Uist. There it woukd have the glory of twisting the tail of the arrogant little country that had dared to ignore the extra-territorial rights of the greatest superpower on Earth and, what was worse, had taken its Consul General into custody.

As three bells struck, the Master Sergeant of Marines, as was the tradition, poured out a triple measure of Bells Whisky for each of his men. By the time eight bells tolled, they would be well and truly ready for battle.

'Have you got the bomb casing?' said Miriam Katzenellenbogen.

'*Chut,*' whispered Alsace.

'*Sch...,*' hissed Lorraine.

'Hush,' murmured old Mrs McTurk.

'Be quiet!' snarled Lady Lucinda.

'Will you shut up,' yelled Miriam Katzenellenbogen.

They had crawled through the bog to within three yards of the North Uist Police Station, and were ready to begin the operation to release Mary Lou Krantz and the Consul General. Everything depended on calmness, silence and accuracy. As the false dawn brought a gleam of light into the eastern sky, Lady Lucinda began to add sugar to the sodium phosphate.

'One lump or two?' she asked.

* * *

CHAPTER 28

In which the lance is boiled.

'*Ah so*, it is beautiful!'

'What wondahful breaches! What a prace for a gorf course!'

'How lomantic!'

The party from Omeiwaku Denki had bagged all the best seats in the Sikorski helicopter which flew them from Achnasheen to North Uist, but Donald was glad that they were appreciating the view. It was one more thing which would help land the project for Scotland, and one more thing that would help gain his promotion. The weather too was helping – instead of the habitual rains and south westerly gales for which the Outer Hebrides were famous, the sun shone out of a clear blue sky and the winds of yesterday had abated to a gentle zephyr, in keeping with the rusting Fords which were to be seen scattered about the machair.

Behind him, strapped into their seats, were the Permanent Secretary and the Minister. Sir Terence had been trying, unsuccessfully, to argue that the success of the visit would demonstrate the perfection of the present structure of local government and prove that there was no need for reform or amalgamation. The Minister had argued, equally strongly, that if the visit was successful it would necessitate reform, since there was no way in which the North Uist Urban District Council could cope with an inward investment the size of the Omeiwaku Project and oversee the construction of the Feelgood factory, particularly if it was led by Provost Farquhar Urquart and Chief Executive Hamish McTurk.

'Besides,' he said, 'My colleagues in the Scottish Cabinet will never wear a U-turn. The Scottish Parliament would unleash the hounds of hell. It would set a most unfortunate precedent. It will make it impossible for Penicuik to take over Edinburgh.'

'Those are no parallels whatsoever,' responded Sir Terence.

'I am not talking about parallels. I am talking about politics. Farquhar Urquhart is an independent, and it is not the job of the North British Office to support dissenters.'

Their argument was cut short by the Captain, who announced that he was about to attempt a landing. The engine noise increased, and two minutes later they bumped onto the Field of the Gathering of the Clans of North Uist and Pabbay.

Hamish McTurk had deployed all his organisational skills in arranging the welcoming party on the Field of the Gathering of the Clans. The Provost was resplendent in a kilt of the Hunting Urquhart tartan. Pipe Major Hector Mackinnon, hereditary piper to the Chiefs of the Clan Donald, was warming up his pipes for his rendition of Provost McFee's Return to the Isles. A Guard of Honour consisting of policemen in blue tunics and soldiers from Cook Sgt Carrier's platoon in battle fatigues and chef's hats was lined up behind Sgt Stripe on the greensward. An elderly man in a black suit, black homburg hat and dog collar was clutching a bible and muttering to himself.

Behind them, held back by a red and white tape of the sort used by the fire brigade to keep crowds away from major earthquakes and cats stranded up trees, was a throng of schoolchildren waving Japanese flags and a group of elderly ladies in black raincoats and headscarves. They were led by a swarthy man wearing mirrored sunglasses, a black shirt, a white tie, and a five o'clock shadow dating back to 5 am the previous Tuesday. And overlooking them all, on a little knoll revered by the natives as being the home of the fairies and behind which the island's small gay community was wont to go cottaging, stood Amaryllis Squaff and her cameraman. Amaryllis was speaking earnestly into the camera for the benefit of Joe Ordinary of Boise, Idaho.

Hamish McTurk ushered the visitors away from the chopper and presented them to the Provost, who bowed low and introduced them in turn to Hamish McTurk. Sgt Stripe steeled himself for his great moment. The time had come for him to save his nation. Hidden in the heather, the rest of his troop awaited his signal.

'Platoon, shun!' he yelled above the sound of the rotors.

The soldiers shuffled to attention, while the policemen ignored him. No-one had told them anything about drilling; and most of them didn't know how to anyway.

'As you were, you horrible bunch of wankers!' shouted Sgt Stripe. 'Ooo do you think you are, a bunch of fucking fairies. Any of you want to prance about on top of that there fairy knoll, fall out! We're 'ere to impress the little yellow men, not to make a laughing stock of the great British Army. Once again, Platoon 'shun! Pres-e-e-e-e-e-e-nt Arms!'

The soldiers snapped smartly to attention and presented arms. The policemen shuffled their feet together and raised their truncheons to a position which in other circumstances would have rendered the Feelgood ToyBoy™ redundant. Provost Farquhar Urquhart removed a crumpled sheet of lined paper from his sporran and began to read.

'Minister, President Yamamoto, distinguished guests, *ceud mile fàilte gu Ubhist Tuath,* a hundred thoussand welcomes to North Uist. On behalf of the people of North Uist I welcome you to our beautiful island. But before I do so, I invite the Reverend Torquil MacCorquodale of the Free Church, Lochmaddy, to pray for God's blessing on our proceedings.'

The Reverend Torquil MacCorquodale was under strict instruction from McTurk to pray for no more than forty minutes at the outside. He was also under instruction to avoid controversy. He had, if the Lord spared him, some intention of complying with the first instruction, but – as a result of a brief discussion with Donald MacDonald about a contribution to the Gospel Hall Roof Repair Fund – none whatsoever of complying with the second. He stepped forward, removed his Homburg, clasped his Bible firmly between his hands, and began:

'Oh Lord God of the Heavens and the Earth, of the sea and the sky, of the land and the waters, of the trees and the grass, of the infant and the....' The Rev MacCorquodale paused for a moment while trying to find something decent to pair with infant, then continued: 'Lord God who hast been made manifest to us through thy holy word, who hast given us thy commandments to rule us and thy rod for our chastisement, miserable sinners that we are, who hast ordained that those who are ignorant of thy bountiful mercy shall burn for ever in everlasting fire and brimstone, torment and agony, look down, we pray Thee, on the Feelgood Project, that it may be a source of succour to thy afflicted people of North Uist and of bringing thy salvation to the heathen Japanese, whose fashion it is to come bearing swords and waving them about.'

The Minister was appalled. Hirosiguchisan was muttering into President Yamamoto's ear, doubtless giving him an accurate translation of the Wee Free Minister's words. The expression on Yamamoto's face resembled that of an Air Chief Marshall welcoming a returning kamikaze pilot back to base. Donald Macdonald was equally concerned. How the hell was he going to land the project if this old git continued to insult the visitors. Donald MacDonald, by contrast, observed the proceedings with delight. The Wee Free Minister was earning his contribution to the roof repairs, and handsomely.

Five hundred yards to the West, three landing craft were disgorging a platoon of heavily laden US marines onto the silver strand under the command of Master Sergeant Capote. And behind the police station, Miriam Katzenellenbogen was struggling to light the fuse of her home made bomb with Alsace's Zippo lighter.

The Minister turned to the Provost and McTurk. 'Can't you shut the man up?' he hissed. But neither the Provost nor McTurk had been listening. The Provost, like a dog trained by Pavlov, had switched off his hearing aid the moment he heard the Reverend Mr MacCorquodale say the words 'Oh Lord'. And McTurk had no intention of losing the skill, hard won through many a five hour sermon, of not attending to the Minister's homilies. 'It would be most discourteous to do so,' he hissed in reply. 'And besides, it iss the Lord's blessing that we are needing to win the Project. He will not be more than another hour.'

The Minister had a quick and not altogether reassuring vision of the second coming before realising that McTurk was referring to Mr MacCorquodale, who was in full flight.

'...the Japanese, who came first bearing swords and waving them about but now hold out the tools of friendship, the yellow devils whose swords have been fashioned through thy bountiful goodness into ploughshares and other instruments of thy grace.'

Stuart MacLellan wondered briefly how the Feelgood ToyBoy™ could be regarded as an instrument of the Lord's grace.

'And next we pray that the Project will not bring succour to the people of Benbecula, who have turned from thy word to the pagan falsehood of papistical masses and the painted statues of saints and idols...'

'Say, what's this jerk saying,' muttered Brother Loyola out of the corner of his mouth. 'I'll ram his papistical masses straight down his throat. You girls ready, Mother Superior?'

'Sure thing. We're ready to kick ass.' The Mother Superior had discovered that the only way to communicate with Brother Loyola was in his own coinage.

'Wait my signal.'

'And let it be a sign, a sign of all thy blessings,' concluded the Reverend Mr MacCorquodale. 'Amen and again I say Amen.'

The word Amen prompted the Provost to reconnect his auditory nerve to external stimulus. Salivating mildly, he moved forward. 'And now,' he said, 'on behalf of all the people of North Uist I should like...'

He was interrupted by the braying of Hector Mackinnon's pipes. Hector Mackinnon, while not averse to prayer, did not like speeches, and he had a particular aversion to those of the Provost. He put his chanter to his lips, squeezed the bag fiercely beneath his elbow, and launched into the ground theme of *Provost McFee's Return to the Isles*. The Japanese, mistaking it for the National Anthem, stood stiffly to attention as the Provost lapsed into silence.

Those of you who are acquainted with the classic works of the *piobaireachd* will know that the fifth variation of *Provost McFee's Return to the Isles* bears a remarkable resemblance to Colonel Bogey and is played, as it is termed in the Gaelic, *pianissimo* and without use of the drones. It was while Hector Mackinnon was engaged in the trickiest passage of this section, and President Yamamoto was trying to recall which film it reminded him of, that Miriam Katzenellenbogen finally produced a flame from Alsace's zippo lighter. The bomb surpassed all her expectations. With a flash of flame and a thunderous crash the gable end of the police station disappeared in a cloud of dust, and a splinter of wood from the eaves was projected straight as an arrow into Pipe Major Mackinnon's windbag. His pipes deflated with a hiss, and Pipe Major Mackinnon wheezed into silence.

Mary Lou Krantz and Henry J Klassinger III emerged, triumphant if a little dusty, and set off at a run across the Field of the Gathering of the Clans towards the Fairy Knoll on which they could see a TV camera set up to record their escape. They were closely followed by Lady Lucinda, Miriam Katzenellenbogen, Alsace, Lorraine and two barking Pekinese. *'Ils sont libres,'* yelled Alsace. *'Sie sind frei,'* screamed Lorraine, not to be outdone.

'Now!' shouted Brother Ignatius Loyola, taking advantage of the confusion. The Sisters of the Immaculate Contraception cast their black raincoats to the ground, revealing that they were clad in nothing but black stockings and red suspender belts. They began to chant 'Hey nonny no to the Feelgood ToyBoy,' in their habitual Gregorian plainsong, but not in the Phrygian mode.

'Now!' shouted Sgt Stripe. The troops of the Guard of Honour cocked their rifles, and the reserves emerged at the double from the heather and rushed down the hill towards the Japanese, firing bursts over their heads with their sten guns.

'Now!' shouted Master Sergeant Capote, and his platoon discharged a volley of smoke grenades into the mêlée.

The schoolchildren threw their flags to the ground and ran screaming from the field through the choking orange smoke. Lady Lucinda's Pekinese hurled themselves barking at Private Krunt, and Tse Tung was shot. The Dog Bran, who had been skulking in the heather after rabbits, burst out, tail wagging and mouth foaming, and leapt at Cpl Snodgrass's throat. Cook Sgt Carrier and Cook Cpl Roux, inflamed to a fury at the thought of Japanese cuisine, threw President Yamamoto and Hirosiguchisan to the ground and stood above them, brandishing bayonets. Alsace and Lorraine began fighting in the machair, pulling at each other's plaits and demanding the return of their homelands, thus finally proving Lady Lucinda's hypothesis that linguistic differences were the cause of war. Lady Lucinda did not, however, notice the success of her experiment – she had run howling to the dead Pekinese and was clutching it to her far from inadequate bosom when she was bitten in the rump by its sister, who in its doggish brain blamed her for the whole episode. Sergeant McPloud looked round for someone to arrest and was bowled to the floor by the Dog Bran. 'In the name of the Lord,' thundered the Reverend Mr MacCorquodale, 'be still!'

An uneasy silence fell, broken only by the occasional whimper or snarl and the scream of gulls returning to the municipal tip. The Japanese lay face down on the ground, experiencing a mixture of rage and humiliation, and vowing that, whatever else, the Feelgood factory would not be built in Scotland. From time to time, Hirosiguchisan stole surreptitious glances at the Sisters of the Immaculate Contraception who, in the interest of public decency, had been lined up with their hands above their heads in order to prevent further disrobing. The Reverend Torquil MacCorquodale sank to his knees, praying for guidance. And the Minister, remembering his Bagehot, realised that he would be expected to take control.

'What in the name of heaven is the meaning of this?' he shouted at Sgt Stripe.

Sgt Stripe swelled his chest, as if expecting the Minister to pin on a medal.

'It's a conspiracy, see Guv, innit,' he explained. 'These Japs ain't wot they seem. They ain't businessmen – they're a highly trained group of crack troops under the personal direction of the Emperor what 'ave come 'ere to capture the Islands as a first step to world domination. Me and my mates 'ave saved you all from a fate worse than death, that's wot we've been and done. Classic example of the military in support of the civil arm.'

The Minister, remembering his Bagehot, looked round for Sir Terence to give him guidance. But Sir Terence had turned on his heel, and was surreptitiously leaving the field.

Ignatius Loyola unwrapped a Havana cigar and handed it to Donald MacDonald. The day had exceeded his wettest dreams. Donald MacDonald took the gift with relish. It had his too.

From her fairy knoll, Amaryllis Squaff had caught the entire proceedings. She was now interviewing Mary Lou Krantz and Henry J Klassinger III about their ordeal. 'Tell me,' she asked for the benefit of Joe Ordinary in Boise, Idaho. 'Did the British authorities subject you to any form of sexual harassment?'

* * *

CHAPTER 29

In which we take our leave.

Six months had passed. Dwight Dildenschneider sweltered under a Californian sun. Beside him stood Megan Morgan Thomas, sporting a diamond the size of a sparrow's egg on her left hand. They had come to California for the official opening of the biggest inward investment that had ever come to Montery County. Dildenschneider pulled on his cigar, squeezed Megan's hand, and turned his attention to the speeches.

'And so, *ah so*, say Plesident Yamamoto,' translated Hirosiguchisan. 'It is with the gleatest pressure that I decrare the Feelgood Factory open. May those employed in the Prant adopt the total quality plocedures that have made our company gleat, and may those who employ our ploducts enjoy the benefits of our inclemental implovement ploglammes and our commitment to total product safety.'

'Safe sex, in other words,' whispered Dildenschneider. Yamamotoasan added a few words, grinning broadly at Dilldenschneider and Megan Morgan Thomas.

'I wish to pay particular tlibute, say Plesident Yamamoto, to the contlibution of Miss Megan Morgan Thomas, who had test driven our ploduct with the assistance of Mr Dildenschneider and made many suggestions for inclemental implovements, and to that of Mr Dildenschneider himself, but for whose enthusiastic help and support this ploject would have gone elsewhere. So lift your glasses of Sake, and dlink to the success of the Feelgood Factory.'

Dwight Dildenschneider reached for his glass and swelled with pride.

Five thousand miles to the East, Dudley Scrope was also reaching for a glass and swelling with pride. Following the Japanese debacle, Sir Terence Mould had been powerless to prevent the amalgamation of the Benbecula and North Uist Urban District Councils, and Dudley Scrope, as promised by Donald MacDonald, had been made the first Chief Executive of the new Metropolitan Council. In the interest of inter island harmony, he had shifted his headquarters to North Uist where, since the Council Offices were not wired for the new technology, he had discovered the pleasures of the quill pen.

He lifted his eyes from the article he was perusing on *The Modern Council Chief Executive, Where She Went Wrong* and gazed at the stags' heads mounted on his office wall. Now which the hell was the one in which Provost Urquhart had hidden his corkscrew?

Two hundred miles to the south, Sir Terence Mould was swelling, but not with pride. He had been examining a long list of names, published that morning in the *Scotsman*, of those who had been honoured by Her Majesty for services to effective government in Scotland. Now he was re-examining the list with the aid of a magnifying glass. One name in particular was bothering him. He had written the citation in his own hand before passing it to Dibbs for typing and onward transmission to Holyrood Palace. 'Donald MacDonald,' he had written, 'for services well beyond the call of duty to the restructuring of local government in Scotland.'

He examined the name a third time. Sure as hell, the letter 'd' was a minuscule.

He stabbed his finger angrily on his intercom.

'Yes, Minister?' lisped his private secretary.

'Get me Dibbs,' he snarled.

* * *

Hugh Morison

Lightning Source UK Ltd.
Milton Keynes UK
02 December 2009